THE SWORD AND THE CROSS CHRONICLES

REVELATION

OLIVIA RAE

Books by Olivia Rae

The Sword and the Cross Chronicles

SALVATION

REVELATION

REDEMPTION
(Coming Soon)

Contact Olivia at
Oliviarae.books@gmail.com

For news and sneak peeks of upcoming novels visit:

Oliviaraebooks.com

Facebook.com/oliviaraeauthor

*To my critique partners who stood by me
year, after year, after year...
Mary Brady, Victoria Hinshaw, Donna Smith,
Kathy Zdanowski*

*And special thank you to the two writers that never let me
quit no matter how hard I tried.*

*Pamela Ford & Laura Scott
Your words of wisdom and unending support
made this book possible.*

And to the glory of God

One

Think not that I am come to send peace on earth: I came not to send peace, but a sword.
Matthew 10:34

Tyre, Outremer, August, 1191

"JULIAN, THE MASTER WISHES TO SEE YOU." Lying prostrate in the position of his crucified Lord, Julian de Maury pressed his cheek firmly against the cool marble floor to block out the intrusive voice interrupting his prayers.

"Brother Julian, the master said 'twas urgent. I am to escort you to his quarters immediately."

Julian ceased his chant and opened his eyes. He waited for his sight to adjust to the dusty beam of light which filtered downward onto the makeshift altar. "I am conversing with God, Andrew."

"We have visitors who cannot be detained."

He flattened his fingertips against the stone floor, then submerged himself into a final prayer. Upon completion of his petition, Julian slid his hands across the smooth surface until his thumbs touched the sides of his chest. He waited for the blood to rush through his numb forearms, then pushed himself onto all fours.

The muscles in the back of his neck and shoulders ached as he raised his head until his gaze fixed on the golden crucifix above the altar. The emerald in the center of the

1

cross glittered boldly in the streaming sunlight. Julian never tired of staring at the blessed stone that had come from Solomon's crown.

His heart ached. The cross belonged in Jerusalem above the granite altar where King Solomon's temple once stood. Not above a shabby wooden structure in a home once owned by a wealthy Muslim merchant.

"Please Julian, these are *important* visitors," Andrew urged.

Rising to one knee and with precise movements, he signed the cross on his chest. "Are they more important than God?" Julian asked before rising to his feet.

Andrew rushed over to help brush out the creases pressed into Julian's white tunic during hours of meditation. "God is patient, but *Richard Coeur de Lion* is not."

Julian's hand stopped on the large red cross that covered the front of his tunic. "The king is here?"

"Aye, and he seeks the help of the Order of the Templar."

Julian's heart began to race. Why would Richard come north when he prepared to march his troops south from Acre? It could only mean one thing. The Templars were needed. *He was needed.*

With each rapid breath his chest expanded. He slapped the smaller knight between the shoulder blades. "I cannot believe God has answered my prayer so quickly. Lead on, Brother."

The warm summer air swept through the large arched windows as they strode down the aged corridor toward the master's chamber.

Andrew looked about without breaking his stride. "I am glad God has given a swift answer to your prayers, but be careful how you greet Master de Sablé, lest he mistake your joyous mood as a result of an unclean thought."

"Nay, Brother, my mood is caused by a righteous request. Many times I have wondered why I was not at Hattin when our Templar brothers perished at Saladin's hand and why the fight was taken from me in Jerusalem and again at Acre.

God denied me the chance to fight thrice for one purpose only. He wishes me to march at King Richard's side to the gates of the Holy City and crush Saladin, sending him to the fiend once and for all."

"I often wished God allowed us to slay Saladin while we still controlled Jerusalem," Andrew said.

Julian's chest tightened. The battle at Hattin had marked the end of the Christian reign in Palestine. Almost all his Templar brothers had fallen beneath infidel swords. Even the True Cross had been lost. Twelve weeks later, Saladin and his army stood at the gates of Jerusalem demanding surrender. Julian would have fought to his death before turning the city over to the vile infidels, but the perfidious master, de Ridefort, ordered the Templars to lay down their swords and give up the city. Julian's ears still rang with the curses and jeers that accompanied their retreat from the Holy City.

A mild breeze swept through the hallway, ruffling Julian's hair. He took a deep breath and confessed, "At least you were in Acre when the city fell back into God's hands."

"Why punish yourself? The siege of Acre was long. The capture and subsequent death of Master de Ridefort had brought chaos to the army. To leave and travel through enemy country alone, to bring back food and reinforcements was courageous."

Julian's throat dried. Only Andrew would turn his shame into courage. He shook his head. "Nay, not courageous, but impatient. Had I waited another week, King Richard and Master de Sablé would have arrived with both."

Andrew stopped and placed his hand on Julian's shoulder. "We lay siege to the city for ninety-eight weeks. None knew the king would come."

"Perhaps, but now the time has come to prove my worthiness and loyalty. To heed Saint Paul's words and put on the full armor of God. Come, we have tarried long enough."

True enough, Saint Paul spoke of a spiritual battle and

3

not a physical one, but Julian believed at times they were both the same. For how else could the Lord work in men's hearts if they were being persecuted by others? But if the threat is removed then surely the Word would flourish.

With strong purposeful steps, Julian made his way down the hall to the master's chamber. When he reached the door he placed his hand on his belt. *He had left his sword in the dormitory.* A fleeting panic reverberated through his chest. Julian took a deep breath. He was not a vain man who needed a steel object to bolster his courage before a mere king. He knocked briskly on the door before folding his trembling hands.

"Enter," bellowed an unfamiliar voice.

Julian opened the door and crossed the threshold. A bright light streamed through the diagonal windowpanes, momentarily blinding him.

A tall man with red-gold hair and piercing eyes stood near the window. The cross of his arms and the width of his stance personified strength and power. Julian swallowed hard and bowed low before King Richard the Lionheart.

"Arise, man," the king ordered. "So you are Breanna's brother, Julian de Maury. I have heard much about you. Master de Sablé, is it true the Saracen curse the name of this man?"

The elderly master moved to the king's side. "Aye, Your Majesty."

Richard grunted and looked Julian over. "I see your sister in your eyes. But her jaw is set with a softer line. She is indeed a comely wench, and from what Royce tells me she is even more beautiful now that she is a mother."

The king's frankness and comparison irritated Julian. After all, she was a woman and he was a knight in God's army.

Richard brushed a hand over his short beard. "It has been a long time since I have seen them. I shall have to make a point to visit when I return to England. They have proven to be very loyal servants to the crown."

4

Julian nodded. Royce had been wise not to protest when Richard seized the throne from his father, Henry II. But then, Royce did have a good head on his shoulders. Julian knew such when he sent his friend to help Breanna after she had become a widow. Their marriage was a surprise, but Julian could not have been more pleased.

"But that is not what I came here for." Richard narrowed his eyes and again took in Julian's full measure. "Are you truly God's Avenging Angel as every Christian knight claims?"

Julian's skin grew warm under the king's scrutiny. "Your Majesty, you honor this humble knight. I am merely a servant of our Lord."

"What say you, Baldwin? Does he gain your approval?" the king asked.

A thin sour-faced man moved from the shadows. "Good God, he won't do, Sire!"

Julian straightened his shoulders and raised his chin. He dug his fingernails into his calloused palms. Who was this man who judged him so hastily? "You are fortunate, sir, I do not have my sword in hand or your tongue would be lying at your feet. God's name is holy. 'Tis blasphemy to use His name carelessly."

The man cringed. Richard exploded with laughter, then waved toward the colorless man. "This is my most trusted counselor, Sir Edward Baldwin."

Baldwin nodded. Julian ignored the feeble greeting by directing his attention back to the king.

"Recant your words, Edward. You have offended a knight of the Templar," Richard ordered.

"He has offended God, Your Majesty. Not me." The muscles in Julian's body tensed, his fingers itched. 'Twas a good thing his sword lay upon his bed. "He should do penance for his sin against our Creator."

Richard tipped back his russet head and guffawed again. "So he shall, noble knight. So he shall."

Julian let his last breath out slowly. He took no pleasure

in instructing the King that 'twas God who should receive the glory. "Nay, Your Majesty, not noble; I am but a humble servant of our Lord."

Julian knew to disagree with the King could mean death.

The room became instantly quiet; even the few insects that buzzed near the closed window took refuge against the pane, as if the serious mood that had descended upon the room's occupants had also fallen upon their wings.

Richard sat in Master de Sablé's chair. He leaned forward, his eyes hooded behind thick bushy lashes, his face unreadable under the wiry beard. "Is it true, Brother Julian, you have never broken a single article of The Rule?"

Julian lowered his chin and quietly answered, "With God's help."

"Impossible! There are over six hundred of them," Baldwin blurted out.

Gritting his teeth, Julian responded to the black soul who rested his hand casually on the back of the master's chair. "Keeping The Rule is easy if one meditates before one commits a rash act or utters witless words."

Julian raised a brow and hid a frown when a low rumble escaped Richard's throat for the third time. How could he find humor where there was none? 'Twas a Templars duty to correct the faithless.

Richard slapped his knees then stood. "I think he is perfect. I know the family and if Master de Sablé trusts him completely, then so do I."

"Well, I do not," Baldwin said, with a wave of his hand. "He is much too fair of face. We must consider his attitude toward women. When was the last time he had a dalliance? Julian de Maury, how long have you been a member of this order?"

Julian could smell the acid of this demon's blood. How dare Baldwin question his purity? He purged his lungs with a cleansing breath, seeking the restraint his faith always insured. Sure as he stood in God's grace, someday the king would realize he harbored a serpent in his midst.

"I have been in this order for almost ten years," Julian answered.

"Ten years without a woman! Good God, he will ravish her before they reach Antioch."

Every muscle in Julian's body ached to lash out at this blasphemer. He took another calming breath. "Never in my entire life have I defiled myself with a woman."

Again the room became deathly still; Richard moved close until he stood toe-to-toe with Julian. "Are you saying you have never lain with a woman?"

Julian nodded, refusing to release the rage Baldwin had planted.

Master de Sablé stepped to the King's side. "Your Majesty, Julian never speaks other than the truth."

As if he sensed the volcano bubbling beneath Julian's calm exterior, Richard backed away until at least four hands separated them. "Yes, of course."

Julian raised his eyes heavenward in prayer, pleading for control, then looked upon Richard. "Your Majesty, let me burn in the fires of hell if I should ever love another soul more than my Lord."

"Aye, burn you shall," Baldwin taunted. "Not in hell's fire, but in a blaze just as consuming, just as condemning!"

"Quiet, Edward. No one is judging Julian's loyalty to our God," Richard reprimanded. "In fact, I am more than satisfied with him."

Julian lowered his head, trying to contain his exuberance and find his humility. He locked his knees and pressed his feet against the floor for fear he would forget his place and jump for joy. Richard had selected him. He would be sent on a glorious mission and escape the mundane tasks of polishing the marble floors. He would ride beside the king into blessed battle.

His Majesty walked to the window and squashed a still beetle against the pane with his thumb. "Many years ago," Richard continued, "relatives through marriage of my dear deceased brother Geoffrey came to the Holy Land on a pilgrimage. Muslims set upon them before they reached Jerusalem. We believed the whole family perished. Then came reports that a girl resembling Geoffrey's niece lived among the Muslims near Acre."

Richard coughed, clearing his throat. Julian waited respectfully for the king to finish his tale and speak of the great holy battle before them.

"When the city fell to the armies of God, we found Lady Ariane. She had been living with the infidels these past ten years. Now listen carefully, Julian, for this concerns your mission."

Julian straightened his shoulders. Whatever the test, God would find him true.

"When we found her, one of King Philip's cousins was with us. Jacques de Craon became smitten by the girl. Since I refused to marry Philip's sister, Alice, the bond between France and England has been unstable. I proclaimed, de Craon could only have the girl through holy matrimony. Fortunately, in his lust, he has agreed to my terms. A marriage between de Craon and the Lady Ariane would heal many wounds. Unfortunately, the girl lived as a concubine in the house of a man named Abi Bin and has accepted heathen ways."

The King droned on. Julian swayed slightly. Visions of conquering the Muslims thundered through his mind—the clang of armor, the screams of the infidels as they tasted the steel of his sword. Finally, the fight would be his. This time he would march into Jerusalem and smite the wicked.

Richard's voice boomed above the battle cries. "What say you, Julian, are you up to the task?"

Julian widened his stance, pulled back his shoulders and laid his palms flat against the sides of his white tunic. His glorious mission was at hand. "Aye, Your Majesty."

"Good. I need a trustworthy knight to convey the Lady Ariane to England and train her in the ways of a good Christian."

What is this? Before Julian could give voice to his question the king spoke again.

"Also, while you are there, keep a sharp eye on my brother, John. I have received reports he is misusing his power and has designs on the throne."

England? The banners of battle Julian had created in his mind crashed to the ground. Surely there must be some mistake. Richard wanted him to return to England while playing nursemaid to some girl?

"Your Majesty, The Rule is very clear about dealing with children. No knight of the Templar is allowed even to be a godparent for fear of wanting a family of his own. Is there not someone of a lesser order who might school the child?"

"Child?" Richard crossed his arms in front of him. "Haven't you heard a word I said? The girl has seen at least seventeen summers. She is a woman."

Julian stared at the King. This was not a test worthy of a Knight Templar. He glanced at the Master and noticed the severe frown creasing his face. Did the Master truly expect him to carry out so trivial a task?

"Bring the girl in," Richard roared.

Across the room a door that led to the Master's sleeping compartment burst open. Flanked by two knights stood a slender girl draped in a drab hooded cloak. When one of the king's knights tried to usher her forward, she retaliated with a swift kick to his shin. Her hood fell away, revealing a girl, nay, a woman with flawless skin, perfectly sculptured cheekbones, and bright green eyes that sparked pure hate.

But it was her hair which caused Julian to fight the urge to cross himself. For before him stood a siren whose rich wavy tresses matched the consuming fires of hell. Edward's earlier words cried out in his mind: *Burn you shall. Not in hell's fire, but in a blaze just as consuming, just as condemning.*

Ariane took great pleasure in the insolent knight's howl even as pain shot up the foot she had slammed into his grimy shin. The weeks of trying to escape these Christian monsters had left her bone-tired and bruised, but no less determined.

The knight reached for her again. When she jumped away from him, her slipper caught in a large crack in the stone floor. She stumbled and raised her hand to brace herself for the inevitable fall. Swift feet crossed the room. Her hands landed against a solid chest adorned with a blood red cross. Ice swept through her veins when she noticed the white background of the tunic.

The red cross turned thick and sticky underneath her fingers. Blood covered the hilt of a glittering silver sword. High shrills pierced the air.

"My lady, are you hurt?"

The harsh, strong voice broke through her nightmare. The tight grip on her sides reminded her where she was—in the arms of a Templar. A murderer of the children of Allah.

With a shudder, Ariane spun away. She brushed her riotous hair from her face and spit a few strands from her mouth. She raised her gaze three hands. The tall knight's strength, his broad powerful chest, seemed to make the room shrink. Ariane pulled back her shoulders, meaning to hurl a string of Arab curses at the arrogant Templar. But the curses died on her lips as she saw the savage storm ready to break in his fair colored eyes. Even the firm set of his cleanly shaven jaw indicated the tempest brewing beneath the controlled exterior.

Queasiness engulfed Ariane. His face seemed familiar and then again not. She fought the fear brewing in her belly. Surely he was just one more of the countless filthy Christians who shoved her about in her captivity. And yet, this man would never be only one of many. His beautiful, hard, stern face was like none other.

"Lady Ariane has forgotten her English tongue so we will address her in Arabic." The choppy Arab words of the dog,

Richard, drew her attention from the imposing knight. To the left of the Anglo ruler stood the cobra, Edward Baldwin and two other Templars, one of strong build and elderly, the other of slight frame and young. The older knight had a face of a weasel, sly, with thin eyebrows. The other resembled a dog's whelp, scrawny, with mud-brown hair.

What was the dog king up to now?

Ariane squelched the smile, which begged to cross her lips. Little did the dolt know she understood every syllable he uttered. She had been wise not to reveal her knowledge of the English language.

"Lady Ariane," Richard said in Arabic, waving to the older knight. "May I present the Master of the Temple in Jerusalem, Robert de Sablé." The seasoned monk bowed slightly. Richard ignored the younger knight and waved to the golden Templar with the puzzling face. "Before you stands Julian de Maury."

She had heard many tales about the Christian's Avenging Angel, who killed those who followed Mohammed and served Allah. Julian de Maury looked like an angel, but she knew the truth of it. He was a demon. A butcher who murdered harmless eunuchs such as faithful Isam. Is that why his face made her wary?

Screams mixed with the thunder from horses' hooves. A silver sword slashed.

Ariane shook the thought away. She matched the Templar's even glare. He offered no greeting, but wiped his hands on the side of his white tunic as if he had touched a leper. She longed to tell him what she thought of him in a language he understood, but she clenched her jaw to keep from shouting at him in English and giving herself away.

Abruptly the man turned to face the King. "Your Majesty," he said in English. "Forgive me, but 'twould be unwise for me to leave the Holy Land. Soon God's army will recapture Jerusalem. Surely you will need my sword in the fight."

Color crept up the king's neck. He crossed his arms and

planted his feet firmly. His face took on a fierce, wild look. The weasel's and whelp's eyes widened. Yet the butcher seemed unaffected. He stood before his king like a cold and unyielding castle tower.

"Take her to England," Richard grated out in Arabic. "Stay there until the lady is safely wed to Lord de Craon."

The mention of the beady-eyed Frank who ransacked her home freed Ariane's tongue. "I will not wed that worm!"

The cobra Baldwin hissed in English, "I know not what the lady said, but she sounds distressed. Perhaps she would be more at ease if I escorted her home."

Home. Baldwin had destroyed her home. Ariane chewed on the inside of her cheek, to keep understanding from showing on her face. If only she had a dagger, she would slit the belly of this snake that murdered her faithful Isam.

"Enough," Richard roared. "All leave except Julian and the lady."

The weasel, the whelp, and Richard's two mongrel knights scurried to the door like a pack of animals fighting for table scraps thrown on the ground. Baldwin slithered behind, then turned and bowed to his king. Richard waved him off. Baldwin straightened slowly, his gaze slid to her and crawled up her body. She wished she stood close enough to spit in his face. Instead she spat on the ground.

"Leave us." At the force of Richard's command, Baldwin jumped. He spun about and hurried out the door.

The room grew cold with silence. Ariane glanced at the king whose face bore deep crooked lines of disapproval. His eyes fixed on the closed door while his chest rose and fell with exaggerated breaths.

Ariane had seen Richard this way many times before, his anger boiling beneath a fragile calm. She meant to look at the floor until the King's rage ebbed, but a strange force pulled her gaze in another direction, into cool ice-blue eyes. A chill pricked her spine.

An ice-blue jewel sparkled in the hilt of a broadsword, floating downward.

"Brother Julian," Richard said in Arabic. "The marriage between Lady Ariane and de Craon is extremely important to the Crusade. Sir Baldwin does not speak the infidel language, and in truth, I do not trust him in this matter. When he looks upon Lady Ariane the flames of desire burn hard and fast in his eyes. I promised Lord de Craon she would remain untouched from the day he set eyes on her and by God, he shall have it. It is the least I can do since he has agreed to marry the soiled lamb. But be careful. She is a crafty one. Already she has tried to seduce two of my knights into helping her escape. Luckily we got wind of the plan before it could be brought to fruition. I trust this will not happen with you, de Maury?"

The Templar nodded, but looked like he had just eaten a spoiled date.

Ariane balled her fists at her side and stamped her foot. "I refuse. I will not wed that slimy worm nor will I go anywhere with this...butcher."

Richard walked over to stand in front of her. He placed his hands on his hips, his gaze traveled her body as if she were a mare to be auctioned. She well expected him to examine her teeth or slap her thighs to check her strength. He switched to his English speech. "Julian, you will take the girl."

Ariane lowered her head, certain comprehension of his words could be seen in her eyes. Waves of anxiety rushed through her, she would need all her wits in order to escape this knight.

The Templar cleared his throat and spoke in English. "Your Majesty, she may not be Lady Ariane. Many young Christian children have been abducted by the Muslims."

Richard motioned the Templar knight to his side. "She wears a necklace given to her by my brother Geoffrey at her baptism. The front carries our family crest; her name is engraved on the back with a tiny cross above the script."

Richard backed away allowing the Templar to move forward. Her skin crawled when his fingers grazed her neck. She slapped his hand away and stepped back.

"Keep your filthy hands off me, Templar butcher," she spat in Arabic.

He inched forward. "I won't hurt you," he said fluidly in the same tongue.

She took another step back. "Nay, you will. I feel it... I know it."

Ariane heard the grind of his teeth through his insolent smile. Surely he wished to wring her neck. "Never have I raised my sword against a lady."

A strong hand gripped the hilt of the sword. The blue stone flashed in the late afternoon sun. Falling downward, downward...

She gulped hard. He had no sword on his hip, yet she felt—"Yea, you have, I know it. I know it!" Her back came up against the cool chamber wall. He advanced slowly until his shoes touched the tips of her slippers. Her heart thudded wildly. There was nowhere to run. No chance of escape.

He touched her again, then hesitated, holding his trembling fingers before her. He flexed his hand then gently slid his fingers down her neck. They were not cold as she suspected, but radiated warmth. She stood paralyzed on the spot when he raised the chain that hung about her neck. She could do naught but watch the small heart glint in his large palm.

The king's face loomed near the Templar's shoulder. Quietly he said in English, "When we sacked the house of Abi Bin, a eunuch died protecting her. With his last breath, he begged us to spare her life. He claimed she was of noble English blood. I believe he spoke the truth for every time someone tries to take the necklace from her she fights like a wild animal. How many infidels would cherish a necklace inscribed with the cross of Christ? I believe that deep in her soul she begs to be saved. 'Twas God's will we were sent to the house of Abi Bin."

The Templar butcher took his time examining the heart. Then he raised his gaze to meet hers. "Perhaps you are right, Your Majesty." His warm English words washed over her throat chasing away the chill. "But she may have stolen the charm from the true Lady Ariane. By chance she could be a skillful thief."

Ariane grabbed the necklace from his hand and placed it beneath her cloak. Thief indeed. 'Twas Christians who stole the Muslims' homes and lands.

Like a savage lion bored with his prey, Richard shoved the Templar aside and shouted, "Enough of this! Saladin awaits me on the road to Jerusalem. I'll not waste more time on this matter. Her eyes, her hair, even her small stature are similar to Geoffrey's wife. She is his niece!" He drew a deep breath. "I need this alliance with Philip. The French grow weary of the Crusade. If they leave, Jerusalem will be like the Star of Bethlehem, beautiful to behold, but unable to be reached. I have not come this far for naught. Take whomever and whatever you wish. But you accompany her to England. Is that clear?"

"Aye, Your Majesty. I will do what you and God command," the butcher answered, his voice edged with defeat.

Ariane peered over Richard's shoulder to look directly into the fair, fierce countenance of the Templar.

God command.

God commands me.

The memory flooded her mind. She was but twelve summers when Abi Bin had taken his household to visit relatives in Damascus. On their travels they encountered a group of pilgrims, escorted by Templars. Never had Ariane seen such magnificent men, garbed in white with bright red crosses on their chests and large shiny swords on their hips.

First there were words between the two parties, then shouts and curses. Swords began to clang, both Muslims and pilgrims began to run, while others chose to fight. Frightened, she crawled under a wooden cart and watched the fray.

She saw him. His ice-blue eyes chilled with hate. He wore no helm, his hair hung like a golden veil about his face.

He raised a blue-stoned sword high. It glittered and sparkled in the afternoon sun. The sword glided downward, downward until the blade crashed against the skull of Raya, her teacher. The only woman who bothered to comfort a lonely child in a strange land. Blood flowed freely. His words of vengeance rang loud in her ears.

"As God commands me, I will purge this land with infidel blood."

Allah have mercy! She remembered this face. The golden knight, the Christian's Avenging Angel. Ariane bit her lower lip to keep from calling him a liar. He did kill ladies. He would butcher her like he did Raya. If she could not flee, she would fight.

Ariane pushed Richard, he stumbled backward. She flew at the butcher and drummed her fists on his chest. His hands caught her wrists, subduing her. She struggled to free herself.

The Arabic words rushed from her lips, "Let go! I'll not go! Kill me now, Templar butcher. For I swear, at first chance, I will cut your heart out."

Two

Whereas ye know not what shall be on the morrow. For what is your life? It is even a vapour that appeareth for a little time, and then vanisheth away.

James 4:14

$\mathcal{J}$ ULIAN'S HORSE LUMBERED AIMLESSLY, MATCHING his owner's sluggish mood as they approached the city of Tyre. He had spent most of the day giving escort to King Richard and had hoped during the short trip he could persuade his king to find another to accompany the temptress with the hell-red hair to England.

He'd failed.

The king spent the journey giving specific instructions to Julian on how he should handle Lady Ariane. Every time Julian tried to change the king's mind, Richard would simply raise his hand to squelch Julian's argument. By the time Richard reached safe country and no longer needed Julian's escort, His Majesty had made it clear. Julian would take the lady north.

'Twas hopeless.

With nothing else to do, Julian headed back toward Tyre, making mental notes on what was needed for the long journey. The more he thought on it, the more he was convinced the journey should be as swift as possible. Then mayhap he would be able to return before Richard marched on Jerusalem.

Julian's mood lightened slightly and he urged his mount

forward at a quicker pace. To hasten his journey he would need only a few men. He had already employed Najila to be the lady's maid and companion. If all went well they could leave early on the morrow, well before the sun hit its zenith. At the Templar compound, Julian drew open the heavy wooden door that led inside. An unusual flurry of activity greeted him.

Servants stumbled about, their arms laden with the master's tent. Close to a dozen horses nickered and danced, kicking up clouds of dust. Squires scurried around the yard securing armor and weaponry. Several sergeants, in their black and brown uniforms, carried large baskets of citrus fruit to a wagon loaded with cook pots, bowls, and cups. Knights wearing chain mail, who usually spent the hours after matins honing their fighting skills, examined their broad swords and shields.

Julian's swallowed hard. His belly rolled in a sea of anger and resentment. Only preparation for a campaign would disrupt the Templar's daily routine. Here before him was proof the Templars prepared to fight, while he, Julian de Maury would escort a female from the Holy Land to England.

Near the old well, in the middle of the courtyard, he spotted Master de Sablé speaking to the blacksmith. With strong steps Julian pushed through the sea of chaos.

The master raised a hand in greeting. "Brother Julian, I am glad you are here. The preparations for your journey are almost completed. I have supplied Lady Ariane with one of my tents, along with ample servants to carry her litter. I have also readied twelve knights for her protection. There are reports that Assassin Muslims patrol the roads north of the city.

For a moment, the master's words lay dead in his ears. Surely this commotion could not be for him. "Master, are these not the preparations for a campaign?"

The master tilted his head and raised one questioning eyebrow. "Campaign? We are not going to battle. We will stay here until Richard needs fresh reinforcements to take Jerusalem from Saladin's filthy grasp. There is no need for us to fight at the moment."

Julian waved to the pandemonium. "But all this—"

"This is for you and for Lady Ariane."

Even as relief washed away his anger and doubts, Julian groaned inwardly. The large tent and extra entourage would slow travel and extend the length of his mission.

"Master, I believe God wishes my journey to be brisk and unassuming. I plan to travel by sea, and in the ten years I have been a Templar I have never needed a squire. I prefer to care for my own armor and weapons."

The master waved off his protest. "But you must consider you will not have the time to clean your mail or sharpen your sword. You must use your rest time to educate Lady Ariane in God's word."

Julian took a deep breath of Tyre's warm and obtrusive air. "For the lady's safety the journey should be carried out with the greatest of speed. We will draw less attention if we do not have a large tent and a gaggle of servants. Simplicity is the best way to protect the lady. I thank you for the use of thy tent and servants, but I see no need for them."

The master's face turned sour. "What of Lady Ariane's needs? 'Tis unseemly to have a lady travel without a proper chaperone and the comforts due her station."

Julian planted his feet and folded his arms across his chest. He inhaled slowly. "The lady, has spent ten summers with the infidels without her station considered. I have hired a maid to accompany us, to see to Lady Ariane's needs."

Master de Sablé scratched his gray stubble chin. "Perhaps you are right. The lady serves no purpose if evil befalls her. She must be kept extremely safe in your travel to Marseilles."

Marseilles? He planned to sail all the way to England. "Master, why would I travel to Marseilles?"

The master briefly touched his forehead. "Ah, I forgot to

tell you. You will travel to Marseilles. Lord de Craon will be there on a mission for King Richard and King Philip. Sir Baldwin believes the young Frank may lose interest without a look at his bride before her lengthy Christian training."

So the serpent planned to foil Julian's mission. "Nay, Master," he answered quickly. "I will not go to Marseilles."

"But the king wishes—"

"Nay! Baldwin wishes it. Not the king and not God, whose authority overrules all." Julian unfolded his arms and gripped the hilt of his sword with renewed fervor. "I will not partake in the sin of creating lust in a man."

The master's stern look softened. He lightly grasped Julian's shoulder. "Your words are hard to dispute. However, I have known the king for many years. Be it his order or Baldwin's wish, you will take Lady Ariane to Marseilles. If that is not what God wished He would have prevented Richard or Baldwin from giving the order. I leave it to you to tell her when the time is right. She may not be ready to see her betrothed just yet. We must consider her delicate constitution."

Julian sighed. He could not dispute the master's orders. He must do as he was commanded. But Ariane having a *delicate constitution?* He suppressed the urge to protest this when he recognized the sincerity in the master's eyes. Aye, Lady Ariane was petite in stature; the top of her head barely met his shoulders. She resembled a fragile sea shell bleached by the warm eastern sun, but the way she attacked him yesterday resembled a termagant of a strong, wild, and undisciplined nature.

The master turned and surveyed the courtyard. "I will send Brother Andrew to the docks to make ready the *Knight's Cross* for you and the other Templars."

Julian rubbed his eyes and coughed, trying to purge his lungs of the dust swirling through the air. The master still did not understand. Sailing on the heavy *dromon* would add weeks to their journey. Speed was the essence of their travels. Speed was the key to his salvation.

"Master, I plan to use a swift *lateen*. The vessel will draw less attention and can easily outmaneuver Muslim ships."

The master stroked his beard briefly. "No, Julian, again you forget the lady's needs."

"I think of the lady's protect—"

A clipped wave silenced Julian. The hard lines on the master's face reminded him that he must choose his words carefully or he would be traveling by land accompanied by the entire city of Tyre.

"I think of the lady's comfort and safety," Master de Sablé said. "She cannot travel to England in a ship made for milder waters. Why do you protest so? I would think you would want to use your own ship."

"I have no possessions. The ship belongs to The Order."

The Master nodded. "Aye, Julian, the *Knight's Cross* belongs to the order, but 'twas you who brought the vessel to us, laden with gifts from your home."

"Not my home," Julian corrected. "All was given to God."

Julian lowered his head. Not all was given. He gave a handsome parcel of land to his brother, Hugh. Julian prayed God would understand, for he knew Hugh did not and expected more.

The master placed his hand on Julian's shoulder. "Quite so, but now it is time to give back to God and to England some of the heathens' goods. Take the *Knight's Cross*, take command of it if you wish, for the lady's safety, and the comfort of your fellow brethren."

Julian heard finality in the master's voice. In his mind he saw the large ship filled with cargo, weighed down with knight's mail, swords, and servants. 'Twould take an eternity to arrive in England. His mind raced. He must lighten the load, but how?

Please, God, give me the answer.

A moment passed. Serenity filled Julian's soul. He looked directly into the master's eyes.

"With your blessing, I will take only one other knight, Brother Guy Ashton."

The color drained from the master's face. His eyebrows crept upward. "Guy is a poor choice. Where you steadfastly keep every article of The Rule, I am pressed to find any that Brother Guy has not broken."

"Nonetheless, he is my choice. King Richard has given me permission to select my knights. Having chosen Brother Guy, I need no other."

The master folded his hands. Though many monks folded their hands in prayer, Master de Sablé's hands resembled a stone fist.

"You said you are concerned with Lady Ariane's welfare. Selecting Guy Ashton will place the lady's virtue in great jeopardy."

Julian lifted his chin. "I give my word no man will defile Lady Ariane while she is in my care."

The master studied Julian for a moment. "I would feel more comfort if I had Brother Guy's word. However, I will hold you to yours, and to help you keep it, I suggest you take Brother Andrew de Lynville."

Julian smiled; the master was a stubborn man. "My word is a holy oath, none can make me break it. Yet I will accept Brother Andrew; he is trustworthy and will aid in the education of Lady Ariane."

"Nay, Julian, you are the most pious knight. Her instruction rests squarely on your shoulders. 'Twas why the king and God chose you for the task."

Julian could not argue for he knew the master spoke the truth. Yet hearing another speak of his duty to Lady Ariane made him uncomfortable.

Master de Sablé smiled briefly. "Do this small service for God, and you shall be rewarded upon your return."

"Master, I need no reward. God will grant me that gift on Judgment Day."

"You speak the truth, but allow me to give you that which you earn. Many believed I chose unwisely when I selected Sir Gilbert Bisol to be the military commander of the Templar. You never protested, but defended my decision."

"Brother Gilbert has been a good and just servant. Age and wisdom are always the best choice."

"I agree. However, Brother Gilbert is weary of being marshal and wishes to retire to less strenuous duties. Though you are young, you are the logical successor to the post."

Julian's heart thudded loudly in excitement. This affirmed the answer to his prayers. God truly intended great purpose for him. Never had any master of the Templar chosen a man so young to become the marshal, third in command of the Knights Templar.

He felt the sting of guilt at the proud thought. "'Tis a great honor you wish to bestow upon me, but I do not need compensation for doing the work of the Lord."

"Nonetheless, I wish to bestow this honor upon you." The master placed his hand on Julian's shoulder. "Use this journey to reflect on your new position. You will be taking Lady Ariane to Wynnhurst Abbey. It is close to your home. Ask your family for their advice on becoming military commander. I am sure they will have their opinions, and it is always nice to discuss important matters with family. It will be good for you to see them again."

To see his mother again would be wonderful, but his brother? Hugh had been furious when, upon their father's death, Julian gave the family keep and lands to the Templars. Would ten years have quelled his brother's anger or intensified it?

Dark clouds billowed and swayed, covering the afternoon sun. The wind whipped the sand into small funnels about the yard. A loud clap of thunder resounded overhead.

Julian raised his gaze to the heavens. "God's will be done."

"Lady. Lady, you must rise. We have much to do before we leave."

We? Ariane forced open her heavy eyelids when she heard the feminine Arab voice, only to snap them shut to block out the late afternoon rays that streamed into the bedchamber. Where had the day gone? Sleeping had not been part of her plan. She had intended to slip out of the chamber window as soon as the guards pacing below grew bored with their task. Then she meant to lower herself to the adjacent flat roof and make her way over to the courtyard wall. A short jump and she would be on her way to freedom.

The stress of being handed over to the most ruthless Templar who ever existed and the weeks of sleeping on the hard ground surrounded by stinking Crusaders finally must have taken their toll. A few moments rest on the soft feather bed and her fears melted away. 'Twas she who let her guard down and slept the whole afternoon away. Stupid fool!

"My lady, let us arise. We have little time to pack. We will leave early on the morrow."

Ariane blinked until she focused her vision on a tall, dark-haired, olive-skinned woman who opened a large chest that sat in the middle of the room. The young woman then bent down and scooped Ariane's gray cloak off the floor.

The woman's almond eyes widened as she inspected the garment. "My lady, where is the rest of your clothing?"

Ariane examined the beautiful slender woman who discarded the traditional Muslim burqa of black to wear vibrant red silks trimmed with gold thread. Her shiny black hair was covered with a sheer gold veil. Her skin looked smooth, oiled, and carried a sweet scent. *A clean scent!*

"Who are you?" Ariane asked the vision of perfection.

"I am Najila. I have been hired to serve you."

Cynical laughter bubbled from Ariane's throat as she rolled from the bed to stand in front of Najila. For years she had been trained to serve others, not to be served upon.

"Pray tell for what will I need a servant? The vermin-filled cloak and the drab woolen gown at your feet are all that I own." Ariane placed her hands on her chest and looked downward. "Ah, I almost forgot about this lovely dung-shaded shift that scratches my skin."

Najila lowered her gaze; her cheeks took on a dark hue. "I am sorry."

Ariane reached out to touch the fine linen of Najila's stola. "Do not fret, Najila. I once wore clothing as beautiful as yours, but King Richard did not think it was proper for an English lady to wear such exquisite garments. He thought I would look finer in a camp whore's rags. No doubt he gave my possessions to a woman who caught his fancy."

Najila did not answer, but began twisting Ariane's cloak in her hands.

"Do not feel uncomfortable; my plight is not your fault." Ariane moved over to the trunk and pushed the lid down. "I have nothing to pack in this large chest, and do not take offense, Najila—but I have no use of a servant."

"I could help you with your hair."

Reaching for a tangled lock, Ariane gave a short laugh. "How will you make this unruly mass behave? Truly you would not like to run your fingers through this filthy mess. I will see to my own hair."

"My lady, surely Brother Julian will provide a bath and whatever else you need, if you but ask."

Ariane wrinkled her nose. Was it awe she heard in Najila's voice when she mentioned the butcher's name? "I have been with these barbarian Christians for weeks, and not one has worried about my *needs.*"

Najila placed the worn cloak atop of the trunk, then slid her tongue across her upper lip. "Julian de Maury is different."

The smooth sultry sound in Najila's voice made Ariane frown. "How well do you know this man?"

"My family lives on a large plot of land outside the city of Acre. When the Christians came to besiege the city, my father thought it would be prudent to reject Mohammed and the Koran in favor of Jesus and the Bible."

The words were all too familiar and explained Najila's unusual dress. Many who lived in Palestine willingly sacrificed their souls for the preservation of their homes and families. If Saladin showed up tonight and thrust a dagger into The Lion's heart, Najila's father would again find the Muslim faith of his fathers and wrap his daughter in the acceptable dark burqa.

"Even though becoming Christian saved our lives, many Crusaders still stole our sheep and food. But all that changed when Brother Julian came," Najila continued.

"Did it?" Ariane asked skeptically.

Najila moved closer to Ariane. "Yea, my lady. Once a misguided Crusader tried to defile my sister, Omaria. Brother Julian saved her virtue by fighting and dissuading the wayward Crusader. Since then my father has looked on Brother Julian as a son. Many nights he broke bread with us. He read the Bible to us and brought food to fill our bellies and clothes to cover our backs. Brother Julian found work for my brother Nizam, Omaria and me here, in Tyre. He has been very generous to my family. He even taught me English."

And that's not all he has taught you, Ariane thought. She saw the way of it now. How better to keep her on a tight leash than for the butcher to have his concubine play her maid. Ariane sighed. This woman would not help her escape, unless there was some way she could make Najila distrust the butcher.

A sweet calculated smile crossed Ariane's lips. "You spend a lot of time with Brother Julian?"

The blush returned to Najila's cheeks. "Yea, my lady. We all do."

"We?"

"Nizam, Omaria, and I."

Ariane walked casually over to the trunk where she pretended to examine a hole in her cloak. "Is the rest of your family in Acre?"

"Yea, I have three brothers and four sisters. The oldest is my brother Jeric, then there is my sister Sharar, followed by my two other brothers Rahman and Nizam." Najila lowered her head and voice. "To my father's disappointment the rest of us are girls."

Poking her finger through the hole in the cloak, Ariane gave Najila a sidelong glance. "I am sorry your father does not take pride in having such a beautiful young woman as his daughter. Tell me, are any of your sisters near you in age?"

Najila raised her head and thrust her chin out slightly. "My sister Omaria is a year younger than I and has three suitors already."

Ariane balled the damaged part of the cloak in her hand. This was better than she could hope for. Najila had a pretty younger sister and, by the look on Najila's face, a rivalry already existed between the girls. "Did Brother Julian spend time teaching Omaria English?"

"Yea, my lady, he taught all my brothers and sisters. Twice a week he would give us a lesson after supper."

"Ah, you studied together. You must all be very bright. Did no one need extra help from Brother Julian?"

A deep frown marred Najila's beautiful face. "Omaria did sometimes require extra help. When she had problems with her lesson she would come here for additional instruction from Brother Julian."

Ariane had to turn away, unable hide her excitement. Allah had finally answered her prayers. The seed of jealousy needed but a little water.

"Your father and your sister's suitors are very trusting to allow Omaria to spend time alone with such a handsome knight."

"Brother Julian is a monk!"

Glee bubbled inside Ariane at the stress in Najila's voice. She soon would be free. Swaying Najila to help her escape would be easier than slicing a loaf of bread. "Yea, he is a monk, but he is also a man, and what an attractive man he is. So tall, so strong, and his hair flows about his shoulders like

27

smooth desert sand." Now Ariane would twist the knife. "Your sister must have strong resolve, for I know I would not be able to learn a thing in Brother Julian's presence."

To see the effect of her words, Ariane looked slightly over her shoulder. The lines of worry made Najila resemble a shriveled fig. Again, Ariane turned away to conceal the grin that crept across her lips.

"But then with *three* suitors she may not have that problem. Do you have any suitors, Najila?"

Najila's nerves edged her voice. "Nay, that is why Brother Julian asked me to be your companion."

"That is good, for it may be *years* before you return home. I would not like to think you had a young man growing old waiting for you. Perhaps Brother Julian will find a husband for you when your services are no longer needed. Who knows, mayhap he will wed you to a Norman or Saxon."

The urgency could be heard in Najila's steps as she rushed to Ariane's side. "Brother Julian would not do such a thing."

Ariane shrugged, then purposely allowed her gaze to slide to Najila's belly. "Perhaps not, but one never knows what may develop over the months."

Najila's cheeks flamed as her hand moved modestly to her stomach, confirming Ariane's suspicions. The butcher was indeed dipping into this woman's well.

"Perhaps it would be better if you had a suitor. He would not allow you to travel to a strange, cold land."

Ariane moved toward the chamber window and stared at the horizon. Soon she would make her way back to Damascus and seek Halimah, Abi Bin's sister. Surely aid could be found there. After all, Abi Bin had spent hours making sure she never lost her English tongue. For he had said a concubine could learn many secrets in a man's bed when he did not think his lover understood.

Yea, Halimah would take her in. For she could pay for her keep in many ways. Once she learned how to get close to a man without punching him in the nose. "I know, there are many men in Saladin's army who would consider it a blessing to have a wife as lovely as you."

"And risk her soul. I think not, Lady Ariane. Najila is a Christian now. Your tempting will come to no avail."

The vision of freedom turned to ash in Ariane's mind. Her rising hope fell and rolled deep in the pit of her stomach at the sound of the butcher's voice.

Three

*He is in the way of life that keepeth instruction: but he that
refuseth reproof erreth.*
Proverbs 10:17

*T*HE BUTCHER STOOD BEFORE HER. THE CHAIN MAIL beneath his Christian tunic expanded the Templar's chest, giving the red cross a menacing appearance. A dark scowl furrowed his forehead and hardened his eyes. Even a cold-hearted Assassin would quake before the massive man swallowing up her doorway, but Ariane stood firm and hoped he did not see the shaking of her knees.

Her heart raced like a snared rabbit's when he rushed forward, grabbing the cloak from the top of the trunk. Quickly he wrapped the garment around her bare shoulders. His masculine hot breath swirled around her ear, and a searing warmth poured through her body. What kind of man was this who could mix melting fear with the flames of desire?

"Cover yourself, lady. If you choose to leave your chamber door open please remember your station. You are no longer in a heathen harem."

The icy ruthlessness of his words chilled the embers heating her body and incited her anger, fueling a deep courage she did not know existed.

Even though she had never exposed much of her body to a man, the monk's reprimand and brash attempt to preserve her modesty made her bold. Ariane shook the cloak from her shoulders and planted her hands on her hips.

"What do you know of my life before *your kind* saw fit to save me? More men have fondled me these past few weeks than in all the time I lived with the Muslims. What do you think of that, *holy man?*"

Picking up the cloak, he replaced the garment on her shoulders. The pressure of his large hands sent a spasm of panic through her body.

His gaze locked with hers. "Even though I find your words hard to believe, I must accept what you say, for I have no proof otherwise."

The condescending tone of his voice infuriated her. She stepped away from him, away from his warmth. Briefly, he reached for her, then dropped his hand to his side and gestured the other toward Najila. "Yet, I have witnessed your attempt to sway a Christian from her faith."

The young woman raced to his side with her head bowed and her hands folded. "Brother Julian, please know that I would never forsake my faith."

Ariane rolled her eyes. Najila should have been reared in a harem. Her sheepish ways would have been rewarded.

"Even if I left you behind in England?" he asked, raising a challenging eyebrow in Ariane's direction.

Ariane balled her hands. She longed to slap his smug face. Not only was this man a murderer, he was a spy as well. He listened to her conversation with Najila, then used the knowledge to instruct with fear. His ways were no different than those used by Muslim males. Women in any culture were just tools to be used and tormented.

Najila fell to her knees before him. "Please, do not jest because I entertained the lady's words. I know you would never purposely separate me from my family."

He curled a finger below Najila's chin raising her jaw. "One never knows what God will ask of him. We must always be prepared to accept His will, whatever that may be."

His will? Ariane wanted to laugh at the mockery. 'Twas not God's will the butcher cared about, but his own. He treated Najila as if she were one of his possessions, no better than a clay bowl or his sword.

Nay, not his sword. She remembered his face clearly when he had slain Raya. His eyes held a look of worship as he cleaned the bloody blade. A shiver skidded up her spine. Ariane forced herself to concentrate on the scene before her.

The butcher dropped Najila's chin as if his fingers could not stand to be soiled by the touch of a mere woman. "Arise, Najila. Much needs to be done."

Ariane winced at the adoration she saw in Najila's eyes. The maid might serve Ariane, but her true loyalty lay with the butcher. No one could be trusted. Freedom would be achieved by wit alone.

Alone. Always alone.

For as long as she could remember, her survival depended on her intelligence. After Raya no one cared. Until she met Isam. When the Christians crushed his light, they infused her with determination. No longer would she let others control her life. Muslim or Christian.

The butcher smiled at Najila. The tender scene made Ariane gag. Clearing her throat, she folded her arms across her chest. "If I may interrupt your lesson. I do not need or want a maid. Surely you can benefit from Najila's services much more than I."

His head snapped up and his gaze pierced Ariane. "Your implication is vulgar and a sin. You should beg God's forgiveness for such an evil suggestion."

The muscles in his jaw tightened. So the butcher could be reached. Perhaps she could crush him with his own lust.

Ariane batted her eyes in innocence. "What evil did I suggest?"

"Search your soul, my lady. I am sure you will be enlightened." He then turned and motioned to Najila. "See that a bath is brought for Lady Ariane."

Najila bowed and hurried to the door.

Ariane stiffened. She would not concede to his every whim like Najila. "Halt, Najila. I will not take a bath."

An eyebrow lifted on the butcher's handsome face. "You prefer to smell like camel waste?"

Ariane sniffed slightly, hoping the butcher did not see. Yea, she did smell. A bath would be pure pleasure, but if the butcher wanted her clean, she would remain dirty. Raising her chin, she smiled and strutted around him, flipping her matted hair over her shoulder. "Yea, I prefer the smell of animals to any water offered by a Christian murderer."

"Your preference matters not. Your stench is offensive. You will bathe." His cheek twitched. He flexed his hand, then gripped his sword. A sword with a blue stone in its hilt.

Her memory flashed. *A bluestone sword crashed downward on Raya's head.* She fought back the fear that told her to submit. She could defeat this pious fool at his own game. He was a man; men were ruled by lust.

She squared her shoulders and swayed provocatively in front of him. "Since when does a Christian care about the odor of another? Most, I wager, have not stepped in a pool of water, ever."

His knuckles turned white about the sword hilt. "Many believe bathing is a vain act, therefore a sin."

Her heart hammered against her ribs. She swallowed hard. "Ah, that explains why *you* are so clean."

He dragged in his breath and let it out slowly. She was sure his calm shell was cracking. His voice was harsh. "I, however, *know* that our bodies are God's temples. I believe God would prefer to dwell in a clean body than a dirty one."

Ariane tapped her finger on her chin, praying it did not tremble. She mustered her courage and smiled sweetly at him. "Hmm, is not the cleanliness of the soul what pleases God?"

His blue eyes grew stormy. She watched the muscles in his face contract until his looks hardened like granite. She knew she had pushed too far; the murderer would strike her now. Ariane closed her eyes, drew up her shoulders, held her breath, and waited.

The time dragged. If he did not hit her soon she would pass out from the lack of air. She peeked out of one eye. His one hand still clasped the hilt of his sword. The other remained fisted at his side. His eyes were raised to the ceiling.

Julian's blood pulsed like lava through his body. Eyes heavenward, he prayed, *Dear Lord, give me patience and strength.* He knew not how she managed to rake his nerves raw. She tore at his strength and bled his patience like an open wound.

Even as he prayed, the vision of her standing in her shift filtered into his meditation. When had he become so undisciplined? When had the thought of any woman interfered with his talks with God? Perhaps she was a witch. 'Twould explain his wayward thoughts.

He straightened his shoulders and raised his chin higher. *Heavenly Father, shield me from the evil with which this woman tempts me.*

"What do you see up there?"

Her question startled him. He dropped his gaze to meet hers. She watched him. His breath shook. How dare she interfere with his prayers? He wanted to grab her and shake her until he conquered the temptation to run his hands over her slender shoulders.

Instead he did the next best thing. He returned to the subject. "My lady, you will take a bath."

She turned and gazed out the window. "I cannot bear to take a bath and then wear those bug-infested garments. I do not care if my smell…offends thee."

The lady placed her hands on the windowsill, and leaned slightly forward. She stood on her toes and he noticed the desirable arch of her foot, the delicate turn of her ankle. A youthful warmth sped through his body, pounding his heart, and burning his stomach. What spell did she weave that a simple raise of her heel could resurrect pubescent emotions vanquished with hours of prayer and self-flagellation? Oh, to grip that penitent whip and slash the evil thoughts from his soul.

He breathed deeply and reminded himself the lady before him was part of God's test.

She looked left, then right, then left again. Rapidly she began tapping her finger on the windowsill. She spun about and gave a breathtaking smile that almost brought Julian to his knees.

A very dramatic sigh left her lips. "I can see you will not be swayed. I am tired of fighting. Very well then, I shall bathe."

Julian looked past her at the dark clouds forming in the rumbling sky. Had she taken them as an omen to obey him? Nay, she would not give in that easily. He tipped his head and sharpened his gaze on the lady. What mischief was she up to now?

She dropped her chin to her chest. "The dirt bothers me too. I would love to stay filthy to affront your senses, but I cannot bear the mud and the stench any longer."

"Look at me." He wanted to see the hellfire in her eyes, so that he would not forget who owned her soul.

She ignored his command, staring at the floor instead. No doubt planning another evil deed.

He lowered his voice, digging deep within to maintain his calm. "Lady Ariane, what of your clothes?"

Slowly she raised her head, but refused to look at him. She shrugged. "I will not lie. I wish I had others, but what choice have I?"

Though her words sounded sincere, something inside him said this was all a ruse. Again he looked past her toward the window. A bolt of lightning snaked across the sky. If he were in her position, what would he do? He tried to hide his smile. The lady was quite cunning.

His confidence returning, he answered, "None. Najila, see to Lady Ariane's bath."

The girl rushed from the room, but he did not follow. Ariane meant to escape. He knew it, as surely as he knew his Lord had died for mankind's sins. She believed she could dupe him with charm and witchery. 'Twas time he showed her who held the power and the upper hand. He crossed his arms, widened his stance and kept up his scrutiny. If it was a game of wits she wanted then he would gladly play.

Beads of sweat formed on her forehead. She shifted her stance. "Is there something else you wanted?"

"Yea, my lady, I would have your word that you will not try to escape if I leave this room."

She laughed. "Pray tell, how could I escape with two burly guards at my door?"

He took a patient breath. "Lady, your word or—"

"Or what? You will stay to watch me bathe?"

He remained silent. He had her now. The sparks of shock started in her eyes and shot a blush to her cheeks.

"You filthy pig. You are no pious monk, but a lusty brute." She turned her back on him. "Like every other Christian."

Had some of Richard's men harmed her? For some reason, the thought of any man ravishing Ariane soured his stomach and boiled his blood. He moved until her shoulders were within reach. "Have you been harmed?"

She turned to face him, her eyes cold and empty. "Nay. No one would harm me because of your king."

Relieved beyond measure, Julian's composure returned and he nodded. Yet he could do naught but stare. Could a witch be a fragile female as well?

She shuddered. He reached out wanting to comfort, to chase the chill away. His fingertips brushed her shoulders lightly.

Her eyes flooded with fear. She jumped back and rubbed her shoulder as if he had scratched her with a thorny rose.

"If I give you my word, do you promise to leave?" she asked.

Julian dropped his hand. So the lady witch was repelled by his touch. She did not feel the warmth that burned in his fingertips every time his skin met hers. She felt hate where he felt...he knew not what he felt. She had turned his inside into a torrential mess. Better he focus on her hate.

"Aye, I said so," he clipped. "I will hold you to your honor."

She looked him straight in the eye and answered rapidly, "You have my word."

She lied.

Aye, she lied badly; he saw it in her cunning eyes. Knowing she was a poor liar gave him great satisfaction. If she had a conscience she could be saved, but if he confronted her now she would deny it and drop deeper into sin. "Very well, I shall leave you to your privacy."

Julian strode through the corridor and down the stairs which lead to the hall. He ignored those who greeted him and raced straight for the noisy courtyard. As he expected, no one stood guard by Lady Ariane's window. Instead the guards, knights, and servants raced about trying to complete their tasks before the storm's fury poured upon them. He looked toward Ariane's window. Her bedding being lowered over the window ledge stood out against the black clouds. So be it. Let her education begin.

Pushing through the pandemonium, he headed to the compound gate. She would crawl down her makeshift rope to the roof below. Then she would make her way across the roof to the courtyard wall. Julian stopped and lounged against the wall near the spot where she should appear. She would soon learn that good triumphs over evil, truth over falsehood, the spirit over the flesh.

The first spatter of rain fell from the sky and slid down Julian's cheek as he saw her dainty feet and slim legs dangling from the courtyard wall. He gave a heavy sigh, unfolded his arms, then seized one wayward foot and slid his thumb along the arch. He fought against the heat one little foot created and concentrated on catching the feathery Lady Ariane. Fire swept through his flesh and singed his spirit when he felt the softness of her body against his arm.

"Ahhii," she shouted. Her eyes grew wide and she lashed out at him like a hellcat. She punched and scratched at his face and chest while her legs flailed wildly. "Put me down, you brute."

Nothing would give him more pleasure than to drop her to the ground. He thanked God his chain mail saved him. "Lady, cease thy thrashing."

"I will not. I'll beat your overgrown body until it resembles a mashed pomegranate!"

A rumble of thunder shook the ground. The air whirled about them. Her sweet breath filled his lungs and sought his heart. As if scorched, he dropped the temptress to her feet. Like the flash of light above, she bolted down the street.

Raw rage rushed through his body. He stared at her fleeing back. In a run, he reached Ariane's side within seconds. He grabbed her shoulder and the drab cloak slid away, revealing the scanty shift.

Obviously, the desire to flee was so great that she took no time to dress. Trying to replace the cloak, his fingers grazed the soft flesh of her shoulder. An odd current tingled up his arm. Quickly he removed his fingers from the tempting flesh and circled his hands about the siren's wrists.

"Your evil is powerless against me, witch. You cannot escape."

She paled; her green eyes grew wide and he marveled at their beauty. *The color rivals the emerald in Solomon's cross.* The thought thundered and shook his soul. How could he compare a woman's eyes to a precious holy relic? What devilish power did she use on him?

The wind shifted direction; cool air mixed with the warm. The rain came heavy and hard, pelting the ground, his back, her fiery hair, and the lids above her emerald eyes. He raised his gaze heavenward and thanked his Lord for the chilling effect.

A tug against his hands heated the chill. He looked down at Ariane.

Her brows drew together in determination. "Let go of me. I'd rather *die* than go anywhere with you."

"Do not tempt me, lady. God did not consider thee when he gave Moses the fifth commandment." Julian picked her up and hefted her over his shoulder.

"How dare you. Put me down, ox," she shouted. "I have had enough of your Christian brutality!"

She hammered his back, kicking her legs madly. Years of discipline were about to be shattered.

Julian tightened his grip on her legs and turned his head away from the tempting flesh struggling on his shoulder. He must be strong. "Cease this folly. Your pummeling has no more effect on me than a pesky beetle crawling about. You harm yourself. There is no escape."

"Put me down and I will show you who is the stronger. You may have strength in your body, but your mind is weak. I pray to Allah that lightning strikes thee in thy stupid head."

Julian ground his teeth. Enough of this torture—mental and physical. With strong strides he made his way back to the Templar compound. His feet slapped the muddy ground as he entered the gate. The hard rain pounded his face, clearing his mind.

In the courtyard, she grabbed the corner of a cart laden with cooking utensils. A loud crack on the back of his head sent his mind spinning. Pieces of pottery flew in every direction. His hold on her legs broke briefly. Pain shot through his cheek where a wayward heel struck him in the face. Like a vise, he clamped her riotous legs.

Heaven help him! He suffered more injuries from this hellion than he acquired in all the years he fought the infidels. Before she could assault him with another pot, Julian jerked forward, forcing her to release the cart.

"Ow! Christian brute. I'm bleeding! There is a huge gash in my finger."

He hesitated briefly. Guilt tempered his anger. He had no desire to hurt her. *Nay, 'twas a lie.* She should be forced to feel the raw pain that ripped away his control.

"Put me down. The blood is great. 'Tis flowing all over your white tunic."

Aye, he should stop and check the wound. But if he placed her on her feet, would she try to flee again? The rain gave no signs of letting up. What if she did manage to get away from him? If the cut was bad, she wouldn't last long. Many times he had seen soldiers die from small wounds that festered. He quickened his pace.

"Go ahead, ignore me, butcher. What is one more dead female to you? Yea, you probably relish the thought of my death. Then you would be free to stay with your murdering king."

Her taunts bordered on hysteria. His lack of control had put the lady's life in danger. Crossing the threshold to the hall, he ran straight into Brother Andrew. "Quick, find Brother Stephen. Bring him to Lady Ariane's chamber; his healing skills are needed. Also fetch my robe." With a quick nod, Andrew took off across the hall.

Julian ran down the corridor and took the stairs two at a time. Upon entering Ariane's chamber, he spotted Najila by a tub of steaming water. "Bring me a damp cloth."

Najila hurried to her task. Gently, Julian placed Ariane on her feet, holding her about the waist lest she faint from the loss of blood. "Show me the wound," he said softly.

She held out her hand displaying a tiny red scrape on her finger. In her delirium she must have given him the wrong hand. Julian reached for the other expecting to find a gaping, bloody wound. The hand was cool, her skin unmarred. He looked at her face; she gave him a faint wicked smile.

Striving for a calm that no longer existed, he said, "This is the life-threatening injury?"

"Aye." She laughed.

His blood pulsed, white-hot. In one fell swoop, Julian lifted the witch in his arms and dumped her into the tub.

"Ahhii," she sputtered. "Monstrous pig. I will cut your heart out for this. I will—"

"You will bathe. I order it. If you try to escape again I will chain you to my belt!"

She tried to stand up, but the heavy cloak twisted about her legs causing her to stumble and slip back into the tub. Water flew in every direction. Tearing the cape from her body, she wiped the dripping water from her face. She rose and hurled the cloak at Julian's feet.

"I hate you...you stinking son of a Christian dog!"

He raised his eyes. *Dear God, no more temptation. I beg thee.*

Just then Brother Stephen entered the room carrying his healing tools with Andrew close behind, Julian's robe draped over his arms. Julian greeted the pair by snatching the robe from Andrew's hand. "After you are finished bathing, you will wear this." He tossed the garment near the tub.

"I will not—"

"Silence, lady! You will do as you are told." Julian turned to Andrew and said, "You will bury the filthy garments the lady now wears. Is that understood?"

Andrew opened his mouth then snapped his jaw shut and nodded.

Julian turned back to Ariane. "I have business to attend to in the city. Do not think to escape again. Your window will be heavily guarded, and if you do not cooperate, Brother Andrew will watch you bathe." God forgive him, but he took great pleasure in watching her cheeks turn scarlet.

Andrew rushed forward. "Brother Julian, you cannot mean—"

Julian raised his hand. "The master has given me charge over the lady. If you cannot do what I ask then I shall find someone who can. I need only knights I can trust on this journey. Are you trustworthy?"

Andrew stared at him for a moment, then answered stiffly, "Aye, I am. I shall do as you order."

Julian turned to Brother Stephen. "I was mistaken. Your talent is not needed here."

Brother Stephen did not move, but stared at Julian as if a

strange boil had festered on his face. Najila, who stood near the tub, a dripping cloth in her hand, gawked also as if he, not Lady Ariane, were the problem.

Without another word, Julian pushed between the two knights blocking his way to the door. Upon entering the hallway he heard Andrew say, "Never have I seen Brother Julian lose his temper as he has today."

Julian squeezed the hilt of his sword and gritted his teeth. Andrew spoke the truth.

Four

I lift up mine eyes unto the hills, from whence cometh my help.
Psalm 121:1

HERE HAD BEEN HOTTER SUMMER NIGHTS THAN this; Julian just could not remember when. His body itched with sweat as he tossed about on his pallet. The dark dormitory echoed with the shallow breaths and thunderous rumbles of the slumbering Templars.

A rosary lay heavy and damp in his palm from hours of petition. And still he found no peace. He had lost his temper today in a way he never had before, at least not since his father's death over ten years ago.

The hot stifling air closed in about him. He threw off his cover and reached for a dry linen shirt and braise. He bypassed the tunic marked with Christ's cross and donned a plain brown garment of servitude. Then he reached for his large broadsword and belted it securely around his waist. With deft fingers he wrapped the rosary about the hilt of his sword, making a mockery of his monkish appearance.

He crept from the dormitory through the great marble hall into the sweet jasmine scented courtyard. Striding past the ancient clay well which stood in the center of the yard, he pushed open the heavy wooden gate that gave way to the rest of Tyre.

During the early morning hours only a few oil lamps burned in homes where eastern Muslim and western Christian influences complimented each other in extraordinary harmony. Making his way through the city streets where St. Paul once preached, he left the sleeping city and walked until the nova-filled sky glittered above and a warm, night breeze cradled about him. The unbearable weight of confusion brought him to his knees. He dug his hands into the sandy earth and cried the words Christ used in Gethsemane, *"O my Father, if it be possible, let this cup pass from me."*

More than anything Julian wanted to stay in the Holy Land. Here he trod the ground where Christ once stood, worshipped on the hills where his Lord taught. Here he was close to God. Here he struggled to destroy the dark evil which aimed to reduce Christ's death and resurrection to a myth. Here he knew he served the Lord.

In England, he would be just another Gentile saved by grace. Julian wanted to show God his gratitude for saving his soul, in spite of his past, by fighting the infidels and earning his place in heaven. But in England he would be useless. His past would loom before him for as long as he drew breath. Had that not happened when he visited his sister, Breanna, five years ago? His past sins were ever before him.

He folded his hands in the sand and dropped his head to rest upon them. Surely God had denied him peace for a good reason—to bring Jerusalem back into Christian hands. King Richard was here; the freedom of Jerusalem would be achieved within the year. And he, Julian, would be in England.

Surely this was not what God commanded. With sweat dripping from his brow, he raised his head to the heavens. *"Lord, this cannot be your will. Remove this cup, nevertheless not as I will, but as thou wilt."*

He searched the heavens and waited...and waited. No answer came. The sky became lighter, the stars began to fade. Still no answer enlightened him.

In despair he shouted, "Why?"

A faint star crossed the sky, behind a small hill not far from where he prayed.

Julian stared at the spot as if an answer would rise from there. The early sun's rays began to fill the sky. Suddenly, a small form came over the hill. Julian rubbed his eyes as the figure came closer; a hooded traveler. As the figure approached he dropped his hood and raised his hand in greeting.

Julian came to his feet, his hand falling to his sword. 'Twas a well-known fact that many Saracens had greeted pilgrims in friendship before they slaughtered them like sheep. Though this man hobbled using a large staff to support what seemed to be a frail frame, Julian would not let his guard down. Women, children, and old men had been known to twist a knife in a Crusader's belly. Here in the Holy Land one never knew who his enemy might be.

"Peace be with you," the gray-haired man said.

Julian gave a curt nod and took a step back as the old man sat on a nearby boulder to catch his breath.

The man removed a small bag from his shoulder and opened it; Julian drew his sword. The elder man cocked an eyebrow and stilled his hand. "Do Templars make a habit of killing the weak and helpless?"

Julian lowered his sword slightly, but did not lower his guard. "Many so-called weak and helpless have been strong and powerful when a man's back is turned."

"You have nothing to fear from me. I seek only to find my wineskin to quench my parched throat." The old man held out the sack to Julian. "Perhaps you would like to search for the object I require?"

"Nay, empty the bag on the ground. Often I have seen Saracens slip deadly serpents into their sacks in hope that one greedy Crusader will meet his death."

The man dumped the contents of the bag onto the ground. "But surely there is no greed among the Templars?"

Julian knew a comment laced with sarcasm when he heard it, but he could not contradict the words. Many of his Templar brothers had sworn loyalty to The Order in hopes of becoming rich men from the booty taken from the infidels. In some ways

The Order had become a mockery. Some monks had wives conveniently forgotten back home. Julian winced. Even Brother Guy practiced weekly debauchery, and Julian would call Brother Guy a friend if God allowed him to have one.

"Ah, your silence gives way to the truth of the matter." The old man waved his hand to the contents on the ground. "Do you see any serpents?"

Only two things lay in the dirt before Julian, a wineskin and a loaf of unleavened bread. Julian still refused to sheath his sword; instead he lowered the tip to the ground and rested his hands on top of the jeweled hilt. "You travel light old man."

"Aye, much lighter than you, Templar."

"Thrice you have called me a Templar, what makes you think such? I could be a humble pilgrim such as you."

The old man's eyes swept Julian's form. "Aye, you wear nothing but a plain robe such as mine, but only a Templar would carry a sword such as that." The man gestured toward the skin on the ground. "May I?"

Julian frowned and nodded. "I could just be another Crusader taking a few hours rest and solitude before today's trials begin."

The old man held the skin upward and gave it a slight squeeze. Wine washed over his lips. He sighed and wiped his mouth with the back of his sleeve. A few droplets of wine glistened on his white beard. "Aye, you could be, but you are not. Crusaders wear their hair short and cropped, most have beards such as mine."

"Templars wear the same, old man—"

"And you have neither. Aye, your point is well taken. Your hair flows like golden shafts of wheat about your shoulders and you scrap your face daily like the heathen do. A penance of some sort? I wonder."

Julian tensed his grip around the blue jewel in the hilt of his sword. How could this man have ascertained the truth? He began to shave his face after his father's death, hoping the small act of penance would blot out some of the sin

Julian bore when his father died. Yet none but God knew the reason why he performed the act daily, nor would he discuss it with this stranger. "Do you have business in Tyre?"

The old man rubbed his beard and his dark gaze seemed almost to pierce Julian's soul. "Nay, I am on a journey, much as you shall soon be."

This was highly irregular; how could this man know about his journey? Perhaps he had been sent by Baldwin to prove Julian was of faulty character, or perhaps King Richard had sent him to make sure Julian fulfilled his duty. Surely Master de Sablé would not send such a man?

The old man bent down and picked up his bread. "Will you break your fast with me?"

"Nay, I do not eat before morning prayers."

"But you have been praying all night."

This man's knowledge shook Julian's control. How could he know such a thing unless the man saw him on his knees before Julian noticed him? Surely that had to be the answer. "I fast twice weekly and today is a day of fasting."

The old man took a bite of his bread. "And why do you do this?"

Julian narrowed his eyes. Any good Christian would know why he would fast. "Because it is pleasing to God."

"Is it? I wonder."

This man could only be an infidel to say such a thing. Julian shifted the sword in his right hand preparing to strike if necessary. "Wonder what?" Julian snapped.

The man took another bite, seemingly unfazed by Julian's threatening stance. "If you do it for God or for yourself."

'Twas almost certain this man was an unbeliever, but was he just a lost soul or a spy for Saladin's army? "You are bold, old man. All Christians do penance to God. Do you believe in God?"

The stranger took another swallow of wine then leveled Julian with his gaze. "Aye, there is a God. Rest easy, Julian, I have not come to judge your faithfulness."

A slap across the face could not have left Julian more

senseless than the words this man uttered. "How do you know my name?"

The man removed his sandals and began to massage his feet. "The hair, the face, the blue stone in the sword—you are Julian de Maury, the Avenging Angel. Any man with a keen eye would know who you are. You make yourself different to stand out. You tell yourself it is God's will, but I think you set yourself apart in hopes of being a target for an early death. Rest easy, I am not one of Saladin's minions. Sit, have some bread and wine. I think God would like you to start your journey with a full belly."

Totally disarmed by this man's words, Julian sheathed his sword and sat. If this man was an enemy, then he was a worthy adversary, and for some strange reason Julian knew that if this man had come to kill him, he would be already dead. He thought of the man's words. *Was all this for God or himself?* Such a question had pricked into his consciousness before.

"Who are you, old man?"

"Who I am is of little importance. Let us discuss that which is of grave importance, your journey." The stranger offered Julian a hunk of bread. "Here, take and eat."

Without thought to his fast, Julian took the bread. "I cannot speak of my journey."

"I do not wish to know the particulars of it—only why you fret so."

Julian bowed his head and aimlessly drew with his finger in the dirt. "The journey takes me away from the Holy City, which will soon be ours again."

The old man offered Julian a drink. "Now I understand. Perhaps God does not want King Richard to free Jerusalem. Perhaps this journey you are about to begin will enlighten your mind and turn you from the man you are today to the man God wants you to be. Answers come to those who are patient."

Julian took the wine. *Patience!* A skill he struggled with daily.

Understanding energized his body. God had ordained this journey to teach him patience. The fight would be his if he completed this simple task. He would spend this journey in reflection. Hours of prayer would strengthen him for battle. Once in England, he would deposit the girl with an order of holy sisters and be back in the Holy Land before the king purged Jerusalem of the evil Saladin.

Julian handed the skin back to the old man without taking a drink. With renewed strength and vigor he rose to his feet. "My thanks, sir. Our talk has been an answer to my prayer."

"Be careful Julian, your thoughts could still be clouded. Take a drink, it may clear your mind."

"Nay, sir, my mind has never been brighter. I must return to the city. I know what God wishes."

"Do you?"

"Aye, many thanks, stranger." Julian offered his hand, but the old man waved off.

"Do not thank me until you have learned what is in store for you. Go in peace, Julian, and remember to listen to your heart."

Julian walked a few paces toward the city. "I shall. Come walk with me into the city. There are those I would like you to meet."

He turned back to beckon, but the old man and his bag were gone. Julian walked up to the crest of the small hill and yet the man was nowhere to be seen. The man had disappeared just as mysteriously as he had appeared.

Julian's spine tingled. Did he speak to the man in Arabic, English or the Frank's tongue? For a brief moment he thought he used all languages, even Latin.

Julian shook his head. No matter, his mission was clear. The sun had just started its ascent in the sky. Perhaps he had not missed matins. Patience! He headed toward the city, his duty firm in his mind.

49

"This is the vessel we are to take?" Ariane stared at the large *dromon* before her.

"Aye, Lady. The master insists we use the *Knights' Cross*. 'Tis large enough to insure your comfort," Andrew answered.

Ariane cast a sidelong glance at the young knight. *Comfort indeed.* Once before she had seen a vessel this size, King Richard arrived in Acre in such a massive ship, and with him came a great army. Faithful Isam had counted seventy knights on horseback disembark that ship, along with a gaggle of soldiers and servants.

Why would a great ship be used to transport one female? The warm humid air left by a summer's storm squeezed her lungs when she spied hordes of food and baskets brimming with fine silks and linens being loaded into the hold of the ship. Servants pushed large trunks across the pier, no doubt loaded with jewels and gold stolen from the Muslim faithful. Why, even a set of fine Arabian horses was being ushered onto the ship.

Christian monsters! Not only did they rape Muslim women, but they raped the land as well. Why had Allah turned his back on his people? Why had Allah deserted her?

Because you never were a true believer.

She could recite Mohammed's revelation by rote, but she never understood the fervor to die for the Muslim faith.

She watched two men on the dock drop one of the heavy chests. The Christians died for possessions and dominance. That she could understand. Perhaps that is why Allah put her in the hands of those who killed for profit, because her own soul was empty.

Ariane dismissed the abhorrent thought by concentrating on the anger brewing in her belly. Her gaze drifted up the two large masts that dominated the ship. She blinked against the brilliant sun. A curse upon the bright orb that chased the storm away.

The weather worked against her. Ariane had hoped it would rain for days, delaying their departure, giving her time to escape. Yesterday during her bath the storm had raged, battering the buildings without mercy. She thanked Allah every time thunder shook the earth. She had barely stepped from her bath when the winds ceased, the clouds broke, and the sun shone brightly through her window. Despair flooded her body. Even the weather had done the butcher's bidding. 'Twas all his fault. By now she could have been halfway to Halimah's had the butcher not interfered. He had outsmarted her, read her thoughts like a Bedouin reads the stars.

Andrew laid a gentle hand on Ariane's shoulder. "Come, my lady. Brother Julian does not wish to tarry longer."

Her breath became short; a sickening ache damped her previous anger. The wind rushing through the palm trees swallowed up the noise on the busy dock. Ariane turned slightly, to drink in the sights of her homeland for the last time.

Two merchants haggled over a basket of olives, a young girl ran past, sprays of sand rising from her heels. A large lump formed in Ariane's throat when she raised her gaze to the hills behind the flat roofs. Never would she forget the comfort of eastern rays warming her cheeks or the luxury of soft Arabian silks brushing her legs. Never would she forget the nomad's gentle song or the camel's stubborn cry. Never would she forget Isam or Raya.

Andrew nudged her shoulder trying to usher her toward the boat. "Come, we have made comfortable arrangements for you. Your maid is already below deck."

She mutely followed until the meaning of his words took their full impact—*below deck!*

"Nay! I will not go below! Better to die here and now than to be dragged into a dark smelly hole." She wiggled her arm free from Andrew's hand and turned to run. Unfortunately, two large Templars blocked her escape.

Andrew grabbed her forearm and tugged her toward the ship. "My lady, the hold is not so smelly and one becomes accustomed to the darkness."

"Not I. I have spent too many nights in stinking ships and hellish holes to ever enter one willingly."

She kicked Andrew in the shin, and shoved her fist into his belly. The two infernal lackeys grabbed her arms stretching them from her body trying to dance away from her riotous kicks.

Red-faced, clutching his stomach, Andrew stumbled before her. "P-p-please, my lady, you must go below. Brother Julian has ordered it."

Brother Julian has ordered. Of course, *he* controlled everyone. Even this simpleton before her. "Nay. Tell brother butcher I intend to stay here. And tell these Christian backsides to unhand me."

Andrew's face twisted with pain as he tried to straighten his back. He stretched his neck and tried to puff out his chest like a ferocious lion, but instead he resembled a long-necked camel. "We sail shortly. You must go below deck, now!"

She all but laughed at the ruby tinge of his cheeks. The young Christian pup could not scare a mouse. In fact, she suspected he would run for the nearest stool if a small creature scurried between his feet.

"I will stay here," she snapped back. "I have sailed with Abi Bin's family to Crete many times. The air below is always foul and the corners are filled with long-tailed vermin." She stamped her foot and tried to twist free from the Templars' grasp. "I will not be trapped below."

Andrew drew a thin hand through his hair. "Th-this time will be different. Your maid is making comfortable quarters; she is arranging your things right now."

The coarse robe she wore itched her neck and scratched her arms. "*Things?* I have no things, except the rough robe on my back." A mild breeze ruffled the robe, disturbing the butcher's male scent buried within the folds.

He is here even when he is not.

She tried to concentrate on how pungent the odor was, but his smell sent warmth through her body that she did not desire. Ariane frowned. "Nay, I do not own this sack either. Make these brutes release me now. Is this how you treat ladies in your barbarous country?"

Andrew's face flamed. His Adam's apple bobbed wildly in his throat.

Good. The knave should feel foolish. She was in control, not Andrew, not the butcher. She must keep the upper hand.

Another knight casually strolled up to Brother Andrew's side, and draped a forearm on the younger knight's shoulder. His black hair glinted in the sun, and his dark eyes shined with mischief. A lazy smile crossed his lips, displaying a set of pearly teeth.

"What is this, Brother Andrew? Having trouble with the lady?" the dark knight asked in English.

Andrew shrugged the man's arm off his shoulder. "Nothing I cannot handle."

The knight threw back his head and laughed. "Aye, Andrew, you always know how to handle the ladies."

Andrew's lips thinned. "This is not your problem, Guy."

The cur, called Guy, ignored Andrew's remark and swept his gaze over Ariane's face and body like she was a tasty delicacy. "So, this is Richard's package. If her body is anything like her face, then Lord de Craon is a very lucky man."

Package indeed. Who was this arrogant swine? Ariane itched to slap his face, but doing so would expose her knowledge of his language, and the pig was not worth losing such a valuable weapon.

Andrew straightened his shoulders. "Brother Guy, I see no need to insult the lady."

"Come now, Andrew, she knows not our tongue." Guy smiled at her and leaned forward. "If she wears a scowl, it is because you do not *know* how to handle a woman. Not because of anything I have said."

Ariane deepened her frown, mustering her most hate-filled look. He backed away.

"Ah, see, Guy, your charm does not work on her," Andrew said.

"Perhaps, or perhaps it is your bungling about that has raised her wrath," Guy answered briskly.

Andrew lowered his chin to his chest and did not respond. Ariane wanted to shake him. Why did he not defend himself? He was like the new girls that entered Abi Bin's harem—meek and weak. She closed her mind to the compassion.

"Release the lady," Guy ordered.

Immediately the lackeys dropped her arms. She sagged and rubbed her wrists as the blood rushed to her hands. Guy gave her a brilliant smile. Bah! Did he think she would be grateful? The fool was as transparent as a piece of glass.

Guy addressed her in smooth Arabic. "Lady Ariane, I am Brother Guy Ashton, and if there is anything I can assist you with feel free to ask."

"I would like assistance away from this dock," she answered sharply.

He cleared his throat and crossed his arms. "My lady, you know that is not possible."

She raised her chin and mimicked him by folding her arms. "Then I shall stand here."

"My lady," Guy said. "We shall set sail soon and you must board."

"Why?"

"See," Andrew said in English. "She is very determined."

"She is stubborn," Guy responded in the same language. "No doubt because you started this encounter in the wrong manner. Watch, and learn."

Ariane fumed. What a rude insolent dolt. He was almost as obnoxious as the butcher, but no one was as conceited as he.

"Dear lady, I think only of your health. I know this has been a weary ordeal, and I am sure a good rest will help preserve your flawless beauty." His Arab words were thick and sultry and had absolutely no effect on her.

He gave a crooked smile when Ariane's disapproving gaze roamed over his body. "Nay, I choose to stay here. I do not wish to be in close quarters with homely Christians."

Guy threw back his shoulders and breathed deeply, he

looked at Brother Andrew and then back at her. "Not all Christians look like Brother Andrew."

Oh, this one loves himself. Again she allowed her gaze to travel slowly over his body. "I spoke not of Brother Andrew."

Her comment did not have the desired effect. A slight smile eased onto Guy's face as if he was enjoying the banter. "Lady, you have no choice. 'Tis time to leave."

"Please, Lady Ariane, allow me to escort you," Andrew added shyly.

"Hush, Andrew, her unwillingness is your doing," Guy reprimanded in English. "Let me take care this."

Andrew shifted from foot to foot; he opened his mouth, but no words came out. Then he snapped his jaw shut and looked away. Why did he not stand up to this hound?

The look in Andrew's eyes was similar to that of the young harem girls; trusting, honest, unspoiled by position and power. She gritted her teeth. His kind was always her downfall. How many times had she gone to Abi Bin's punishment hole defending and protecting the innocent? She could hardly suppress the urge to defend this young knight.

Allah save her from her own soft heartedness! Andrew was none of her concern. She must concentrate on her hatred of all Christians. She must concentrate on her hate of Julian de Maury, the monster who wished to take her away from the only home she remembered. But when she looked into Brother Andrew's eyes...and then at the arrogance in Guy's face...

"Very well, Brother Andrew. I see you are determined. Lead on." Ariane almost bit her tongue as the words she wished to hold rolled from her lips. Covering her nose and mouth she added, "Let us hurry. The sheep dung smell of your friend is offensive."

A swarm of bees could have buzzed into Guy Ashton's gaping mouth. Andrew bowed slightly and smiled. He offered his hand to Ariane which she accepted.

Putting Guy in his place made her feet feel lighter. She

was in control. By the time they reached the next port she would stroll off this ship with every Templar's blessing. Be it using her charm or her wit, she would have her way.

Andrew opened the hatch to the hold. The heavy stench of past voyages twisted like a serpent through the air and slithered into her nose. Grabbing at her throat, she gasped for air. Her mind began to float, her heart thudded in her chest, what a fool she had been. To thwart Guy, she had stepped into her greatest fear.

"This way, my lady," Andrew pointed to a narrow ladder.

Ariane tried to yank her hand from Andrew's grasp. Her future would be blacker than this ship's belly if she remained on her present course. Yet Andrew's grasp was firm and she found herself being pulled down into the desolate hold, further into the darkness. Groping in the blackness was her reward for pitying this whelp. Her throat became tight. Yellow-eyed rats scurried and squeaked in every bleak shadow.

Memories of past voyages and the punishment hole seeped into her mind—dark, hungry days spent in chilling dampness. The vermin with their sharp teeth gnashing at her food. Her clothing. Her arms and legs. Anxiety prickled her skin. Grabbed at her lungs. This time they would forget her. She would rot in this tomb. Perhaps that had been the butcher's plan all along. To leave her in the darkness. Alone. Forgotten. Forever.

She spun about. Her heartbeat matched the thump of waves against the hull. She ran toward the ladder.

"My lady, where are you going?" Andrew shouted from the abyss.

"I cannot stay. Let me off." Her lungs burned. Pain split and shattered through her mind. She ran blindly. Through the veil of darkness. Unable to find her way. Alone. Lost. Forever.

Something circled her waist, squeezing breath from her body and Ariane cried out. Allah have mercy! Death came to crush her life.

Five

*He brought me forth also into a large place; he delivered
me, because he delighted in me.*
Psalm 18:19

*J*ULIAN QUICKLY SUBDUED THE SCRATCHING NAILS OF
Lady Ariane. The woman fought as if she were
possessed. His stomach rolled when he crushed her
shaking body to his chest and felt the pounding of her
heart. Her trembling told him this was more than just an
idle attempt to escape; this was flight brought on by dark
fear.

Brother Andrew appeared from the shadows, breathing
heavily. "She was following me, then suddenly bolted."

Giving Andrew a silencing reprimand, Julian eased his
hold to peer down at Ariane. "Lady, what ails you?"

"Let me go," she sobbed, renewing her struggle. "I
cannot stay here."

The boat jarred slightly against the dock. "Nay, we are
about leave."

She cried out. The shudder of her body tore at his heart
and he knew not what to do, but hold her tight.

"Please," she begged. "I cannot stay. There is no light."

His gut twisted. He glared at Andrew. "Seek out a
tallow." Her tears of terror spilled onto his tunic. "And be
quick about it."

Andrew brushed by him, and headed up the ladder. Julian
shifted Ariane's body in his arms to release one of his

57

sword-worn hands. Lightly he stroked her hair with trembling fingers. What past hell tormented her now?

"Hush, there is nothing to fear," he whispered in her ear. His lips quivered as they brushed against her luxuriant hair. "You are safe in my care."

"Nay, you shall kill me or lock me in this hellish hole," she cried as she wept.

Kill her? Lock her in a hellish hole? "Lady, I will not harm you."

She balled her fists then feebly let them slide down his chest. "You will. I have seen you kill before."

The events of the past weeks must have addled her mind, for never had he set eyes on her before yesterday.

The boat lurched again. She cried out, "I do not want to die."

Her raking sobs lanced his heart. "I have told you. Never shall I raise my hand against thee."

He placed his palm against her wet cheek, wishing he could draw the fright from her body. Not knowing how it happened, he found his cheek resting atop of her head, rubbing against her satiny hair. Thoughts of comfort mixed with a strange desire to protect her cloaked his mind.

Andrew returned with a candle in hand. His eyes widened when the light fell upon the tender scene of Lady Ariane wrapped in Julian's arms. The young knight coughed and dropped his gaze to the floor.

Andrew's embarrassment angered Julian. Surely 'twas obvious he only tried to calm the girl, nothing more. He straightened his shoulders and released Ariane, but she clung to his chest, desperate. He fumbled to dislodge her, but she wrapped her arms around his waist and gave a cry of distress. He was at loss. How could he compose the lady when his pulsed raced as if he was going into a holy battle? He raised his eyes in supplication, but the dark planks above him killed the petition on his lips. God truly had sent him into the bowels of hell.

"Raise the tallow so the lady can see there is nothing to fear," Julian snapped.

Andrew complied without a word. Julian placed his fist below her chin to raise her face to the light. The candle accentuated the tears glistening on her cheeks, accentuating her lovely lips. Julian let out a long breath. By all that he held holy, he ached to kiss her tears away.

Disgusted at his lustful thought, he curled his fingers around her upper arms and pried her from his body. "Lady Ariane, look about you. There is nothing to fear here."

She cast a woeful gaze around the hold. Her shoulders quaked. "'Tis dark and narrow. You will lock the door. I will be alone in the dark."

Aye, the hold was dark, but narrow? A *dormon* had the widest hold in all Christendom. She looked about, but did not see. The pit of his stomach went cold. He had seen the same look in soldiers who had lost their wits because of the horror of war. What monster had instilled such fear? Julian vowed to strike the man dead if he still drew breath. "There are no doors here, and I promise a light will always shine by your side," he said gently.

She began to twist in his grasp. "I want to go above. The walls are close; I cannot breathe."

Shouts from above and the sway of the boat told him they were underway. The sailors were securing the sails; Ariane would be in their way. If she saw the land slip away, he feared she might try to jump into the sea.

He could not let her go above. How did one calm a woman's fear? The sword, the scripture, he understood, but dealing with a woman was beyond him. Most of his life he had tried to avoid women and their erratic moods. The women back home had been possessed with fits of giggling whenever he came into their presence. All that had stopped when he became betrothed to Jane. Then the women wept for days, but their tears were not shed in vain for the marriage never took place. When he gave his life to God he expected them to rejoice. Instead they wept again. Aye, he knew little of women; most were like weeds squeezing the life out of their loved one.

He looked down at the delicate flower in his arms. "'Tis time to settle in for the journey."

"Let go of me. I'll not go in the hole again. 'Tis dark. The ladder is but a pace away." She twisted from his arms, and like an arrow, her hand found its mark across his face.

He winced. Delicate flower, bah! More like a flighty bird that swooped to and fro depending on her mood. First she clings and then she strikes.

Scooping her up in his arms, he headed for the stern of the ship. "Follow me, Andrew."

By the time he drew back the heavy curtain raised for Lady Ariane's privacy, her screams had reached magnitude proportions. Besides testing his faith, did God wish him to be deaf too?

Relief swept through him when he saw the area had been readied according to his instructions. Najila sat on the pallet nestled against the wooden hull. The other pallet had been placed closer to the curtain. A lamp filled with oil stood on a large trunk that separated the pallets, giving the area a warm glow. Julian had intended Ariane to have the pallet near the wall, but given her fear of close dark places, he almost fell to his knees praising Najila's choice of selecting the more private bed.

He looked at the thrashing form in his arms. "See, my lady, a light shines brightly so there is naught to fear."

She stopped her struggle and glanced about. Suddenly her fist raced forward and smashed him in the nose. 'Twas as if an ax had split open his face. Pain curled around his cheeks and thundered through his head. He stumbled forward. Fearing he would drop Ariane, he rounded his shoulders to cradle her more securely. Like a giant oak, his body crashed against the floor.

When the ringing in his ears stopped, his gaze focused on two beautiful emeralds sparkling with innocence. A warm flush penetrated his body at the feel of the lady lying atop him. If he but lifted his head, her lips would join his. Something warned him a kiss from her lips would not be like those he received from Jane or other females who boldly tried to give him their affections.

Julian closed his eyes and inhaled her sultry desert scent. He swore he heard the devil laughing at his dangerous and damnable predicament.

His eyes flew open as her body seemed to soften. A tiny smile twisted the corners of her lips. Was this all a cunning act? Did she try to deceive him again? Obviously her fear of dark, close places had disappeared. Now he prayed to God her malady would return.

Julian grabbed her shoulders and shoved her off his body, then rolled to his feet. Najila's gaping and the scarlet color dotting Andrew's cheeks compounded the awkward situation. Quickly he rearranged his tunic.

"Brother Andrew, remain here until Lady Ariane is reconciled to her situation," Julian said.

"Oh nay, do not leave me," Ariane cried. She rose to her knees, lurched forward wrapped her arms about Julian's thighs.

Furious at the intimate gesture, Julian unwrapped Ariane from his body and jerked her to her feet. He would not fall for her evil tricks. When he looked at her he expected to see her sneaky smile, but instead horror framed her face. Once again she had slipped back into her own personal hell. This time he knew no soothing or persuading would conquer the demon who tortured her.

Julian lifted Ariane into his arms and headed for the ladder. "Andrew, bring the trunk to the captain's quarters. Najila, bring your pallet."

After he had arrived in the Holy Land, Brother Randall had assumed command of the *Knight's Cross*. Since Master de Sablé had given command back to Julian, Brother Randall would have to understand the lady needed his quarters. Brother Randall could use the modest adjacent room, the compartment offered to Julian and he would sleep with Guy and Andrew in the hull.

By the time Julian reached the ladder, Ariane had clasped cold clammy arms about his neck and pressed her face deeply in his shoulder. No longer did she cry, but neither did she respond to his voice. Circling one arm around her waist, he used his other arm and hand to climb the ladder into the sunshine.

He paused only briefly, thinking the light would return the heat to her skin, the sparks to her eyes, and the snap to her tongue. But she remained mute and did not give up her hold about his neck.

With a brisk knock, Julian entered Brother Randall's quarters and stopped. For a moment he thought he had stumbled off the ship and into an infidel's harem. The simple bed and modest furnishings, which had served Julian well on his journey to the Outremer, were gone. Soft fabrics and silks lined a pillowed bed; goblets of gold stood on a table etched with eastern designs. Next to the table stood a pair of ornate chairs with ivory sculpted arms and legs. Brightly painted tapestry hung on the wall. It seemed Brother Randall thought himself more important than God to keep some of the goods many fellow Templars had given their lives for. Julian inhaled deeply. The room smelled of sweet jasmine and…sin.

Any regrets for forcing Brother Randall from his bed quickly fled Julian's mind. In fact, the captain could sleep with his men instead of the adjacent quarters. The master and King Richard had not entrusted the lady to his care only to be deviled by a misguided brother.

Julian walked over to the plush bed and began to unwrap the lady from his body. His breath caught in his throat; her skin was ghostly pale and cool to the touch. Panic shot through him when he grasped her wrist and felt the weak flutter of her heart. He removed her sandals and tucked her feet under the bed covers. Pushing up the bulky sleeves of her robe, he began to rub her arms.

"Lady Ariane, do you hear me? Look about you. You are safe."

She did not acknowledge his words. 'Twas almost as if the shadow of death hung upon her. In desperation, he pulled down her sleeves and wrapped the remaining linens around her body. He moved down to the foot of the bed and reached under the covers and began to massage her frigid feet.

Dear God, please spare her life. Do not give the devil another misguided soul.

"Lady Ariane, you must fight the darkness. Do not let the devil win." He blew warm breath on the delicate digits in his hands, then continued his administration.

Seeing no change in her condition, Julian again began to massage her toes, her arches, the heels of her feet. Slowly he worked in a circular motion up her ankles and calves. Though sweat formed on his brow, he could not remove the icy feeling from her feet and her limbs. Her complexion remained gray, her eyes empty and distant.

I beg of thee Lord, do not let the lady die. Not knowing what else to do, Julian pulled up his tunic and placed her frozen feet against his warm belly. The life giving heat flowed from his body into hers.

"Lady Ariane, look at me. I'll never let anyone put you in darkness again. You'll always be safe with me. I promise."

She blinked.

God be praised. She blinked.

A tingling sensation traveled up Ariane's limbs, sending small quivers through her thighs. Her cloudy vision swept about the strange room. Images of silks and linen-lined walls shimmered through the fog and mixed with air perfumed with a sweet flowery scent. Stellar beams of light drifted from the side of the small room and rested on a golden figure sitting across from her. Ariane closed her eyes and reveled in the relief flooding her body.

She was dead.

Her soul had passed on to eternal peace. Perhaps the angel sitting at her feet was Gabriel, who had spoken to Mohammad centuries ago. Allah be praised, the Muslims were right and the Christians would rot in their devil's hell.

"Lady Ariane, you're safe."

The words from the angel's lips were sweet and soft like a tender melody sung by a lover. She was safe in the angel's care. No more dark closets. No more leering men. No more Templar butcher.

"Ariane, I promise no evil will befall you."

The sound of the ethereal voice sent the tingling in her body upward, soaring through her stomach and chest to cradle her heart with gentle care.

A promise from an angel. Safe. Forever.

"In the name of your son Jesus Christ, dear God, let her open her eyes once again."

In the name of Jesus Christ. Nay, it could not be.

Ariane opened her eyes and abruptly focused on the angel's face. The starry particles in the beam of light about his head turned to motes of dust. Two blue orbs that she knew well stared at her. The sweet voice did not belong to a heavenly angel, but to the Christian's Avenging Angel. She had not passed to the land of milk and honey, but remained in the land of strife and torture.

The planes on his face were drawn downward. Many would think it was a look of concern. Yet many did not know him like she did. She was not deceived. 'Twas the look of anger and contempt. And then he did the cruelest thing.

He smiled.

A smile brighter than a candle's glow. A smile deep and wide like the heavens above. A smile that transformed a monster into a caring, loving human being. She tried to close her eyes to focus on her hate, but she could not. The smile revealed a compassionate soul and made him even more beautiful.

Bah! She must have lost her wits. That was not

tenderness glittering in his eyes, but a cunning twinkle. Nor was it affection that softened his face, but sly deceit. 'Twas his evil that made her heart race and her breathing short.

Ariane looked down at her linen wrapped legs. Why even her tingling limbs rose and fell with fear. She could feel her heart pound in the balls of her feet. Fright warmed her feet not security.

"My lady, can you hear me?" the butcher asked taking in a deep breath.

Odd, but her legs seemed to rise with each breath the butcher took. And the rapid pounding on the balls of her feet began to slow to a rhythmic thump. She wiggled her toes. The blanket was quite coarse. Every so often her toenails caught in its long pile.

Then suddenly something grabbed her feet and began... Rubbing? Massaging? What manner of blanket was this?

Ariane threw back the covers. 'Twas not the blanket that wrestled with her feet. The butcher's tunic was bunched up beneath his shoulders and the balls of her feet rested against his beating heart.

Heat shot through her body.

"Good, there is color in your cheeks," the butcher said.

And everywhere else as well, she thought. In a moment she would boil with color.

"How do you feel?"

Feel? The heels of her feet lay in the palms of his hands. Her limbs were bare and exposed for his perusal. Her heart raced hot blood through her body. To make matters worse, she had no desire to pull her feet away from his attentive administration. And he asked her how she felt?

He was winning. She could see it in his proud eyes, in his conceited smile. If she did not get the upper hand quickly all would be lost.

Ariane tore her feet from his grasp and tried to flee the room. She had not gone a pace before her wobbly legs collapsed. Suddenly she found herself cradled in two masculine arms that gently placed her on the bed.

The butcher stood sentinel. No trace of the smile remained on his lips. No outward sign of confidence lingered in his eyes. His face hardened with lines of annoyance.

"My lady, you are safe in my care. I would not harm you in any way."

Just when Ariane opened her mouth to voice her disagreement, the door crashed open. Andrew walked backward into the room directing two burly sailors who struggled to get a large chest through the doorway. Najila followed, her arms overflowing with bedding.

"Just place the chest…" The words died on Andrew's lips as he looked about the cabin. His skin pinked. He gave a questioning look to the butcher.

"Aye, Brother Andrew," the butcher said in English. "It looks as if Brother Randall does more than meditate when he is on his journeys. It would be wise to post a guard outside the lady's door."

Andrew nodded slowly. "I will seek a few trusted men, Brother. If I cannot find any, then I will stay at her door the entire journey."

Ariane almost openly refused the young whelp's offer, but quickly reminded herself they spoke in English.

"Nay, that will not be necessary," the butcher said. "If there are no trustworthy men on this boat, you, Brother Guy, and I will share the duty."

"Not Brother Guy," Andrew protested.

The butcher stayed any further words from Andrew with a slash of his hand through the air. "He has given me his word."

Ariane could see the doubt in Andrew's eyes when he looked away. Oh, she hoped Andrew's fears were right. If the arrogant Brother Guy was ruled so strongly by lust, she would use his weakness to obtain her freedom.

"Should I have men dispose of these infidel trappings?" Andrew asked still using his English tongue.

Light flooded the room when the butcher pulled away a tapestry covering one of the small ports. "Nay, perhaps the familiar objects will calm the lady on the voyage."

"I do not think a constant reminder of her life with the infidels is good for her Christian education."

"Her education is my concern, not yours," the butcher grated out. One only had to look at the tempest brewing in his eyes to know the conversation had ended.

"I stand corrected," Andrew said, his lips thinning. "I shall return to my duties." He gave a slight bow to Ariane and a warm smile to Najila. The smile faded from his lips when he gave a brisk nod to the butcher and left.

Ariane could feel her strength and confidence returning. The two Templars did not agree. She must be the wedge that widened the crack between them. 'Twould not be long before Brother Andrew and Brother Guy would do her bidding. Who knows, perhaps she could convince the two knights that the butcher was not fit for command.

She smiled and reveled in the thought of Julian de Maury in chains.

"My lady, I will leave you in your maid's care. Rest, for tomorrow you will start your training."

The firmness of *his* voice broke through Ariane's musings. Oh yea, it would not be long before he begged for mercy. In chains. Long and thick.

She mustered up her sweetest smile. "My thanks for your tender treatment, Brother Julian."

His eyes widened. He opened his mouth, but could not squeak out a word. With a curt bow he quit the room.

She controlled him! With the simple whisper of his name she had him.

A vision of him caressing her feet speared through her victory. Aye, she controlled him, if she could control her heart.

Julian stormed across the deck, leaving a wake of disgruntled sailors. Where was Brother Randall? No one seemed to know where the captain was. How could a man command a ship if his presence remained a mystery?

"Brother Julian, slow a pace."

The familiar voice brought Julian to a halt, allowing a slightly out of breath Guy Ashton to reach his side.

"Who is your prey that you stalk the deck like a hungry lion?" Guy asked.

Aye, 'tis true. Had he found Brother Randall, he could have crushed the thieving toad with his bare hands. Even though the man deserved to be chastised, Brother Randall was not the source of his anger.

Ariane was.

The thought startled him. When had he begun to think of the lady by her given name? When he placed her feet next to his heart or when she called him Brother Julian? He could hear his name roll of her lips, sweet and slightly exotic...Julian...Juliian...

"Julian! Do ye not hear me?"

The lines on Guy's concerned face focused before him. "I was...searching for Brother Randall."

Rubbing his short beard, Guy stared at Julian. "Aye, you may have been looking for Brother Randall, but your thoughts were elsewhere."

Julian did not answer, but looked about the deck and inhaled the fresh smell of open sea air. Around him the sailors had slowed their vigorous pace. The last sea gull flew from the bow of the ship toward the shore slipping slowly from his view. He would look at anything except Brother Guy's intense stare.

"'Tis the girl, isn't it? She truly must be a witch, to anger the ever-calm Avenging Angel."

Many a time Julian had thought the lady a witch, but to hear someone else accuse her of such turned his insides ice cold. Julian glared at the knight he would call friend if Guy was not such a stupid fool.

God forgive him! What was happening to him? Julian leaned against the side rail of the ship. Looking out over the horizon, he shook his head. "I'm sorry, Guy."

"For what?"

Julian gazed at his puzzled friend. "I held an evil thought against you."

Guy's lips twitched followed by a rich laugh. He reached out and squeezed Julian's shoulder. "Brother, that's one to the thousands I've had of you over the years." He leaned closer and whispered, "You should have told Richard to return the wench himself."

Julian straightened his stance. "The lady is neither a witch nor a wench."

Guy's hand slipped from his shoulder and he cocked an eyebrow. "What is this? Defending an infidel?"

"She is not an infidel," Julian said tersely.

"She holds the Muslim faith. Was it not the Avenging Angel who said there is none worse than a traitor to his faith?"

"The lady was but a child when the infidels murdered her family and forced her into submission. She had no choice," Julian hissed.

Guy took a step back and crossed his arms. "Forced into submission? Pray tell, who could force such a termagant into submission?"

Julian felt the anger drain from his tense muscles, a sadness hallowed out his nerves. He envisioned Ariane stubbornly fighting against the infidels, day after day, year after year, until any memory of her past life was erased. Until she could no longer remember her native tongue or her mother's face.

"Nay, you are right. She could not be forced." The sound of his name on her lips drifted through his mind. "But she would conform to kindness and that is why I want you to instruct her."

"What?" Guy moved closer and shook his head as if his hearing had failed.

"You must teach her, Guy, for I cannot."

"You cannot?"

Julian nodded. He turned away and rested his forearms on

the rail, unable to meet his friend's scrutiny. The strong wind whipped his hair back stinging his ears. Waves slapped against the side of the boat asking the question he knew raced through Guy's mind.

Why?

Guy moved to Julian's side and leaned his back to the side of the rail.

"I…"

"She's crawled under your hard shell hasn't she?" Guy muttered.

Julian gave a sad smile. Guy had a way with words like none other. Quick, and straight to the heart.

When Julian did not answer, Guy shook his head and began to laugh. "I thought you were made of stone. Not once in the years I've known you did you give a woman a second glance." He nudged Julian with his shoulder and whispered, "That's why I cast my lot with yours. Someone had to comfort those forlorn damsels."

Julian glared at Guy. "Will you instruct Lady Ariane?"

Guy ran a hand through his short locks. "Blast, man. If she quakes your soul, what makes you think I can be stronger?"

"You gave me your word."

"Aye, and I gave the Pope a vow of celibacy, also. And we all know how well I have kept that one."

"You have improved."

"Oh aye, improved. I go wenching but twice a week now. I used to go daily and thrice at week's end before I found God. I am a pious man. I should be honored with sainthood," Guy mocked.

Julian turned to his side and looked at Guy's profile. "You will not break your word to me."

Guy met his gaze. The admiration Julian saw almost choked him. He did not deserve Guy's unfailing friendship. "'Twill not be for long. I will spend my time in the Word and prayer, and surely within a week I will have purged this evil from my body."

Guy nodded as if he had every confidence Julian would conquer this affliction. 'Twas a confidence Julian did not share.

"Very well, Julian, I shall fight off the witch's spells."

"She is not a wit—"

"Aye. Just a cunning maid, which is the same thing."

Six

Take heed, and beware of covetousness: for a man's life consisteth not in abundance of the things which he possesseth.
Luke 12:15

ARIANE SAT ON THE SOFT BED WATCHING NAJILA pile bedding on her pallet, while singing a little song. She had a soft musical voice for the hard Arabic syllables. The cheerful melody did naught but sour Ariane's mood. From the sway of the boat she knew they had set sail. Her chances to escape slipped away with every gust of wind the sails trapped.

"We will travel in style on this voyage. I should do as Brother Julian says when God gives us blessings. I should fall to my knees and thank God. Thank God for your affliction," Najila said.

"I do not have an affliction." Ariane closed her eyes briefly to better enjoy the soft bedding cradling her body. "I just do not like dark, close places."

"I do not care for them much either, but Brother Julian says we should endure all things."

"Does he?" Ariane spoke without opening her eyes.

"Yea, he says the more we sacrifice our needs, the more we please God."

Ariane gave a small laugh. Never had she seen a Crusader or Templar go without having their needs fulfilled. Poor Najila, she put her trust in men who only took, and in a God who did not hear.

Najila babbled on, "Brother Julian is a wise, fair, and courageous man. Chosen by God to teach the sheep."

Opening her eyes, Ariane saw Najila sitting on her pallet, a dreamy look floating across her face. Ariane could not contain the anger bubbling within. *Teach the sheep.* What foolishness was this? 'Twas as if the butcher had washed every thought from the maid's mind and filled her head with nonsense.

Ariane sat up and placed her feet on the floor. "Najila, your Brother Julian is not a good man, but a thief who takes from our lands and a butcher who kills the innocent. He does not care for you. You are but chattel. When he has taken all you have to give, he will toss you out as one empties a chamber pot."

Najila stood and walked over to the large trunk in the center of the cabin. She ran her fingers over the worn wood. "Forgive me, my lady, but 'tis you who does not understand. You do not know Brother Julian. He is all the things I said and more. He is a true man of God, filled with the Holy Spirit, just as it says in the book of Galatians: *The fruit of the spirit is love, joy, peace, longsuffering, gentleness, goodness, and faith.*"

To keep from throttling Najila, Ariane twisted her hands in the bedding. Najila was beyond hope. She could not see the ambition, debauchery, and immorality that were more the true image of the butcher's personality.

Najila unfastened the lock on the chest. "Brother Julian says we should—"

Ariane freed her hands from the bedding, stood, and stamped her foot on the floor. "Brother Julian, Brother Julian! I have heard enough about Brother Julian. Do you not think for yourself? How can you take anything the butcher says as truth? He is a liar, a cheat, and a murderer. 'Tis you who does not see past his handsome face."

Najila dropped the heavy lock on the floor and flipped open the top of the chest. She snatched a gown made of fine green linen and threw it into Ariane's arms. With tears streaming down her face Najila shouted, "You are not deserving of any of these gifts given by Brother Julian."

Ariane met Najila's angry gaze with a glare of her own. Slowly Ariane let the soft linen gown drop to the floor. "I want no gifts that have been stolen from some Arab woman."

Very carefully, Najila picked up a gold girdle embroidered with delicate and unusual flowers. "My lady, I know the woman who toiled over this girdle." She then placed the belt down and grabbed a short, scarlet, silk veil. "I know the merchant who carries these veils."

Najila blew the light fabric at Ariane. The veil sailed gently through the air and landed on Ariane's shoulder. Then she reached deep into the trunk and pulled out a strand of the finest pearls Ariane had ever seen.

"And I know the sailor who harvested each of these pearls. Every piece of clothing and every veil were purchased by Brother Julian. None were stolen."

Ariane moved toward the trunk. A loud gasp escaped her lips when she looked into the chest. There were gowns and veils of many different colors and lengths. Several pairs of linen shoes made of silks and softest leather, ribbons and bands in all sizes and some in very rare shades.

Flabbergasted at the sight before her, it took a few moments for Ariane to organize her thoughts. Surely these were not all meant for her? "You are mistaken, Najila. Some of these must have been purchased for you."

Najila shook her head. "Nay, my lady, all belongs to you. I walked the streets with Brother Julian as he made each purchase. Master de Sablé had supplied enough coin to buy one gown and a pair of shoes. The rest were purchased by Brother Julian using every coin he had and by selling the few meager goods he owned. I believe he would have bought more if he had the means."

Again, Ariane was left speechless. Why would a Templar

buy her such gifts? Especially since she had challenged every word he uttered and attacked every plan he made.

She ran her fingers over the clothing. Now she saw the way of it. He planned to win her over with gifts. She trembled with anger. Did he really think she was that weak and stupid? He would rue the day he tried to win her affections and her control with objects.

Ariane pulled the soft veil from her shoulder and placed it in the chest. She should throw these things back in his face, but she would not gain her freedom that way. A small smile crossed her lips. "Tell Brother Julian that I accept his gifts and I look forward to my Christian instruction."

The hard lines on Najila's face remained, nor could she hide the contempt and jealously in her eyes. "I thought you would, my lady. I am sure Brother Julian will be pleased."

Ariane nodded and picked up the emerald gown resting on the floor. Najila had nothing to be jealous about. Soon she would have her precious Julian all to herself. "Will we make many stops?"

Najila shrugged and once again picked up the golden girdle. "I know only that in a few days we will stop in Cyprus, and then I believe we will travel to Marseilles. This girdle would look lovely with the gown in your hands. Shall I assist you in changing your garments, my lady?"

"Soon," Ariane answered, her gaze drifting over the stolen goods in the cabin.

She knew the story, the wretched fate of that poor island. Cyprus brought great fame to King Richard, but that was where Ariane's troubles began. For 'Twas in Cyprus that Richard married Berengaria of Navarre and not King Philip's sister, Alice. The marriage sealed Ariane's fate, sending her back to a land she could barely remember. A land she had no plans to see.

Richard had conquered Cyprus in three weeks. Emperor Isaac announced he would surrender under one condition— that he would not be put in irons. Richard agreed, and proceeded to make silver chains for Isaac. As a reward for helping him conquer the island, Richard gave the Templar's control of Cyprus.

She could not escape from an island infested with looting Templars, but she could escape from Marseilles. Abi Bin had often talked about the wondrous port city. Ships from all over sailed to trade in Marseilles. She could easily hide there. She warmed to the plan she began to form in her mind.

Abi Bin would brag how he could sail to the city from Arce in fifteen days, but with a large ship like this the journey could be twice as long.

She had to be patient. What was one more month of captivity compared to a lifetime of freedom? She would wait. After all, 'twould not be long.

Julian watched from the shadows of the hold as Brother Randall inspected his cargo. The wayward monk could not hide his joy as he tapped each bag of rare eastern spices. His face grew wide with a wicked grin when he examined the bolts of silks and oils.

None of these goods should be on this ship.

Thankfully, Lady Ariane was not present. In his mind's eye, Julian could see her pointing to Brother Randall and saying, "See, all Templars are thieves."

In this case, the lady was right.

Julian's blood boiled as he watched Brother Randall cover the contraband with large bales of hay. Unable to contain his anger Julian stepped out of the darkness until he stood a breath away from Randall's back.

"Brother Randall, we must speak."

Randall swung about. His face paled and he stumbled backward against the straw bales. "Brother Julian, I was just checking to make sure we had enough hay for the two fine horses Master de Sablé wishes us to sell in Marseilles. The pair should bring a handsome sum. What a fine profit there will be for the Crusade."

Julian squeezed the hilt of his sword. "I have come to tell you that Lady Ariane needs your cabin. She seems to have a great fear of dark confined places and cannot remain below deck."

Brother Randall shifted his feet, moving away from the bales. 'Twas apparent he wished to draw Julian's attention away from his goods as well.

"That be fine. Just fi..." Brother Randall's face flushed as his words drifted to a halt. He rushed past Julian toward the ladder. "Give me a moment to clear away a few paltry items that may be in the lady's way."

"I have already seen your belongings."

Brother Randall stopped his climb and slid back to the floor. He turned and stared at Julian. "Those goods in my quarters are there only until we reach England, where all will be sold."

Julian raised an eyebrow. He could not stand for any of this man's lies. "Pray tell, do you always take and use that which is not yours?"

The liar's Adam's apple bobbed in his throat like a cork. He licked his dry lips. "I am an old man. What is the harm in borrowing a few things to comfort one's brittle bones on a long journey?"

Julian's gripped the front of Randall's robe and twisted the rough material against his chest. "Do not lie, Brother, for your sins against God and The Rule are many. I am not blind. The tapestries have hung on those walls for many a voyage. You should thank God that I do not send you to hell here and now."

Julian pushed Randall away. He stumbled, then fell backward landing in a pile of warm manure.

"All was going to be sold to further the Crusade," Randall cried.

Like a flash of lightening Julian pulled Randall to his feet and aimed the tip of his sword at his throat. "Say not another lie or you shall lose your tongue. I have seen men, women, and children starve while animals like you grow rich and fat at their expense. Your greed has sealed your fate. From this time forth, all that you own will be given to others and that which sits in this hold will be given to the fish. For this journey will be swift!"

"But surely we can come to some understanding?" Randall pleaded.

"Nay! Master de Sablé has given me permission to take control of his ship. I do so now. I will make certain you leave the order in disgrace. Now move up the ladder." When Randall did not comply, Julian pushed the tip of his sword slightly into his neck, drawing a drop of blood. "Move."

Swiftly, Brother Randall ascended to the deck as if he were a young knight. Julian followed and ordered a few crewmen to remove the contraband behind the bales. The commotion on deck brought Lady Ariane and her maid from their quarters.

Julian gritted his teeth. He did not want the lady to witness the disciplining of Brother Randall. 'Twould confirm her belief about all Templars. Nay not all, some. So be it. She would see what is done with a Templar when he breaks The Rule.

When all the loot stood on the deck, the crewmen looked from Brother Randall to Julian. He cleared his throat and purposely spoke in Arabic. "Brother Randall has sinned against our Lord and The Rule. Henceforth, I am taking control of the *Knight's Cross*. He will be stripped of his personal possessions and be returned to England to be judged by his fellow brothers."

Not a single man disputed Julian. Brother Randall's deeds must have been well-known. Some even nodded their agreement.

"Throw the filthy lucre overboard."

The men hurried to their task. Before the ship moved another length, the deck was clear.

Brother Randall fell to his knees and glared at Julian. "You will be sorry for what you have done. 'Twas not only me who benefited. Aye, one close to Richard will hear about this." Randall raised a fist to Julian. "You will be sorry."

How dare this thief raise his fist to him. Julian found it hard to believe a man who had spent years as a Templar did not feel any remorse. Nay, 'twas not hard to believe; there were many others like him. Even Randall admitted those close to the king were entrenched in such evil. "I suggest you spend the rest of this voyage in prayer. Beg that God has mercy on your soul."

Brother Randall's face turned scarlet, but he did not utter another word.

Julian turned and stopped in front of Lady Ariane. His anger intensified when he saw her smug smile. "No man can steal from God. What He has given to others. 'Tis a sin and God will have his retribution."

God forgive him, but he was satisfied when he saw the color drain from her face. Julian stormed toward his quarters. 'Twould be a long voyage and he needed to pray for patience.

Seven

I will never leave thee, nor forsake thee.
Hebrews 13:5

ARIANE RAN HER HANDS OVER THE EMERALD GROWN she wore and adjusted the golden girdle around her waist for what seemed to be the hundredth time this morn. She had Najila braid and unbraid her hair at least a dozen times. Finally she decided to let her locks hang loose, covered only by a thin veil that matched her dress.

The dust from the tapestries made her nose itch. She sneezed. Her nose would be red and swollen soon.

Where was the butcher?

The waves crashed against the hull of the ship. She would be deaf soon.

Where was de Maury?

The heat of the small cabin closed in on her. She would look like a wilted lily soon.

Where was the man?

With nothing else to do, she began to fiddle with the pearls around her neck. "Is my appearance appealing, Najila?"

"Yea, my lady you are extremely beautiful. There will not be one man aboard this ship who would not vie for your attention."

Ariane did not share Najila's confidence. She watched Najila casually run her fingers through her silky black hair.

Perhaps the butcher preferred dark hair and olive skin over her bright hair and fair skin. What then?

Ariane paced the cabin. He was tall and she was short. Mayhap he preferred women who would not give him a backache when he leaned forward to kiss them.

Najila stroked her hands through her hair one more time, and then casually stretched her body. What if the butcher enjoyed women with more curves like Najila? Ariane frowned. She was thin. Perhaps she should eat more.

Najila closed then opened her eyes. Her eyes were a deep brown. Ariane's were sea-water green. What if the butcher cared for Najila more than her? What if the butcher found her homely?

Bah!

What did she care if he found her attractive? Ariane threw her plain red hair over her shoulder. A sharp twinge rippled through her midsection. She did want the big oaf to find her comely. Had not she learned from the other harem girls that seduction was a woman's best weapon? For her sake, Ariane hoped the girls were right. After all, 'twould make her escape easy if he found her too beautiful to resist her needs. Her need to get off this ship!

A quick knock upon the door set Ariane's heart racing. She raised her hands to smooth over her clothing once more, then decided she better not, for her palms were too sweaty and might soil her gown.

"Enter," Ariane squeaked out.

The door flew open. Ariane's heart sagged in her chest. 'Twas not the attractive butcher who stood in the doorway, but his cocky friend Guy Ashton.

"Oh 'tis only you," Ariane said, unable to hide her disappointment. "What do you want?"

Guy stood before her. His mouth hung open like a stupid fish. Yea, even his eyes popped out of his head like the creature.

"Well?" Ariane clipped.

"I-I." Guy looked at Najila and then back at Ariane. He

ran a hand through his hair. "Mary, Mother of God, Julian asks too much of me," he said in English.

"Brother Guy," Najila scolded. "You should not take the name of the Blessed Virgin in vain."

Guy looked back at Najila. "Aye, forgive me. 'Tis just... Oh never mind. Najila, Brother Andrew wishes to see you in the hold. It seems there are a few things left below that belong to Ariane and—"

"Then I shall go at once," Najila interrupted.

"Aye," Guy turned his attention back to Ariane. His gaze traveling over her body. "But please, return quickly."

Najila raced from the room, slamming the door behind her. Ariane eyed Guy warily. For a few moments Guy stood rooted to the spot, staring at her. His thoughts were as transparent as the veil on her head. More things down below indeed. More likely 'twas a ruse to get her alone.

"I am a fool," he muttered to himself in English. "I never should have promised Julian. For now I cannot tumble the maid to ease my desire for this vision before me. Her woman's charms were indeed hidden by the sack she wore earlier. No wonder Julian cannot spend time with her. Yet I do not understand his thinking. If he fears his lust for her, then how can he think I can resist her charms? I will be hard pressed to keep my mind on educating this lovely."

Ariane's insides turned with a mass of confusion. She was elated to find out the butcher found her attractive, but disappointed to find out he would not spend any time with her. Mayhap this was better. She knew she could control the fool before her. His arrogance would ensure her escape. Yet, she wanted to escape under Julian's watch. Where was the satisfaction in knowing that he would blame another for her disappearance? Ariane wanted de Maury to bubble with rage knowing she had outsmarted him.

Guy motioned to the ivory-handled chairs near a small table. "My lady, please sit down," he said in Arabic.

Ariane complied and eased herself into the plush chair. She folded her hands on the table. Guy sat across from her and ogled her again. Nay, no matter how easy it would be to escape from him there would be no victory in it. She needed Julian, not this foolish fish.

Guy fidgeted in his chair, coughed in his hand and then cleared his throat. "Lady Ariane, Brother Julian has asked me to begin your Christian instruction."

"Why?"

"W-w-w," Guy stammered, his lips puckered like a bottom feeder. "W-why?"

"Yea, why? I was told by the king that the straw-hair butcher would teach me."

"Straw-hair? Butcher?" Guy asked, his cheeks puffing out like gills.

Ariane leaned over the table. She curled her finger and motioned him closer. "The one who orders you about."

Guy sat back. "My lady, no one orders me about."

"Then why do you jump and scurry around every time the butcher opens his mouth?"

Puzzlement flashed across Guy's face. "Julian is my friend. He is my only friend. Would you not do anything for your only friend?"

A friend. Ariane slammed her hands on the table and rose to her feet. "Aye, Brother Guy, I would. If I had a friend. Once I had two friends, but murdering Christians took them both from me!"

Guy looked up, but did not stand. "I'm sorry, I know how hard life can be without a friend."

His words of apology and kindness were not what she expected. Could he know what it was like to be all alone? She saw the sadness in his eyes. Was the look of remorse genuine or was he more cunning than she had expected?

Ariane sat down. "Tell me what you know of loneliness?"

Guy took a long breath, then looked away. "I am sure you are not interested in my life. We do not have much time before I return to my other duties. I was thinking we should start with the birth of Christ."

"Nay, we will start with you. For I refuse to hear a word about your savior until I know about my teacher."

Guy returned his gaze to hers. "My lady, we will discuss what I say we shall discuss. Now, Christ was born in—"

Ariane covered her ears with her hand and started humming a tune.

"Stop that," Guy ordered.

She only sang louder.

"My lady, this is ridiculous!"

She upped her pitch.

"All right, all right." Guy leaned forward and pried Ariane's hands from her head. "You win. What do you want to know about me?"

Ariane gave him a lazy smile. "Tell me of your loneliness."

He sat back and began to stroke his short beard. She thought he planned to avoid her request.

"You ask me to give you the story of my life. A life I have left far behind. A life I care not to resurrect."

His words did not surprise her. Christians came to the Holy Land for one of two things, sometimes both; to plunder the land or run away from a troubled past. His words drew no pity from her.

"I was born a bastard son of a noble. My mother was his favorite slut. My father took great pleasure in ridiculing my every act and extolling the good qualities of my legitimate brother."

Guy rose and began to pace the room. The hatred for his family raged across his face. "Besides being the favorite target for my father's wrath, I assisted my brother in his knight's training. Actually, I played the fool who stumbled about and lost every sword fight so that my brother, Hubert, could look like the great warrior my father so desperately wanted."

"You lost the fights on purpose?" Ariane asked.

"Aye, I knew my place and held it well. A great many ladies took pleasure in giving me comfort." Guy gave a stony smile. "They would run away from Hubert, the ugly pampered puff. However, once in a while he would catch one…once in a while."

Guy stopped pacing and gave Ariane a cold look. "This conversation bores me. I am here to teach you, not pour out my soul to a heathen."

"Then you had best leave now, Templar, for I will not listen to a thing you say." Ariane covered her ears with her hands and began to hum again.

Guy circled the table and pulled her from her seat. He shook her until her hands dropped to her side. "Have you not had enough pain in your life to kill your wish to hear of more?"

Ariane raised her chin. "I enjoy hearing about Christian pain."

Releasing her, Guy stumbled back to his chair. "Very well, my lady, then I shall continue with my tale. Not because it gives you pleasure, but because of a promise I made to Brother Julian."

She folded her hands on the table. "Please continue."

"When my father became tired of my mother, he married her off to the cook. From that union came my sister, sweet Sara. When Sara reached thirteen summers she caught the eye of Hubert." Guy turned sideways in his chair and rested his head in his hands. "And one day he…raped her. My father laughed. He found it very amusing that his son would enjoy the daughter of a woman he fancied in his youth."

Ariane sat rigid. The tortured look on Guy's face drew deep pity from her soul. She had no desire to pity a Christian, yet if he continued she knew she would.

She rose. "I do not wish to hear more of this."

Guy reached across the table and grabbed her wrist. "A few moments ago my tale intrigued you. Now it is too gruesome. Nay, my lady, you will hear all. For now I have the need to finish it."

The coldness of Guy's words crept through Ariane.

Slowly, Guy eased Ariane back into her chair before he released his grip. He watched her for a few moments, then settled back into his seat.

"I went to the armory and stole a sword. I found Hubert training in the courtyard. The idiot laughed when I came at him with a devil's cry and the sword high above my head. He truly believed he could beat me as he had done in past fraudulent practices. I had him on the ground begging for mercy faster than a falcon could take flight. I was ready to pierce his heart when one of the other knights cracked me on the back of my head with the hilt of a sword. I woke up in chains. I am only alive today because Sara offered herself to Hubert in exchange for my life."

It was then that Ariane realized the contempt she saw in Guy's eyes was directed at himself. Instead of defending his sister's honor, he cast her into a whore's life.

"I was banished. I spent the next few years drinking and whoring around the countryside. One day I received word that my beautiful sister died trying to bring Hubert's bastard into the world. After that I cared naught what happened to me. I drowned my sorrows with daily drink. Even the whores didn't want me anymore."

Ariane wondered briefly if Guy spoke the truth, for most men held by the allure of strong drink looked worn even after they had changed their ways. "You look too vigorous to ever have been a drunk."

Guy gave her a bitter smile. "I was at death's door when Brother Julian picked me up out of the mud."

"Brother Julian is the reason for your change?"

"Aye. He cleaned me up, fed me, and never asked what sin I had committed in order to wind up in such a wretched state. He gave me the sword I wear today. He gave me an honored place in his home. He gave me my life back."

This made little sense to Ariane. Why would a man take a complete stranger into his home and exalt him to such a high level? Ariane narrowed her eyes. "What did he want from you in return?"

"Nothing. I had turned my back on God, yet Julian did not chastise me for my lack of faith. In fact, he said one day God would find a way to return me to the fold."

Ariane looked at the large red cross on Guy's chest. "When did this transformation from sinner to saint take place?"

Guy laughed. "I am not a saint." A wicked smile drifted across his lips. "But my belief in Julian's words were fulfilled in the most unusual way. For one crisp autumn day, Hubert and his pretty new wife marched up to Julian's home seeking rest from their travels."

Ariane leaned forward, certain she had heard wrong. "You jest?"

Guy raised his hands, a look of pure sincerity on his face. "Nay, I fell twice as I ran for my sword, I could not contain my excitement. But Brother Julian stopped me."

"Of course he did," Ariane said dryly.

"He made me promise not to shed blood in his home."

"And you agreed?"

"Aye."

"Why?" Ariane asked, astonished.

"Julian gave me a second chance on life and had never asked for anything in return. I could not refuse his request."

Once again she saw the unquestionable admiration in his eyes. Perhaps she could not be the wedge to break the strong bond between Guy and the butcher.

A grin of satisfaction broke across Guy's face. "So I did the next best thing."

"What would that be?" Ariane asked.

"I had carnal relations with his wife."

Ariane inhaled sharply. Guy's laughter echoed off the chamber walls.

"Hubert walked into his bedchamber and found me with his wife. I thought for sure I had forfeited my life when Julian followed Hubert into the room."

Ariane's mouth went dry. She had seen firsthand Julian's

wrath. *The stone in his sword matching the ice-blue color of his eyes. The cries of dear Raya.* "What happened then?" she croaked out.

"Hubert went into a rage and reached for his sword. Like a lightning bolt, Julian withdrew his sword and crashed Hubert's to the ground. By then I had left his wife—" Guy blushed slightly. "Julian dismissed me from the room. Being nude and totally defenseless, I found his words quite intelligent. Later, I discovered Julian had ordered Hubert to leave and not return. He gave no apology for my indiscretion."

"But what did he expect from you, to follow him on this foolish Crusade?"

"Nay, he said naught to me about my recklessness, but went to the priest and gave confession for me."

"He confessed your sins?"

"Aye, and did my penitence."

Ariane's lips thinned. "He rules you by guilt then?"

"Nay, by love. For never have I found a more giving man. He paid the Templars large sums of gold to accept me in the order. For no bastard is allowed. You do not believe me, but in time you will learn his true nature."

"I have seen his nature when he carried me like a sack of grain over his shoulder and threw me in a tub of water. He is not loving."

Guy laughed loudly. "The whole order gossiped about how you had broken Julian's control. I would have given my teeth to have been there."

Ariane joined in Guy's infectious laughter.

Suddenly, the door crashed open. The so-called loving Julian stood before them. A deep scowl marred his usually handsome face.

"The lesson in over," he announced.

"But we have yet to begin," Guy said lamely.

"Then what have you been doing in here?" Julian thundered.

88

Giving him her sweetest devilish smile, Ariane answered, "Love. We were discussing love."

We were discussing love.

The waves slapped fiercely against the fast moving ship, and the wooden boards groaned. Julian raised his eyes heavenward and thanked God he had survived the voyage this long. Cool sprays of sea water stung like ice on his cheeks. He inhaled the fresh air that had delighted Mariners through the ages. A gull squawked overhead.

They would be in Marseilles by midday. A fifteen-day voyage had turned into months of living hell.

The time on Cyprus resembled a bad dream. He had spent most of his days keeping an eye on Randall and his slow moving crew. The unloading and loading of goods should only have taken a few days, but for these slothful sailors, it took an eternity. Julian sighed. While he played guard to an old man and a dim-witted crew, Guy instructed Ariane.

His mind did naught but revisit every moment he had seen the pair, whispering and laughing with their heads together. The thought still grated his nerves. Yet Guy insisted he was but building a friendly bond with the lady so he could teach her God's word more easily.

We were discussing love.

He believed Guy. He trusted Guy. Guy had never lied to him in the past. Yet when Julian tried to test Guy's instruction, Lady Ariane seemed to know naught. He even tried to take charge of her education, but found his thoughts constantly turning unclean. His temper would flare and the battle between them would ensue, which made his mind weak. He would roar and she would threaten to cut his heart out.

Even Andrew seemed bewitched by her charms, for he spent more time tagging behind Ariane and Najila than he did reading scripture. Nay 'twas not true. Andrew would daily read passages to the two on deck, and Lady Ariane would fuss over the exquisite tone of his voice. She seemed to have good things to say about everyone. Except him.

She liked nothing about him. Julian ran his fingers through his hair. She enjoyed Andrew's voice, and Guy's wit, but she said he was a bellowing butcher with straw-colored hair.

We were discussing love.

He slammed his fist on the mast. *Those words.* His mind always returned to those words as if they were a rote prayer.

What had she meant? Guy told him the words meant naught but love of family long lost. But her eyes did not have the look of family devotion; they burned with the fire of sensual desire. Whom did she desire? Guy? Yet he gave his word not to know her. The thought of Guy's possible betrayal bothered him, but the thought of Ariane's love for Guy sliced through his body like a jagged edge sword.

Julian grimaced into the sea spray. She called him an oaf, a clod, a fool. Aye, she was right. He was a fool. For his mind and body dwelled upon her jewel-green eyes, her bright glowing hair, her lush red lips, and her strong, determined spirit. When he ate he thought of her. When he worked he thought of her. When he prayed he thought of her.

He wanted this nightmare to end. In England, things would be different, when she was gone from him.

A soft musical laughter swept across the deck and twirled through his body. Julian turned, Ariane stood near the bow, in light conversation with Najila, Andrew, and Guy. Ariane gave an angelic smile to the trio.

We were discussing love. Oh, that such words would include him.

They had docked over an hour ago. Ariane traced her steps across the cabin. The knots in her stomach jumped with each drop of her heel. The plan she had devised seemed so easy a month ago, but now she wondered if she would be allowed out of this cabin while they were in Marseilles.

Before the sailors had finished rejoicing over the sight of land, the butcher grabbed her around the waist and carried her back to this God forsaken cell. If he planned to lock her in this prison until they set sail again then he was a bigger fool than she had thought. Did he really think a flimsy wooden door would prevent her from escape? Bah!

Ariane walked over to the door and rattled the latch. She placed her foot on the door and pulled the handle. The door did not budge. A large board slammed against the wooden frame on the other side.

"My lady, 'tis no good. The door is barred. They will come for us when the ship has been secured," Najila sat calmly on her pallet, brushing her long dark hair.

Ariane tugged on the latch one more time. "What makes you think they will come for us at all?"

"We were allowed off the ship in Cyprus, so why not here? Besides, Brother Andrew has promised to show me the town."

Ariane gave the door a swift kick. "Cyprus crawled with Templars. It is easy to let a fly loose in a spider's web. As for Brother Andrew, remember he is a Templar and all Templars lie."

Najila's fingers drifted through her long mass hair. "Nay, not all Templars."

Ariane looked through a crack between the door boards. "Brother Guy can recite a lie faster than he can utter a prayer."

"Aye, but Brother Andrew and Brother Julian do not lie."

Ariane shook her head. Najila sat with a dreamy look on her face...a look Ariane had come to know well when Najila talked about the butcher. Many nights Najila had slipped out of the cabin. Where did she go? To the butcher's bed? Ariane had thought about following her, but every time she planned to, her courage failed. For in truth, she did not want to find Najila wrapped in the butcher's arms.

Ariane wiped a few strands of sticky hair from her sweaty forehead. "Brother Andrew is young and will learn the ways of his order, and I have seen with my own eyes the deeds of Brother Julian. He lies."

Najila opened her mouth, but the sound of the heavy board being lifted from the door ceased her protest. The door swung open and the butcher filled the entry. His white tunic strained against his chest.

Most would fear his presence. His wild sun-kissed hair hung long. His shoulders emanated brute strength. His towering height created fear. Ariane feigned indifference and gave a loud sigh.

"My lady, I will escort you about Marseilles. Mind you, I will watch your every step so do not attempt to escape or your time on dry land will be short. First, we shall visit your betrothed."

"What?"

"Lord de Craon is here on the king's business. His Highness thinks it is wise for his cousin to see you again."

Ariane's stomach tilted. Her mind filled with past thoughts of fighting off the filthy little man the night she was captured. Had not Richard intervened, placing her under his protection, she certainly would have lost her virginity. 'Twas something she had fought to keep intact for many years. Ariane had lost count of all the times she had spent in Abi Bin's punishment hole for not giving herself to his guests or, more truthfully, to his enemies. He had always said her knowledge of English made her a valuable weapon, but his patience to put her learning to the test had almost run out.

Then Richard had come and saved her from a life of whoring and spying. Instead she would be one man's property. Wedded or not she would still be a whore. Ariane saw no difference between Abi Bin and Richard. Both were greedy men with only their own interests at heart.

She crossed her arms over her chest. "Nay, I will not let that slimy worm touch me."

"Nor shall he," Julian agreed.

"What?" This man talked in riddles. She was beginning to get a headache. "Did you not say, I am to see him?"

"Aye, see you, but not touch you."

Ariane threw her arms in the air. "I give up. I cannot understand you. How will he see me and *not* touch me? 'Tis an impossibility with the man. Believe me, I know."

Julian frowned and grabbed the hilt of his sword. "He will not touch you because I will remain in the room. There will be no touching!"

The sincerity in his words almost made her laugh. "You will not leave me alone with the worm?"

"I gave you my word."

She tapped her finger against her lips. "And you never lie."

He nodded.

This might prove to be a worthwhile outing after all. Mayhap she could use what she learned in the harem to provoke de Craon to touch her and when the butcher attacked the wretched worm, she could escape.

A not so innocent smile slipped across her lips. "Then I shall see the worm. You will not leave me alone?"

The muscles in his jaw grew taunt. "Nay, my lady, you are always safe with me."

"Then lead the way. For I am anxious to see the city."

They joined Brother Andrew and Najila on deck and followed them to the dock. Ariane glanced up at de Maury. His eyes kept moving about, scanning the dock. Deep lines creased his forehead as he began to frown. Something troubled him, and she just couldn't help adding to it. Just a little dig of jealousy would add to his worries.

"Where is Brother Guy?" she asked sweetly.

The lines on his face deepened. He looked like an old man. "Guy is checking the cargo. We will need to do some trading. Dry meats will not maintain your beauty for your betrothed. Fear not, Brother Guy will have time to explore the city later. Your mind should be on your betrothed, not on what Brother Guy is doing."

The butcher's words struck Ariane like a lance to the heart. How could she have been so wrong? During the past few weeks, Ariane had interpreted his anger for jealousy over her relationship with Guy. Aye, he was jealous, but not for himself, but for her betrothed, Lord de Craon.

She should have known. Had not Guy given her tale after tale over the weeks about Julian's brave character and unselfish nature? 'Twas foolish of her to think his blood boiled with lust. Why, come to think about it he avoided her as if she carried the vile plague. She had been the fool, not he. Mayhap he would let Lord de Craon touch her after all.

She did not care to find out. She needed to escape, now.

Ariane surveyed the dock. Young sailors yelled and struggled while herding smelly livestock onto various ships. Others strained to carry heavy trunks into the city's marketplace. The sun glinted off brass bowls as traders and merchants haggled over linen scarves, leathers shoes, dried thyme and other herbs. Pure pandemonium. Surely she could slip away.

His large hand circled her wrist. When she looked up she saw his determination. "Nay, I will not have you flee from me."

Her heart hammered in her chest and probably pulsed in her wrist as well. She wanted to run from the cold, hard look of him, yet stay in the warmth of his firm grip. What was the matter with her? She must keep her mind sharp if she wanted to gain her freedom.

He pulled her forward through the crowd. His long gait and fast pace separated them from Najila and Andrew.

"Stop. We have lost Najila," Ariane shouted.

The butcher pulled her forward. "She is safe with Andrew."

"Slow down." The quick beat of her heart and her shallow breathing sent a rainbow of colors before her eyes. "Stop! I can hardly breathe."

He kept his pace. "We will stop when we are safe."

From the corner of her eye she learned the meaning of his words. Three men broke from the crowd and fell upon Julian, tossing him to the stone pavement. His hold on her arm broke. She looked down at the red marks circling her wrist, a symbol her captivity had ended. She was free.

She was free.

Eight

*Intreat me not to leave thee, or to return from following after
thee: for whither thou goest, I will go; and where thou
lodgest, I will lodge: thy people shall be my people, and thy
God my God.*

Ruth 1:16

ROZEN TO THE SPOT, ARIANE WATCHED AS THE MEN
pummeled Julian's back and his face. Each and every
blow caused her to wince.

She should run; this was her chance for freedom.

Julian struggled to ward off their attack with a quick slash
of his sword. The butcher barely made a sound as one
assailant kicked him in the stomach and another thundered a
fist in his jaw.

*Run. He murdered Raya. Run. He will give you to de Craon.
Run. He cares naught for you. Run!* She turned away. Her
ragged breaths became loud sobs as she ran down the street.

What if he is killed? She ducked behind a slow moving
cart, then ran up another street filled with merchants
examining and hawking wares.

He needed her help. A shepherd herded a flock of sheep
down the street toward the docks upsetting carts, tables, and
baskets. Dodging sheep she slipped between two buildings.
Tears stung the corners of her eyes.

He does not care about you. She leaned against a wooden
structure to catch her breath.

She should go back. The more she tried to justify her

thoughts, the more she realized the futility of it. She could not save him. She was no match for three massive thieves.

Neither was Julian. What if they seriously injured him? Left him bleeding, dying? Andrew and the others would find him. *What if they were too late?*

She knew what she must do. Ariane inhaled deeply, trying to slow her rapid breath. She pushed herself away from the wall and turned to enter the street. She had barely rounded the corner when she saw a familiar face.

"Brother Randall," she practically shouted. "Follow me, Brother Julian needs our help."

The large monk stepped in front of Ariane blocking her passage. "Is he in danger?"

"Aye." Ariane tried to skirt his beefy form. She had no time for this chatter. Did he not see they must find Julian before it was too late? He could be dying as they speak. "Three men fell upon him and I foolishly ran away."

Brother Randall backed her further down the narrow passage, rubbing his massive belly against her stomach. "Fear is nothing to be ashamed of, Ariane."

The use of her given name sent spikes of apprehension up her spine. He flashed a rotting smile; his breath smelled like horse manure.

With every step Ariane took backward, Randall matched it with a forward move. "I do not understand why you want to go back and help him."

His hand lashed out and grabbed her around the neck. Her head exploded with pain as Randall slammed her against the wooden building. Splinters pierced her back when he threw his full weight against her body.

"Your precious Julian is dead. Soon his friends will follow." Randall reached up with his other hand and ran a grimy finger across her jaw. "Ye have soft skin."

Ariane squirmed against his weight, trying to free her legs. He squeezed her throat; she gasped for each tiny breath she could steal into her lungs. She tried to cry out, but she could not manage one meager sound.

"Ye have cost me a lot, girl. If not for thee, Richard would have stayed in Acre. If not for thee, Brother Julian would still be lying on the chapel floor in Tyre. If not for thee, I would still have my own ship."

Randall removed his hand from her chin and planted it on the side of her breast. He gave the soft flesh a painful squeeze. Ariane gasped and renewed her struggle.

"What is so special about ye that make so many willing to throw away their lives?"

He grabbed the material above her breast, rending the gown in half to her waist. "Perhaps I should take a look at what de Craon wants and Baldwin wants to destroy. Perhaps I should see what distracts the great Avenging Angel."

She tried to clutch the remnants of her gown together. "Are you mad?"

Randall slapped her across the face. Again he pushed her against the wood structure. "Aye, mad with grief since all that I had has been taken away. Years of savings gone. All because of ye. But that will change the minute ye are dead."

Ariane struggled, squirmed and twisted against his rotund body. Her lungs burned. She was not ready to die. Not here, not at the hands of this stinking mule. Think. She must use her wits. She forced a smile to her face.

"Why would you want to kill me? I have been trained to pleasure a man in many ways."

Randall pushed his arm against her throat. "Save thy words girl. I am not interested in thy charms."

Ariane gasped for air. There had to be a way out of this. "You could trade me for a handsome price."

Randall laughed. "Not interested. Baldwin will give me my weight in gold for thy corpse. I will claim that by the time I found thee it was too late. Julian will be dead and I will have my ship back. Aye, no one will gainsay my story."

Quickly, Randall shifted his arms until his hands circled Ariane's neck. Ariane could not break free. She felt herself become lightheaded. Allah, have mercy, I cannot move. Save me. *Send me a savior.*

A blood-chilling cry pierced the air. Ariane tried to focus her eyes on the source, but she could not find it. Randall let go of her neck; Ariane crumbled to the ground. Metal mated with metal. He screamed, pleading for mercy. Then she heard nothing but a gurgle from his throat.

When her vision set itself right and she had enough strength to raise her head, she saw the blue-jeweled sword dripping with blood. Above the sword stood Julian de Maury, his white tunic torn and muddy. A deep gouge above his left eye turned his golden brow red. His bottom lip bled more with each labored breath he took. He looked broken and bent.

He was the most beautiful thing she had ever seen.

"You found me. You saved me," Ariane said.

"Aye." His gaze passed over her body. His blue eyes became fiercely dark; his mouth took a hard bent. "I wish I could kill the pig again. Did he harm you?"

Ariane looked down. She tried to put the two pieces of torn cloth back together with little success.

"Here." He pulled off his tunic and handed it to her. "Put this on. 'Tis ripped, but will cover your…protect your modesty."

Ariane took the tunic covered with the red cross of Christ and slipped it over her head. She reached for his extended hand, her feet wobbled as she gave Julian a weak smile. "My thanks," she said before blackness over took her.

Once again, blurred images swam in front of Ariane's eyes. Just when she thought she could reach the surface, someone would force a warm thick liquid down her throat. Then darkness floated forward.

"She has had enough of that," a stern voice insisted from the mist.

This time she intended to fight the darkness. A foggy image began to form.

The sweet smell disappeared and the unseen hand lowered her head. "She still has marks. The poison continues to lurk in her body."

"Woman, the bruises have faded. The only poison that remains in her body has been placed there by your blasted potion."

Ariane did not recognize the scratchy old voice, but the stern voice flooded her body with familiarity and relief.

"I have seen many women go mad when they saw the marks of ravishment upon their bodies," replied the old woman.

"And I have seen many men become slaves to the evil liquid you hold in your hand. She has spent two nights in darkness; it is time she arises and faces the light."

"As you wish, Brother Julian." The fuzzy image retreated and a much larger one loomed over her.

A warm hand brushed her forehead. "Ariane, it is time to wake up. You have slept long enough."

The image before her took focus. Her breath caught in her throat. His bruised, beautiful, smiling face looked down at her. "Where am I?" she asked.

"We are still in Marseilles. In the home of a well-known healer. Though, over the past few days I have wondered about her methods. She seems more interested in keeping her patients in a stupor than curing their ills."

Ariane looked about. The narrow area boasted of nothing but her pallet and a small wooden stool. A worn brown curtain blocked further view.

She turned her attention back to Julian. Someone had mended his Templar tunic. A healthy scab had formed above his left eye. His bruises had faded to a faint yellow. She wanted to gently rub her fingers over those bruises. "She seems to have had some success with you. Najila will be glad that you are still pleasing to the eye."

He furrowed his forehead. "I do not care if Najila finds my looks pleasing. I do not care how I look to anyone."

Ariane's finger fell from his face. "Well, nonetheless, you are quite handsome."

A light flush colored his cheeks. "My features please you?"

She smiled. Could he possibly not know the effect he had on women? How many times had Guy sworn that Julian was truly celibate? Considering the source, she'd denied the truth of the statement, but the boyish look of innocence did naught but confirm Guy's words.

Ariane could not hide her mischievous nature. "Since you do not care if others find you comely, it matters little what I think."

He looked disappointed. "True. What matters is that you recover from your ordeal."

Her ordeal. A plain white tunic rasped against her sore flesh. Shame flooded her body. Not because of what Brother Randall tried to do, but because she had left Julian when he needed her the most. He had repaid her betrayal by coming to her aid.

Ariane bit her trembling lip to force back the tears that begged to flow. "I am sorry. I should have stayed to help you, but... I wanted my freedom."

Julian brushed a few strands of hair from her cheek. "You did what any warrior would do when held captive by his enemy. I praise you for your attempt."

"But I failed."

"Aye."

Ariane lowered her eyelashes. What good would it do if she told him Brother Randall prevented her return? The outcome would still be the same. She knew what Julian must do. "I hope you will seek mercy in your punishment."

"Punishment? I seek no retribution. Did you not understand my words? I applaud you."

She looked up. Irritation laced his voice and his features. "But you must. It is expected. How will you save face among your fellow knights if you do not punish me? A good punishment may prevent me from escaping again."

Julian cocked his wounded eyebrow. "As I told you

before, I care little about what others think. As for preventing future escapes, I truly doubt any punishment would prevent such an act."

He knew her too well. Surely he did not know about her punishments from Abi Bin? The thought of nights in the black hole caused her to shiver.

"Are you cold?"

"Nay, just taken by an unpleasant thought from the past."

Julian narrowed his gaze as he reached out and began to rub her arms. "Long past or recent past?"

She knew he spoke of what happened with Randall two days ago. "Long past," she answered quietly.

A deep breath escaped Julian's lips. "Do you wish to speak of it?"

His concern and diligent ministration to keep the chill away almost brought the smile back to her lips. Had she not seen him murder Raya, she would have believed him incapable of such a horrendous deed.

"Nay, just keep me out of dark places. Like this room," she teased. "When do we return to the ship?"

Abruptly, he stopped rubbing her arms. His eyes clouded from a brilliant blue to a gloomy gray. By the look of him, one would think she had asked him the gravest question ever given since the beginning of time.

"I will return to the ship shortly. You will not," he answered solemnly.

Ariane groaned as she raised herself to her elbows. "I am fit to return now. Surely you do not wish to delay our voyage any longer?"

Julian put his hands on his knees and straightened his back. "The ship will set sail within the hour."

Ariane shook her head. She must still be under effects of the potion. "But you said I am to stay here."

"Aye." He looked away as if the sight of her pained his eyes.

"Then you will stay behind with me?"

"Nay."

Ariane shivered again. Only this quake did not come from her past, but from the cool tone of his present voice. "I do not understand. How will I get to England if you leave me behind?"

He stared at his thumbnail as if it had some special secret. "You shall not continue onto England."

A cold sweat broke at the nape of her neck and chased another shiver down her spine. "Then where shall I go?"

"Wherever you choose."

This meant one of two things; either she was dreaming or he had lost his mind. She raised herself to a sitting position. "What say you? Are you giving me my freedom?"

"Aye," he growled.

"Why?" she asked bewildered.

He rose and paced the small confines of the sleeping chamber. His shoulder brushed the curtain with each step he took.

"My error in judgment harmed you. Brother Randall and a few crew members loyal to him disappeared shortly after we docked. I knew he would try to take control of the ship again. With Guy remaining at the ship and Andrew at my back, I thought all was safe. Foolishly, I let my guard down, endangering your life."

"My life? As I remember, 'Twas you they fell upon. I ran. I should have stay—"

"The outcome would have been the same. To run was very intelligent."

"But—"

He stopped his pacing and waved her to silence. "We have discussed this matter already. I will hear no more of it. Andrew came to my aid. Within minutes we had the upper hand, but you were missing. Since Randall was not among the scurvy bunch, I realized the true target of their evil plan. 'Tis by the grace of God I found you." A sly smile splayed across his lips. "That and the fact you left pieces of dress and veil on every wagon and merchant booth you passed."

The smile disappeared and he continued, "Brother Randall's loud voice led me to you and revealed a very interesting point of his plan.

"Baldwin! Upon further inquiry I have discovered Lord de Craon was not expected in Marseilles. 'Twas Baldwin who told Master de Sablé we should stop here at the king's orders. I believe that was a lie. Obviously, he is not truly loyal to King Richard. I can only assume your demise was his main goal."

Julian's body shook as he spoke, a look of pure fury in his eyes. He gripped the hilt of his sword until his knuckles turned to a ghostly white.

"I knew then what must be done. At dusk, a man by the name of Robert de Cantelle will come for you. He is an honorable man who sailed with me when I was captain of *Knight's Cross*. He could not stomach the deeds of Brother Randall when he took over the ship. Robert's complaints fell on deaf ears, so he left the order. He lives in Marseilles. You will be safe in his care. Arrangements have been made to take you back to Tyre. I am setting you free."

Freedom. She would be owned by no man. Her life would belong to her. Freedom. She should be overwhelmed with joy.

But she was not.

Julian. What of *his* life? Before the thought had taken full form, Ariane realized the source of her panic. "What will happen if you do not complete your mission?"

"That is my concern, not yours." He pulled out a small dagger from under his tunic.

"But Julian—"

"Hush, my lady. You must listen carefully if you wish no ill to befall you." Julian flipped the dagger over in his hand examining the blade. "You will take this dagger. My sister had one once and it became very useful. It is a small weapon, but if used wisely, it can save your life."

"But—" She kicked the cover off her legs and tried to stand.

He planted his hand on her shoulder and pushed her back down on the pallet. The blade glittered in his other hand, less than a hand's width from her chest. "Ariane, listen! It is important that you know the proper use of this weapon or it will bring about your death. Many times when I assisted pilgrims into Jerusalem, we met Muslim traveling parties. Some greeted us with kindness, others with swords drawn."

Julian lowered his head and tapped the dagger against the palm of his hand. He hesitated. Then raised his glassy gaze to meet hers.

"Often they had women and children in their parties. Once a woman attacked me with a small dagger. She slashed the blade through the air like a crazed animal. Charging at me like a wild boar. So foolish. Such a waste. The only way to fend off her attack was to place my own blade into her breast."

The agony in his eyes ripped Ariane in half. A memory flashed before her eyes. *Raya gripping a paltry dagger, waving and lunging at Julian.* She had forgotten about the weapon in Raya's hand.

His shoulders slumped. He sank heavily onto the stool. "If I could change anything I have done in my life, I would change the death of that poor woman. God forgive me."

The hatred Ariane had nourished so diligently against this man began to fade. He gave out a long sigh, which tore at her heart. She reached out to him, but he pulled away from her touch.

"I did not tell this story for pity, but to educate you. If you find yourself threatened, wait until your enemy is less than a hand from you, then thrust with all your might, here." He pointed to his heart and smiled sadly. "Then you will be able to do as you have always wanted to do to me...cut his heart out."

He grabbed her hand, shoving the dagger's hilt into her palm. Without warning he leaned forward and placed a lingering kiss on her forehead. An odd current drifted down from her head and seeped its way through her eyes, her nose, and her mouth. 'Twas almost as if she could taste the kiss on her lips.

Then suddenly he stood and made his way over to an opening in the curtain. "Godspeed, Lady Ariane." He gave her one last breathtaking smile and left.

Numb, Ariane stared at the fluttering curtain. She was free. The butcher had released her. The butcher...the butcher. The words rang false in her ears. He killed Raya to protect himself. He saved her from Randall. The Avenging Angel had become her guardian angel.

Gone. She would never hear his strong determined voice or feel the warmth of his touch. Never again would his gentle lips linger against her skin.

Her gaze drifted to the dagger in her hand. The handle possessed the same blue stone she had seen in the hilt of Julian's sword. So much like the color of his eyes...when he smiled.

Her stomach ached. Her heart felt like every mule, horse, and goat in this town had trampled across the fragile body part. There could be only one cure for what ailed her.

She clutched the small weapon in her hand, jumped from the pallet, and pushed back the curtain.

"Mademoiselle, you should be in bed," the old woman chided.

Ariane brushed by the woman and stopped in the doorway. She looked left then right. A man struggled to move his cart through the street which had turned muddy and rutted from a recent rain. She saw a group of dirty children playing in the puddles and a woman chasing a renegade goose, but she did not see Julian. She stepped into the street.

"Mademoiselle, ye have nothing on your feet! The chill will pull the poison through your body again."

Ariane ignored the old woman and made her way further into the middle of the road. Again she looked left and right.

Nothing.

Sickness rolled like sea waves through her stomach. The harbor! He headed for the harbor.

"Which way is the harbor?" she called to the old woman standing in the doorway.

"Mademoiselle, your death—"

"Which way?" she shouted.

The old woman pointed her finger to the right. Ariane ran down the sloppy street, sharp stones cut her tender feet. Then she came to a halt. She raised up on her toes.

There. Less than a furlong ahead she could see his broad shoulders above the crowd. She pushed and shoved her way down the road. Cold mud splattered her calves as she ran.

"Julian." Her breath ragged, her lungs weighted and spent, the word came out a few tones above a whisper.

She pushed onward.

"Julian! Julian!"

Her legs ached and she stopped. She took a deep breath before racing forward again.

"Julian! Julian!"

He turned slowly. Her heart leapt in her chest.

"Julian! Julian!"

Closer. Clearer. She could see the lines of his jaw. She slid to a halt with a pace between them.

He said not a word, but stared at her as if she were a few bushels short of a boll. "Julian, I—"

"Came to finish me?" His gaze narrowed on the dagger in her hand.

Ariane looked at the dagger. Mud splattered the blade and the front of her white tunic. She inhaled when he came forward until less than a palm separated them.

His large hand wrapped around hers, lifting the dagger until the blade rested against his heart. "Then take the trophy you have always wanted. Cut away, dear lady."

She tried to pull away, but he would not release her hand. "Nay, I have not come to kill you, but to go with you."

His face flooded with confusion. "My lady, you are ill?"

Arian stamped her foot in the mud, splattering the brown slop over his boots. "I am well enough to know what I want. I want to go with you."

"Why?"

What could she tell him? That she would miss his rich voice, his intriguing looks, his appealing touch? Nay. "What will happen to you if I stay?"

He shrugged and let go of her hand. "I will deliver the cargo and seek out Richard's brother, Prince John."

"What will you say about me?"

"I will tell the truth. That I let you go."

Her heart thundered in her chest. "You will be killed."

His fingers lightly brushed her cheek. "Mayhap. What matters is you are safe and happy."

She turned her head toward his fingers. "I will go with you."

"If you do, I will turn you over to Lord de Craon," he said softly.

"I know."

"It would be better if you cut my heart out."

She looked at the dagger and gave it to him. "Nay, I have grown fond of it where it is."

He gave out a long sigh and gazed down the street. "Ariane, leave."

"Nay."

"Leave!"

"Nay!"

He looked down at her and brushed back a wayward strand of hair with a trembling hand. "Then we must go."

"Aye," she whispered.

A deep frown settled on his face. "Where are your shoes?"

She shrugged.

He shook his head and swiftly lifted her in his arms. "You will catch a chill."

"So I have been told." The heat of security radiated from his arms to her cradled body.

He shifted her in his arms until he could place the dagger in her lap. "Better that you keep this also. Someday it may be your best ally."

Ariane closed her hand around the hilt of the dagger and placed her head against his chest. Whatever you say, Julian."

Nine

Sanctify them through truth: thy word is truth.
John 17:17

ULIAN INHALED THE COOL CRISP AIR OF LATE AUTUMN and scanned the English coastline near the home of his youth. Moss frosted the ancient rocks protecting the shore. Only a few brown leaves clung to the barren tree branches, and the grass had already taken on the look of winter sleep. More than a year had passed since he started this task. By now he had hoped Lord de Craon's desire for Lady Ariane would have faded, but no missive came freeing her from the marriage contract.

He thought he would be elated to return home to see his mother again, knowing that half of his journey was over. Julian folded his hands on the rail and bowed his head. God forgive him, he wished his travels were just beginning. He squeezed his hands together until his nails dug deep into his flesh.

What had become of him? His mind was a jumbled mess, much like this journey had been. One minute he would be irate over the time they had lost due to minor details, and then the next minute he would fear they would reach their destination too soon.

Now the time had come. He had to turn Ariane over to the nuns at Wynnhurst Abbey. Then perhaps he could calm the emotional wave he had been riding. When she angered him, this thought brought relief. But again, she would call him by his given name and he wanted nothing more than to hold her in his arms forever. Julian unfolded his hands and slammed his palms against the rail. Oh, the devil knew how to torture a man. Why did God stand aside and let the wretched torment continue?

Guy came up beside him, clasping and rubbing his hands together. "Julian, we should wake the others. We have much to do this glorious day. By God, I had forgotten how cold this land could be."

"Do not use God's name in vain, Guy."

"What is this? My ears do not sting from the loud reprimand I am accustomed to receiving when I offend God. Instead you utter the words so softly one wonders if the breath you drew to say them was worth it."

Julian turned away from his friend's intense scrutiny.

Guy let loose a low whistle. "As captain, I would think you would be running from stern to bow shouting orders that would wake the dead. Instead you stand here like a moonstruck cow. She's wiggled her way deep into your heart, has she not?"

Julian turned until his back rested against the rail and crossed his arms against his chest. "You speak like a fool."

"Fool, am I?" Guy tapped his temple. "Then I am the smartest fool that has ever been born. Your eyes all but roll from your head and jump into her lap whenever she is about. Admit it, you have found something you can love almost as much as God."

Julian grabbed the front of Guy's tunic and twisted the material until Guy's eyes grew wide with fear. "Say not another word, friend, or I shall have to cut your tongue from your mouth. No one. No one! Will take the place of God in my heart."

"That is not what I me—"

"Cease your prattling!" Julian released Guy with a shove. "Go wake the others. As you said, much needs to be done."

Guy stumbled back and rubbed his chest where Julian had grabbed him. "As you say, Brother Julian."

Julian's throat became tight, his blood chilled at the cool tone of Guy's voice. He clenched his hands. What was happening to him that he would lash out at his only true friend? A friend who did naught to offend him, but spoke the truth.

Ariane wrapped the warm cloak about her as she stood at the rail and watched several small boats travel back and forth between their ship and a weather-beaten pier. They had taken a small river off the channel to this obscured spot. Nothing but a few wooden buildings stood back from a rotting pier. "Why have we landed here and not at a familiar port?"

Guy stood beside her his brow furrowed as he checked the cargo list. "Because, my lady, Brother Julian is a wise man. If we travel on to Dover or London most of the goods we carry would be confiscated by Prince John, or another order of monks."

"I can understand his fear of John, but of another order of monks? I find that hard to believe. Who would want to anger the Templar's Avenging Angel?"

"True, the Templars are a powerful order and Julian's reputation is well-known, but greed and sheer numbers will change even the most pious man into a murdering thief."

Ariane nodded. "Aye, I know the truth of that. For I have stood here this past hour and watched boat upon boat being unloaded filled with loot taken from my homeland."

Guy threw back his head and gave out a loud laugh. "My lady, with all due respect, this is your homeland."

Ariane shivered and glanced at the dark clouds billowing above her, and then at the molten brown earth along the shore. The land looked hard and unyielding. She blew a puff of warm air into the frigid day and watched it take a smoky form. She buried her cheeks deep in the cloak. "Nay, this is not my homeland—'tis too cold."

Guy inhaled deeply of the crisp air. "Aye, 'tis cold, but smell the freshness. It is good to be home."

She peeked her nose out of the thick cloak and took a small sniff. Freshness? She smelled naught, except the beginning of a sneeze. "So this is winter? I do not care for it."

Another chuckle escaped Guy's throat. "Nay, this is autumn, my lady. Winter brings winds and cold that will rattle your teeth."

Whatever did Guy mean? Her teeth chattered now, surely it could not get colder, and yet, somewhere in the recesses of her mind she remembered being very cold, her feet being warmed near a large fireplace while her father spoke—of what? His words, what were they? Murdering—what?

Must have been a dream. She clutched the tiny heart necklace that held a small carving of a cross. A necklace from her father when she had been little. The only murderers she knew were Christians. Her father had been a Christian. Surely he could not be talking about his own people that way?

Guy pointed to the shoreline. "Look yonder. There stands Julian and, by the cross, that looks to be his mother beside him."

She turned her gaze to follow Guy's outstretched arm. Julian did stand on the shoreline with a woman finely dressed. Ariane's blood began to move in her ears as loud as the wind roared against the coastline. She strained against the cold wind for a better look. What kind of woman would give birth to such a magnificent man?

Magnificent? Where had that thought come from? He was exasperating, demanding, stern, and ill-tempered. And yet he could be good, giving, gentle, handsome, and aye, magnificent.

"Come along," Guy said. "Our boat has arrived."

Trying to make sense of her thoughts, Ariane followed as Guy helped her down the rope ladder until her feet safely landed into the small rowboat. What if Julian's mother did not like her? *Why should she care*? After all she was not marrying Julian.

Ariane's heart gave a small lurch. There lay the problem. Whenever she thought of her coming marriage, it was Julian's face she saw, not Lord de Craon's. Allah have mercy, she must get a hold of herself or she would go mad.

The boat swayed against the pier and she looked up to see Julian standing there, his hand extended. "There is someone I wish you to meet."

Dumbfounded, Ariane took Julian's hand and stepped ashore. Her breaths became short as she saw the dignified dark-haired woman watching her.

Julian gave Ariane's palm a gentle squeeze. "You are so cold. Your eyes are as wide as those of a rabbit caught in a snare. You have nothing to fear here, Lady Ariane. I am here, you will be safe. Come." His voice though soothing offered her no comfort.

She managed to propel one wobbling leg forward. Julian dragged her along as if she were a sack of wheat at his side. Her whole body felt numb. Surely her breath would cease at any moment and she would collapse like a fool before this lovely lady. Blast it! Why should she be afraid of one old lady, even if it was Julian's mother? Ariane swallowed, knowing full well she wanted this woman to like her.

They stopped, her mind a jumbled mess. What possibly could she say to this woman?

At the last minute, Ariane lowered her head and pulled the hood of her cloak as far as possible over her forehead. 'Twould be better to play the shy innocent instead of blurting out something stupid. After all, this was Julian's mother. Mayhap if she made a good impression on his mother, she could make Julian realize that it would be a sin to give her to Lord de Craon.

"Mother, may I present the Lady Ariane, niece of the late Geoffrey, Duke of Brittany," Julian said in English. He then repeated the same greeting to Ariane in Arabic.

The older woman reached out and removed the hood from Ariane's face. "Oh my, look at her hair."

Ariane's blood ran cold and then hot and then seemed to drain from her body all together. The woman's voice had the air of aristocracy and made Ariane feel more insecure. She kept her head bowed, but the woman gently raised her chin. Ariane squeezed her eyes shut. Think. How do you address a lady again?

"Look at me, child," Julian's mother said tenderly.

Julian translated the command.

Ariane blinked. She was greeted with a warm smile and eyes that matched the shape and color of her son's. Aye, Julian's eyes and smile came from his mother, but that seemed to be it. She was petite. Yea, almost half the size of her son. Her deep, rich, black hair with a few strands of gray was pulled away from her forehead. Her calm voice and warm fingers seemed to pull the chill from her bones.

"You say she is related to the royal family through marriage?" Julian's mother said in English. "If I did not know any better I would say she was Richard's own. Have you not noticed how beautiful she is?"

He cleared his throat. "Aye, mother, I have noticed."

Julian's mother gave her son a peculiar look. "Really, have you? I have never known you to notice any woman." She turned her attention back to Ariane and gave out a sigh. "She will make beautiful children."

The praise was all too much for Ariane. Never had anyone fussed over her so. Yet, the more Julian's mother talked the more Julian frowned. Mayhap he did not agree with his mother. Aye, that had to be it, for not once during their voyage had he given comment on her looks. He talked about her instruction and her health, but never about her appearance, except when she was without shoes and one very off-putting comment about her hair.

Julian's mother released Ariane's chin. "Tell her, I think her hair coloring is beautiful."

Julian repeated his mother's request. Even though Ariane

understood every word Julian's mother said she waited for his translation.

Ariane feigned surprise. "I have been told it is the color of the flames of hell."

Julian hesitated then translated.

"Pray tell, who would say such a thing?" Julian's mother quickly turned a hard gaze on her son.

Julian said naught.

She gave her son another stony look. "Tell her, we will have to change your thinking on that matter. Tell her, that her hair is the color of the sun on a warm autumn day."

Again Julian said naught.

"Tell her, Julian." his mother ordered.

He shook his head. "Nay, Mother, I cannot say that."

"Why, Julian, since when do you disobey your mother's wishes? My, things do seem to have changed."

Julian lowered his head without comment. Ariane's heart plummeted. He could not give her a compliment even when the words were not his.

"The unloading is all but completed, Julian," Guy shouted as he strode up the pier. "The men will tighten up the ship. They wish to be finished before evening prayers. Baroness, how good to see you again."

"Sir Guy, I should have known that you would be with my son. He is lucky to have such a loyal friend."

Guy bowed his head and took Julian's mother's hand in his, giving it a brief kiss. "It has been a long time, Lady Catherine. I have returned your son as I promised, free of injury."

Ariane watched intently. Julian's mother, Lady Catherine, acted like a true lady. All about her treated her as one. Despair swept through Ariane. When had Guy ever bowed or kissed her hand? Never. When had Julian treated her with such respect? Never.

True, Julian probably showed respect because Lady Catherine was his mother, but yet there seemed to be more than just the devotion a son gave to his mother. In fact, the only time he did defy his mother was when he was expected to translate a compliment. How civil and polite Julian and Brother Guy were around Lady Catherine.

Julian grunted. "'Tis more likely I have kept Guy's tunic from being ripped."

Well, mayhap not totally polite with each other.

Lady Catherine pulled both men to her sides and wrapped her arms around them. "It matters not who took care of whom. You both have come back to me, and I thank God for that."

Ariane wanted to crawl under the frozen rocks. She felt like an outsider. She was always the outsider; she was always alone. Both men looked at Lady Catherine as if she were a queen. Was that it? Mayhap that was why Julian respected his mother so, she acted like a queen.

Catherine turned her attention back to Ariane. "How is the girl's education coming along?"

"She is a quick study, my lady. Though her English tongue is slow," Guy answered.

"She has a strong mind. She will do well at court," Julian added.

Do well at court. Ha! They talked as if she were a child. Slow to her English tongue indeed.

Ariane crossed her arms. They may think 'Twas all right to speak as if she wasn't there, but she did not. Ariane spun about and made her way back to the small boat.

Julian came up behind her and grabbed her by the shoulder. "Where are you going?"

"I am returning to the ship. You were right. I should not have come here. I do not belong with baronesses and ladies. I am naught but chattel to be given to whomever the king decides." Ariane shouted in English.

Julian released her arm and stared at her as if he had never seen her before.

Guy rushed forward and stopped at Julian's side. "By God, Julian, did you not hear her? Her English is flawless! Her lessons must be taking hold. I take full credit for that."

Lady Catherine came to stand next to her son. "Not a word of English before your trip, you say?"

Guy smiled. "Mayhap 'twas Julian threatening to use the lash on her when he was angry that improved her mind."

"Really?" Lady Catherine gave her son a curious look.

"Well, I do not think he really would have. 'Tis just that Lady Ariane seems to bring out the worst in Julian."

"Really?" Lady Catherine repeated.

Julian stood in stony silence. Ariane chastised herself. Not once had she slipped on this journey, and now in one brief moment of anger and insecurity, she had blurted out in English like a knave. Ariane looked down, she could feel Lady Catherine's intense gaze and Julian's frozen stare upon her. The ruse was up. The only one still in the dark was Guy, for he prattled away.

Finally he stopped. "By the cross, Julian. I think she knew English all along."

Ariane glanced Julian's way. 'Twas a mistake. For he stood like a warrior ready for battle. Pure fury darkened his eyes.

He grabbed her arm and dragged her up a steep incline from the pier.

"Where are you going?" Guy shouted. "The abbey is to the south of here."

"'Tis too unsafe. I am taking the lady to Crosswind Keep." Julian snapped over his shoulder.

"To your home? Do you think that is wise?"

"I think 'tis a wonderful idea," Lady Catherine called out in a voice filled with amusement.

Men and beasts alike gave way as if a blazing fire was hot on their heels. Julian ignored every friendly greeting in the bailey and strode to the hall. Still he did not ease his pace, but yanked her up a set of crude steps to a room near the end of a narrow hallway.

He slammed the door and released her. She saw the rage roar across his face. He would beat her now. In her haste to get away from him, she stumbled over a wooden stool and landed bent in half over a small table. Ariane heard Julian coming up behind her. Quickly she straightened and her head flew back against a hard surface, followed by a loud crunch.

"Ow! God Almighty, I think you have broken my nose!"

Did her ears deceive her? Did he say what she thought he said? Did he use God's name in vain? A sin against the second commandment? Oh, he was angry. She spun about hoping to block the blows that surely would fall upon her. Instead Julian stood there cupping his nose, a small trickle of blood filtering through his fingers. Oh dear, she had done it now.

She looked about for something to stop the blood. The room was not without comforts. Besides the table and stool there stood a fine chair and a very large bed. An old tapestry of a young man on his knees in prayer hung above it. Underneath a small window stood a simple stand with a basin and a pitcher, but there was not a rag in sight.

Another loud moan left Julian's throat as he slid down to sit on the floor, tilting his head back against the door. Ariane rushed over to the basin. Allah be praised, there was water in the pitcher. Julian gave out another groan. Quickly Ariane poured the water into the basin. She removed her cloak and dipped a corner of it into the water. She ran over and kneeled next to Julian.

"Remove your hands so I can take a look," she said.

"Nay, I fear you will plow your fist in my face again and finish me off for good."

"Don't be foolish, 'Twas an accident brought on by your own stupid act." Ariane pulled his hands away, dabbing at his nose and chin.

Julian sniffed. "My actions were brought on by deceit. I should have known you remembered English. What better place to hide a spy than in a man's harem. How many men did you deceive?"

After clearing the blood, Ariane examined his nose. "Does not appear to be broken. 'Tis as straight and noble as before, only larger and much redder."

"Aye, I can feel it grow wide across my face. How many, Ariane?"

"I have lost count." Let him think what he wanted. He would not believe the truth anyway. Ariane pressed lightly against one side of his nose to pinch off the flow of blood.

Julian's body tensed. "And French, you speak that tongue as well, do you not?"

"Oui, je parle Francais."

Julian grabbed the cloak from her hand and held the material to his nose. "Aye, I suspected as much."

Ariane reached for the cloak again. "Here, let me help you."

"Nay, you are too harsh. You are not a tender, compassionate nurse." He sniffed, lightly patting the corner of the cloak against his nose.

"You are truly a powerful warrior, to crumble under the pain of a bruised nose. Here, let me help you to yonder bed. Mayhap if you lie flat the flow of blood will stop." Ariane placed his free arm over her shoulder and began to push up. He did not budge.

"I can stand on my own," he said stiffly.

"Are you sure? 'Tis a grave wound you have."

Julian pushed himself up against the wall. "Do not jest with me. You do not know the pain of this injury. How many times have you been smashed in the nose?"

Ariane guided Julian to the bed. "I have never been smashed in the nose. I'm usually the one who does the smashing."

Julian lay down and all tension seemed to leave his body. "Aye, I can believe that. Ariane, I want no more lies, no more secrets. I cannot protect you if there is no trust between us."

She sat down next to him and began to smooth his hair off his brow. Aye, as she suspected 'twas soft as a bird's feather. She became more bold and let her fingers float through the soft strands. He closed his eyes.

"Protect me? I do not need any protection, Julian. I can

take care of myself," she said softly, using her index finger to tuck his hair behind his ear, gazing at the softness of his ear lobe.

He dropped her cloak from his nose. The flow of blood seemed to have stopped. Yet, he did not open his eyes. "Aye, you are strong and beautiful, but you still need my help."

Her heart skipped a beat. The missed beat fluttered to her stomach and caused ripples of pleasure to move down her spine. He called her beautiful. Her heart seemed ready to burst. If he found her attractive perhaps he felt something else for her. She leaned closer, moving her finger to brush against his cheek. Aye, he was a magnificent man.

"I suppose I could use another lesson on courtly manner. I should not have lost my temper in front of your mother," she said, brushing her finger tips down his cheek once again.

He opened his eyes and gently stayed her hand against his cheek. "Nay, that is not what I mean. Your conduct was fine." The warmth in his blue eyes sent a flutter to her stomach. "Trust me, Ariane. No more lies."

"I will tell no more lies and trust you if you do not use God's name in vain again," she whispered.

He gave a faint smile, then turned his head to kiss gently the palm of her hand. His lips sent a trail of tingling tremors to her hands, her toes, and her heart.

"Aye, you do bring out the worst in me. What shall I do with you, Ariane? What shall I do?"

She could not deny what her heart knew to be true. She loved the sod. Even with his pious pompous manner as well as his kind and caring nature to others. The arrogance and the sensitivity; for all of it was Julian.

Her lips ached to feel his kisses as well. "Whatever you want, my lord. I am yours."

Aye, she was his. Julian placed another gentle kiss on the palm of her hand, then another on her delicate wrist. He took a deep breath and inhaled the soft sweet smell that was Ariane's alone. A smell as fresh as the air after a spring shower. A smell as light as a gentle rain. A smell as delicate as a room filled with jasmine petals. All was Ariane and all was his. He took one more absorbing breath and turned his gaze back to Ariane's lovely face. She moved slightly, revealing the tapestry on the wall above the head of the bed.

The tapestry arrested his gaze, looking as new as the day his mother had given it to him. The yellow of the young boy's hair shown bright. The white of his tunic had not faded. The blue of the boy's eyes were clear and crisp. His mother had taken such good care of it over the many years he had been in the Holy Land. She had given him the tapestry on the same day his father had given him the sword he now carries. Both were gifts to mark the death of his childhood and the birth of his manhood.

He remembered his father had taken him outside where he withdrew the great sword from its sheath. Julian's father waved the sword over his land and said, "I give you this mighty sword so that you may guard and protect that which will be yours."

He had handed the blue-jeweled sword to Julian and slapped him soundly between the shoulder blades. "The blue stone marks the strength of the de Maury family. The same strength I see in your eyes. Be steadfast, for there are those that will wish to destroy both."

When Julian and his father went back to the keep, his mother had greeted him with a large tapestry draped across her arms.

"I made this for you, my son. You are strong of body and mind. God has blessed you abundantly. He has chosen you for some great purpose. Remember to listen to His Word in all things and He will direct your path. Then you will always know what He expects from you."

He remembered the elation he felt when he unrolled the tapestry and saw the image of himself as a youth, praying. Much to his father's dismay, the tapestry became Julian's most prized possession. From that day forth he knew what course his life must take. No matter how hard his father drilled him in the art of combat and the duties of a lord, Julian knew he would follow the path God had laid out for him.

Then you will always know what He expects from you. His mother's words swirled through his mind. He did then, But now...

Guard and protect that which is yours. His father's proclamation followed swiftly on the heels of his mother's statement. Ariane was betrothed to another. She was not his to guard and protect. He had followed his own will over that of God's.

"Julian," Ariane said softly, looming over him blocking his view of the tapestry.

He realized he still held her hand to his face. The warmth from her palm turned from a soothing balm to a heated acid. He curled his hand around her wrist and wrenched it from his face.

Ariane gave a painful gasp which tore at his heart. He eased his grip slightly.

"What we do here is wrong." He released her hand quickly and pulled himself up until he stood above her. "You are betrothed to another, and I am a servant of the Lord."

The smile fell from Ariane's face and was replaced by a look of despair and hurt. He turned away when he saw her eyes redden and tear. Julian stalked to the door.

"But I do not love the man to whom I am betrothed," Ariane cried. I—"

"Do not say it!" Julian tightly grasped the latch of the door. "For what you seek cannot happen. For what you feel must never be returned."

He threw open the door and made haste down the hallway. For he could not bear to hear her wretched sobs without wanting to go back and kiss them all away.

123

Ten

A man's foes shall be they of his own household.
Matthew 10:36

ITH LONG DETERMINED STEPS JULIAN ENTERED THE hall, picked up a wooden chair that sat against the wall, and dropped it down near the large fireplace. He threw himself onto the seat and scowled at the fire, willing it to blaze so hot that it would forever burn away thoughts of Ariane.

Julian's mother lightly planted another chair across from him, and settled herself into it. "Such a sour face. Are you not pleased to be home, my son?"

Julian stretched out his long legs and forced his expression to gentle. His mother could not know of his turmoil over Ariane. "Aye, mother, 'tis good to be home. Little seems to have changed."

He looked at his mother's delicate features. The years had agreed with her. The lines on her face and about her eyes were still fine. Her skin held tight to her chin and her cheeks held good color. Mayhap there was a little more gray in her hair, but her eyes still sparkled as they had when he was a boy.

Julian took a deep breath. Aye, little had changed since he left. The rushes still smelled fresh as they did ten years ago. The hall was still orderly. The trestle tables and benches were still stacked in the same corner. The servant's pallets were neatly stored in another. Except for an occasional monk that hurried about, all was the same as the day he left.

The Templars had kept the promise they had made to him when he had joined the order. Before turning over his holdings, Julian drafted a document ensuring his mother's welfare. The Templars would not take full control of the lands until his mother's death. Father Bethal, the family's religious counsel would be the controlling clergy, and his brother, Hugh would be given a third of the land. Though the Templars had protested, they had no choice but to agree. Two-thirds was better than nothing, and a healthy tithe made the Templars more than agreeable. His mother had been overjoyed with his decision. Hugh, on the other hand, was not.

His mother gave a warm smile and folded her hands on her lap. "Yea, little has changed here, but much has changed with you. Has it not?"

He thought about ignoring her comment, but she held his eyes fast with a determined look. A look he remembered well; she demanded an answer. A diversion would not work, but he tried a feeble attempt anyway.

"I am tired from the long journey. Mayhap I should retire for a few hours."

His dear mother cocked one eyebrow. "Retire, where? You have given your chamber to Lady Ariane.

She paused. He knew her next remarks would be carefully worded. Like a skilled swordsman, she would aim straight at her mark. Julian prepared himself for his counterattack.

"Unless, you have some agreement with this girl?"

"Agreement?" As always his mother's first blow of words knocked him senseless.

"Yea Julian, to share things."

Julian bolted from his seat knocking over the chair. "What are you suggesting?" He cringed slightly when his voice came out a little less than a roar.

"Why, I suggest nothing. I just find it a little unnatural for the son who left years ago to become a Templar to step off a ship and drag a young woman though the village, through his home and up to his chamber."

Warmth spread over his body. He was a grown man, yet his mother had a way of making him feel like a runny-nose lad. "Mother, surely you would know me better. I would never compromise a lady. Nor would I jeopardize my soul."

"Sit down, Julian and lower your voice. Do you wish to make this family the center of peasant gossip?"

The brunt of gossip? Nay, never. Here, he was thought of Julian the Pure of Heart. However, things had changed. Now he was called the Avenging Angel or as Ariane would call him, a butcher. But which name fit him? With his wayward thoughts of Ariane, surely he was not Pure of Heart anymore. Nor could he be God's Avenging Angel if he remained here. That left the butcher. Aye, he had killed many and he had butchered Ariane's life by expecting her to marry against her will. Aye, butcher fit him well.

He heard a rustle from the far end of the hall, near the entry, as if someone lurked in the shadows. A servant scurried against the wall and out the door. Aye, even the walls had ears. His mother was right, dragging Ariane to his room had been a foolish thing to do, but she had a way of making him act irrationally.

With a sigh he picked up his chair and sat down. Julian placed his elbows on his knees and folded his hands. "I am sorry. 'Twas a stupid thing to do."

His mother leaned forward and placed her hands over his, her voice quiet and melancholy. "I know you are an honorable man. You were always a serious lad, but you always showed compassion to others. Never have I seen you lose your temper as you did with Ariane. The Crusade has hardened you.

"I have talked to Brother Andrew and I know you are not here of your own free will. But, Julian, you cannot take out your frustration on the girl. She is even more of a pawn than you are. This journey will end for you. You will return to the life you have chosen. You are only inconvenienced for a little while. Lady Ariane will spend her life with a man she does not know and may never learn to love."

Julian glanced up at his mother. Her words had struck like a lance being shoved deep into his heart. *Learn to love.*

Nay, she would never love Lord de Craon.

In his mind he saw himself returning from the Holy Land after Jerusalem was safe, wandering across the countryside because he had no home, no wife, and no family. One day he would come upon the house of Lord Jacques de Craon. Ariane would greet him with a brood of children at her feet. The image became more vivid in his mind. Lord de Craon would come up behind Ariane and embrace her. Then she would turn a smiling face to her husband—

"Nay!" Julian cried.

His mother rose from her seat and wrapped her arms around Julian. "My poor boy. Oh what suffering your tortured mind must bring you." She stroked his hair and planted a tender kiss on his head.

"Ah look, the favorite son has returned to the bosom of his mother."

Julian did not have to look up to know who owned the sarcastic voice. Hugh.

Taking a hard swallow, Julian raised his head and looked at the brother he had not seen for a decade. Though Hugh's lips were drawn tight and his blue eyes shone like a frosted morn, to Julian he was a warm welcome sight. Aside from their differences, Julian's love for his younger brother was so deep it could not be destroyed, even though Hugh loathed him and held Julian entirely responsible for his own past failures.

Julian rose to his feet and moved toward his brother, arms outstretched in greeting. "You look well, Hugh. Marriage must agree with you."

A cold, mean smile spread across Hugh's lips. His back stiffened. Hugh's eyes never left Julian's face as he spoke. "Is that not interesting, Mother? I have not seen my brother in almost ten years and the first thing he comments about is my wife."

Lady Catherine maneuvered herself between her sons. "Hugh, do not start this now. Julian knows naught of your trouble."

Hugh gave out a sad laugh. "He knows naught of what he created. Yet I live with the reality daily."

"Stop this. I will not have you stand here and blame your brother for what you knew was always true. No one else chose your course. You did so by your own free will."

'Twas then Julian noticed the hard lines in Hugh's brow. His brother's torment and hatred had grown since they had last been together.

Julian gently stepped around his mother and stood before Hugh once again, extending his arms outward. "Brother, I cannot change the past, let us not dwell on sad memories and words said in anger. Let us be brothers again in word and deed."

Hugh shook his head and folded his arms in front of him. "Always the pious one. Nay, I will not take you in my arms and give you a heartfelt greeting. I can never forget. Every morn for the past ten years I have prayed for your death."

"Hugh!" Julian's mother cried, clasping her throat. The color drained from her face, her eyes clouded with tears.

His mother's knees buckled, Julian caught her in his arms. His poor mother. He should have thought of what his return might do to her. He should have stayed away. He should have taken Ariane to Wynnhurst Abbey then left.

Hugh rushed over to the chair where Julian had placed his mother. "I am sorry. I should not have—"

Lady Catherine opened her eyes. "I will hear no more of this. Give me your word, Hugh. Tonight we will welcome your brother home. I want naught but laughter in the hall this eve."

Ariane could not bear to stay in that drafty chamber once Julian had left. Restless and in need of a sympathetic ear, she set out in search of Najila. As she turned the bend in the stone stairs, she found Lady Catherine and Julian sitting in the great hall, deep in conversation. He looked so forlorn and in distress. Not wanting to intrude, Ariane turned and started her ascent when a smaller image of Julian strode into the room.

Guy had told her about Julian's brother, but he failed to mention Hugh's looks and demeanor. A half-blind man could not mistake them for anything other than brothers. Even though Hugh stood a hand shorter than Julian, and his hair was dark like his mother's, they both had the same arrogant stance. Try as she might, she could not make her feet retreat. Instead, Ariane pressed her back against the wall and eavesdropped into their conversation.

From the icy words that flew from Hugh's lips 'twas apparent he held no love for his brother. Ariane wondered what had transpired in the past to cause such hatred. She inched closer, hoping to catch more of the discourse.

A small squeak followed by a scamper of tiny feet across her toes sent Ariane shrieking down the stairs. Frantically, she ran past the others and jumped up on top of Julian's chair.

"It ran across my feet."

"'Tis the cold," Lady Catherine waved off and relaxed back into her chair. "The cold weather brings in the mice."

Ariane nodded her agreement then waited for Julian to draw his sword and attack the rodent. Instead he stood with his hands on his hips, staring at her bare feet.

"My lady, where are your shoes?" he asked.

What nonsense was this? He wished to talk about her feet instead of the fortress's infestation. "I am not wearing those shoes. They pinch my feet. You dragged me upstairs with such haste I fear Najila does not know where to find me. She has my silk slippers."

"Oh, oh! What have we here?" Hugh circled around Julian and peered up at Ariane. He held out his hand to help Ariane down.

"Nay, sir, I will not leave this seat until Julian takes care of the furry creature lurking on the stairs."

Julian moved to stand next to his brother. "Lady, I am certain your shrieking has caused the mouse to flee to the next keep. Please come down."

"'Tis all right," Lady Catherine cajoled. "On the morrow we will set traps to catch them."

Julian smiled. "Aye, we will catch every 'furry creature' that dares to cross your beautiful bare toes."

Ariane could not help but return the smile. "Very well, I will hold you to your word and we all know you never break your word." She held out her hand, instead Julian's hands circled her waist and lifted her from her perch. As soon as her feet touched the floor, he quickly released her.

"Do my eyes deceive me? Could it be possible?" Hugh looked back and forth between Ariane and Julian, a twinkle in his blue eyes. "Brother," he threw his arm over Julian's shoulder, "did you bring home a wife?"

Ariane felt the blood rush to her cheeks as she saw the blood drain from Julian's face. Lady Catherine tried to rise, but slumped back in her chair. The only one who appeared to be pleased was Hugh.

He grabbed and began to rigorously shake the hand of the slack-jawed Julian. "Wonderful news. I cannot wait until Jane hears the good tidings."

Lady Catherine had managed to get to her feet, waving her hands frantically in the air. "Nay, 'tis not what you think. They are not wed."

Hugh's wide grin turned to a look of shock, he gave out a loud hoot. "By God, Julian. You have taken a leman. That's even better!" He turned to his petite mother and whirled her around in his arms. "Our angel has grown a tail."

"Put me down. Have you lost your wits?"

The younger brother complied and placed his mother on her feet. He then shouted at the top of his lungs. "Wine! Wine for my prodigal brother. Let us start the celebration now."

A cook and a monk wiping his greasy hands on his robe appeared in the great hall. Both looked at Hugh as if he had taken too many sword blows to his head.

"Hush, Hugh." Lady Catherine waved the cook and the monk away. "This is Lady Ariane. She is betrothed to Lord Jacques de Craon, King Philip's cousin. King Richard ordered Julian to bring her to England for Christian training. She *is not* Julian's leman."

Hugh drooped like a wilted flower. A frown returned to his face. He pointed to his stunned brother, who still had not managed to find his voice. "You mean to say he has not—"

"Watch your tongue, Hugh. Lady Ariane is related to the royal family." Lady Catherine came to Ariane's side.

"What? Royal family?" A look of doubt clouded Hugh's eyes. "I met many and know all the names of the royals. I have never heard of a Lady Ariane." Hugh eyed her boldly. "And I would have remembered if I had seen her before."

Lady Catherine patted Ariane on the hand. "Oh, my, this is difficult to say. Lady Ariane was taken captive by infidels when she was a child and has just returned to us."

Hugh's gaze swept over Ariane again. "She's lived with infidels all these years?"

Lady Catherine gave a quick nod.

"If the woman has been living with infidels, royal or not, she's naught but a soiled tart."

"Hold your tongue, brother!"

The words rolled out of Julian's mouth before Ariane had the chance to speak in her own defense. She flinched. Julian looked as if he could commit murder. Murder his brother? Over her? Nay.

Hugh put up his hands in defense. "I mean no offense, but we all know the truth here. The first thing the infidels do with those on a pilgrimage is rape the women."

Ariane had enough of this oaf's tongue. "'Tis not the Muslims who rape women, but the Christian monsters."

"Oh, the kitten speaks." Hugh walked over to stand

before Ariane. He picked up a lock of her hair and twirled it around his finger. "And what a nice purr it has."

"Enough!"

Julian's roar echoed through the hall. He pushed Ariane aside and grabbed Hugh by the front of his tunic, raising him off the floor. He flexed his arm and Hugh flew across the room crashing into the trestle tables.

"Julian!" Lady Catherine raced to Hugh's crumpled body.

Combing his fingers through his hair, Julian followed his mother and knelt next to Hugh.

Lady Catherine cradled Hugh's head in her arms and gently slapped his cheeks. "Hugh, Hugh, can you hear me?"

Hugh groaned as his eyes adjusted on his mother's face. Finally his gaze set upon Julian. "You lost your temper," he said incredulously. "Nay, never. In all the years...not even when I put the toad in your bed or when I put your fingers in water while you slept—"

"Aye," Julian answered gruffly.

"'Tis the Crusade," Lady Catherine said, helping Hugh to his feet. "The time in the Holy Land has changed him."

Rubbing the back of his head, Hugh looked between Ariane and Julian. His study was so intense that her skin began to prickle. What was he gawking at?

Hugh smiled. "Nay, Mother, 'tis not the Crusade. 'Tis the tart who has changed him."

Ariane cringed as Julian slammed his fist into Hugh's face.

"Julian," Lady Catherine said, shocked as Hugh stumbled back.

Julian shook his head in frustration. "I am sorry."

A tiny secret smile broke across Ariane's face. Julian and she were of like mind. They were perfect for each other. He just did not know it yet.

Eleven

Judge not, that ye be not judged.
Matthew 7:1

"MY LADY, YOU WILL WEAR THOSE STONES THIN IF you do not stop pacing."

"I cannot, Najila. You did not see the disaster this noon time. The way Hugh spoke to Julian! What transpired here in the past that would cause such hate?"

Najila left her seat by the hearth and walked over to the bed. She picked up a velvet sapphire gown. "Oh have you ever seen anything so lovely, my lady?"

Paying no attention, Ariane frowned and steepled her hands beneath her chin as she turned to march once again over the path she had just trod. "Perhaps 'tis because Brother Julian gave all his land to the church. That would sour any man, but according to Guy, Brother Julian gave Hugh a handsome portion to the north of here." Ariane stopped at the end of the room and gazed out the small window. The cold land on this late autumn day gave no answer nor revealed any secrets. "Nay, that cannot be it. There is more here. I just cannot put my finger on it."

Najila placed the gown back on the bed and picked up a soft linen chemise in a light shade of blue. "I have never seen an undergarment as lovely as this."

"Perhaps 'tis just plain jealousy. The second son not being as important as the first." Ariane stopped, turned and continued her tread. "Yet, Lady Catherine seems to love both men."

Najila dropped the chemise, picked up a sheer blue and gold veil. "Oh look, my lady, it is made of gold and blue strands woven together. It will look beautiful over your braided hair and look here, soft stockings with blue garters. Why a queen would not have better."

Ariane frowned her disapproval at Najila. "Mark my words, trouble is lurking in this fortress, and I fear tonight we will see its mischief."

"My lady, oh my," Najila dumped the stockings and garters back on the bed and picked up a shiny golden girdle. "This has sapphires in it. One, two, three. Look, three sapphires grace this golden belt."

Ariane grimaced at Najila's squeals. "How can you discuss clothing at a time like this? First on the boat and now here; your fixation with garments is unnatural."

"My fixation with garments? Nay, I am not the odd one here. I do not run around without my shoes as you do. Most ladies are interested in what they wear so they can please their men." Najila raised the jeweled girdle to her waist. "Look what Brother Andrew has found for you to wear."

Ariane folded her arms and deepened her disapproval. "Brother Andrew? These clothes came from Lady Catherine. I do not understand why she thinks I need more clothing. Mine is perfectly fine."

"Lady Catherine thinks they are not warm enough for this climate. She told Brother Andrew to search the old trunks the monks had hidden away. They belonged to Lady Catherine's mother. I wonder why Lady Catherine would not take this for herself? It looks as if it has never been worn."

"Perhaps because it is too long. I am slightly taller than Lady Catherine." Ariane moved over to the bed and lifted up the sapphire gown. "And 'tis too long for me also."

"That can be easily fixed with a needle and thread," Najila replied.

"Aye." Ariane ran her hand over the soft velvet. Why would Lady Catherine lock up such a fine gown? 'Twas almost sinful to hide such a thing of beauty, never to be worn. Ariane shook her head. *Sinful*. She was even starting to think like Julian. What nonsense was this? Better that he think like her than for her to think like him. "Come Najila, let us try on the dress, for I hear merry voices filling the hall and I can smell the strong garlic from the meat."

"Aye, my lady, 'twill be a night of joviality. Brother Julian has come home."

Joviality. The word rang false in her ears. 'Twas just a feeling, but in her heart she knew tonight would be anything but jovial.

Julian stood in the doorway of the great hall; his mother had outdone herself. The room looked like she was entertaining the king himself. His mother loved revelry. Aye, he remembered she would use any excuse to have a feast. Why once she'd called for a celebration when Father Bethal found his favorite cap, which had been missing for months. But this was not a night for merriment. Nay, something told him this night would bring no good. The shadows from the torches danced off the walls, while a servant scurried about brushing off the benches and chasing the dogs away. One would think a joyous evening was to be had—if one were a simpleton.

Julian inhaled deeply. A familiar smell from his youth. Beef with garlic sauce, his favorite. 'Twas not his day to eat meat, but eat meat he would. He would break a vow before he would break his mother's heart by rejecting her meal this eve. Later, he would do penance and on the morrow he would fast.

"Julian, come and give your mother a kiss."

Julian turned and saw his mother's outstretched arms and a warm smile. "Mother, you are a vision from heaven."

She looked down at her deep scarlet gown. "I am dressed more like a demon from hell, but the color suits me."

Julian laughed and placed a gentle kiss on her cheek.

"Nay Mother, no one would think such a cruel thing about you."

She grabbed his hand and dragged him into the hall. "They have not said as much, but I am sure some of these monks have thought it."

A twinge of guilt twisted through Julian's midsection. "Has it been hard here then? Which of my brethren has caused you pain?"

Her laughter filled the room. "Oh, Julian, rest easy. Father Bethal would cut out the tongue of anyone who would dare speak against me. If anything, since you have left, my life has become that of a pampered queen. The monks have taken over every mundane chore there is and consult me on only the important affairs." She lowered her voice and leaned closer. "Last week I was asked if I wanted wine, ale or buttermilk with my meal. What a stressful task. I wondered how I survived the decision."

"Mother, you jest with me," Julian replied.

"Come, this evening is not for me but for you. Since we are short on nobles, I have invited familiar faces from your youth. See the miller is there talking to Brother Andrew and sitting near the tables is Brother Guy with the miller's daughter, Nell. Oh dear, we must do something about that."

"Aye," Julian agreed warily.

"I thought being a Templar would curb his wild appetite."

"Guy is Guy. He never took the vows to his heart nor did he pretend otherwise. But in many ways he is more of a true Templar than I."

His mother gave him a quizzical look. "How so?"

Julian looked about the room. Aye, this was a celebration and one that should be foreign to a man of a holy order.

Holy order.

The Templars made a mockery of the words. In public they held their heads up high, the vision of piety, but in private…the laughter of women and the flow of wine was heavy. If he were honest, he would admit men like Brother Randall were more common than men like himself. A hand

136

on his sleeve returned his attention to his mother.

"How so?"

"Guy has his faults, but he is no hypocrite. What he does in the dark he does in the light. He took vows to stay at my side and it is a vow he has never broken." Julian gritted his teeth. He should not give voice to the secrets of his order, and yet, he felt his order had in many ways betrayed him, and had betrayed God. "I have said too much."

His mother narrowed her eyes. "Nay, you have only started to give voice to the truth. I have not been blind these last ten years. Tell me Julian, is there any gold left in the Holy Land?"

Guilt consumed Julian. He had given his mother's home to a greedy group and she knew it. "Forgive me. I never wanted you to know about the darker side of the order. I should have listened to Father Bethal and joined the Benedictines."

His mother looped her arm through his. "You wield a sword too well to throw it aside and shrivel up in a dark cell of a monastery. Besides, the Benedictines are no more pious than the Templars. Remember, it was I who encouraged your choice. I am just thankful God did not send you back to me a greedy, blood-thirsty man. I was quite alarmed when I heard they called you the Avenging Angel. I did so prefer Julian, the Pure of Heart."

Julian took his free hand and gently placed it over hers protectively. "I have changed; the blood of many is on my hands, and I would have killed more had it not been for the king sending me here. Then I was angry, but now... I know not what I want or what God wants."

"God gives everything a purpose. Perhaps your purpose lies here and not in the Holy Land."

His mother's words stripped some of the guilt from his soul. For the first time in years a new feeling was taking root. Peace. A fragile peace. A peace that could stand forever. 'Twas good to be home. "Come Mother, let us save Nell before it is too late."

"A wise decision, my son. A wise decision."

Their need to save Nell from Guy became a moot point. By the time they had made their way over to the trestle table a group of peasant children ran up to Guy surrounding him.

"Well Guy, it looks as if you have been saved from the wrath of an angry father," Julian said.

Guy gave a lazy grin. "These lads have been pestering me since this morn. They want to see my famous trick."

Julian's mother raised a delicate eyebrow. "A famous trick? I have never known you to be a magician."

Guy shrugged.

Julian squeezed his mother's hand. "'Tis a trick that saved his life and mine more than once in the Holy Land."

"I am intrigued. Show me this trick," said his mother.

The young boys shouted their agreement, nudging Guy's shoulders.

Guy stood and bowed before Julian's mother. "My lady, your humble servant will now demonstrate the Saladin Scare."

He took a deep breath and slowly began to raise his left arm, suddenly he tossed the appendage behind the back of his head popping his shoulder out of position. Within an instant, his left arm became perpendicular with his right, which he raised level with his shoulder. The dislocation of his shoulder and bizarre position of his arm made Guy's neck look twisted and bent. He ran toward the children screaming at the top of his lungs. The lads and Nell ran screeching from the hall. Then Guy slowly turned about and stumbled forward, his eyes rolling up into the back of his head. He gave out a low moan and collapsed on the floor face down.

Silent terror reigned in the room as the guests began to cluster about the Guy's fallen form. Murmurs of devil possession filtered through the crowd.

"Julian, do you not think you should see to your friend?" Lady Catherine asked.

"Nay, watch," Julian whispered putting a finger to his lips.

Apprehensively, the miller approached Guy and shoved him in the ribs with his foot. "I think he's dead."

With a deafening shrill Guy jumped to his feet, his sword arched high above his head. He twisted the weapon in the air until he brought it down, slicing through a small melon perched on the table's edge.

The crowd roared their approval, Lady Catherine clapped, Julian crossed his arms giving out a loud bored sigh; he had seen this act many times before. He looked about and saw every maid over the age of two and ten gazing wistfully at Guy.

"What a wonderful trick," his mother exclaimed. "Why is it call the Saladin Scare?"

A grim line creased Julian's lips. "Many times while fighting, we were outnumbered. Sometimes we would be surrounded, so Guy would twist his body, scaring many before falling to the ground. The act was enough to alarm the enemy for a few moments. It gave me time to cut down a few more infidels, then Guy would spring to his feet and come up from behind, and together we would finish off the rest."

His mother placed a trembling hand on her chest. Julian almost turned away from the horror and fear he saw in her eyes...for him. He knew what she would ask.

"Julian," she whispered. "I am glad you are home."

"Aye."

"Promise me—"

"Nay Mother, I must return." He could see the tears forming in her eyes.

"Then please, do be careful."

He tried to give a calming smile. "All is in the hands of God."

She placed her shaking hand on his. "What happened to your father—"

"Mother, this has naught to do with Father," he said sternly.

Though she nodded, Julian knew his mother did not agree. Perhaps she was right, perhaps every time he wielded his sword, he did so to slay the demon that lived inside of him.

No matter.

He could kill every infidel that existed and still that would not bring his father back. He could never repent of his selfish act.

Ever.

For his father was gone.

He forced his attention back to the present. He could not change the past, but he could control his present and future actions. Since the day he left a decade ago, he swore he would put the needs of others before his own, and he had done so. The decision had been a good one, one he had been able to live with, until he met Ariane.

The roar of the crowd around Guy gave Julian a reprieve from his troubling thoughts. There stood his friend, the center of attention, men slapping his back, toasting him with mugs of ale.

A hoot came from the entrance in the hall followed by a single hand of applause. "Well done, Guy. Perhaps you should bear the title of the Avenging Angel."

The spite-filled words floated across the room, bringing it to silence. Without cue the guests parted as if they were the waters of the Red Sea. Heads held high, Hugh and his lady floated forward until they stood before Julian.

Jane.

Rich brown eyes with hair to match. A slender shape with dainty hands. She always did give the appearance of a gentle doe in need of protection. So innocent. So unsuspecting. So very dangerous.

In their youth, Jane had been a good companion for his brother and himself. They were nearly inseparable. The three of them would slip into the kitchen and sneak off with a few hot tarts, juggling them between their fingers until the pastry was cool enough to eat. Then they would climb up the nearest sturdy oak and hang upside down until one of them would beg off sick. Sometimes they would take turns slaying the mighty dragon that lived behind the nearest hedgerow. He hated the times he had to play the damsel, but back then, even Jane wanted a chance to be the dragon slayer. Little did he know that she would continue the role into adulthood.

Dressed in a heavily embroidered golden gown with matching veil, Jane stroked the head and back of the small white dog she held in her arms. "It is good to see you home again, my brother." She turned and handed the furry animal to her maid. A look that was anything but sisterly glinted in her eyes when she turned back. Jane notched her chin and raised her slight hand.

When Julian took her hand, her fingers wrapped like a vice around his, rubbing her thumb over his knuckles in an intimate manner. Aye, Jane was still trying to slay dragons and enjoyed leaving their bloody carcasses in her path.

"It is good to be home, my lady," he said shaking free from her dog-scented grip.

Jane cocked an eyebrow and retrieved the tiny animal from her maid. "Still the noble monk knight. What a pity. What shall we do to warm you up a bit?"

"He is not your concern, Jane," Lady Catherine said coming to Julian's side. "Best you worry about your own husband. God and I will take care of Julian."

A chill went down Julian's back when he saw the frigid smile Jane gave his mother and the equally icy grimace his mother returned. So the years had not softened the feelings each harbored for the other. His loving family faded away that frosty autumn day his father died and a thaw had never occurred.

"Sir Hugh and his lady, how nice to see the both of you after all these years," Guy said, coming up behind the pair, throwing his arms over their shoulders.

Julian stifled a laugh as Jane lurched slightly forward,

almost dropping her dog. His mother's features had also softened.

Jane wrinkled her nose giving Guy a look of disgust. "Get your arm off of me, you drunken oaf."

Guy answered her demand by pulling her closer to his side. He turned his head to Hugh and said, "How could you have taken this sweet-tongued maid from me?"

Hugh chuckled. "'Tis good to see you again, Guy."

Jane tried to twist from Guy's grasp, her face redder than hellfire itself. "Ahh, this cow dung mauls your wife and all you do is laugh. You should slit open his navel!"

"This is our good friend, Brother Guy. You would not have me kill our friend, would you?" Hugh asked lightheartedly.

Jane responded by trying to kick Guy. He deftly moved out of her way, bringing laughter and applause from the guests and fueling Jane's bubbling anger.

"I could never understand what you and Julian saw in this pompous bastard!"

The guests gasped. Julian tensed. His mother's hand visibly shook when she grasped his arm. Hugh's face hardened and all jest from his manner fled. Jane's insult would demand satisfaction on Guy's part.

Yet Guy did not release either one, though he fisted his hand and pulled his arm against Jane's neck.

"Apologize, lady, or I swear I'll lash you here in front of all," Hugh threatened.

Casually, Guy turned to Hugh and drawled, "Nay my friend, why waste a good switch. We all know she speaks the truth. I am a bastard and proud of it. My mother had too much sense to marry my father, the ass. But I have one question. Why does your wife carry a mop in her arms? Does she have fleas?"

The room erupted with laughter. Guy placed a juicy kiss on Jane's forehead and released her. She stumbled away shrieking at anyone who came in her path. Hugh threw his arm over Guy and together they stalked off in search of ale.

"Thank God, Guy is a good tempered soul," said Julian's mother.

He heard Guy's laughter from across the room. "He has defused many a conflict with his gilded tongue. Yet one of these days I fear it will undo him."

"Perhaps. Yet it was good to see someone place Jane where she belongs."

Julian frowned at the sharp tone of his mother's voice. "What goes here between you and Jane?"

Her hand on his arm tensed. He could have sworn he heard her teeth grind. One thing was for sure, her soft features had turned stone hard.

"Come we should greet our guest," she said dismissing his comment.

Julian would not budge when she pulled on his arm. "Nay, I will have an answer to my question. When I left you pitied Jane and hoped the marriage between Hugh and her would heal old wounds, but now I see contempt in your eyes and voice. I will have an answer for this."

His mother looked about the room visibly upset. "This is neither the time nor the place to tell you what has transpired since your departure. Please Julian, I do not wish to discuss Jane's torments. We will speak of it on the morrow."

He did not want to wait to discover what Jane had done in his absence, but the desperate look in his mother's eyes quelled any disagreement. Perhaps she was right, enough had befallen this night. One would have to wonder if the devil ruled this eve. What else could he have in store for them tonight?

"Very well, I will not press suit on this."

His mother's arm relaxed on his. "Now then, let us try to make merry this eve for you are home, I pray, for good."

Julian did not give protest. For at the moment he had no intentions of leaving until all was right here. He simply guided his mother through their guests, giving his greeting. By the time they reached the head table, Julian was truly enjoying himself and his mother seemed to be at ease.

Yea, the evil had passed. The devil could do no more to ruin this eve. Julian had just settled himself in the chair next to his mother when loud gasps and whispers rolled across the room. All heads had turned to the stairs.

He could not believe his eyes when he saw the vision. Ariane stood on the last step dressed in a sapphire gown. Strands of lovely red hair escaped her braid and curled around the sheer blue and golden veil. The sapphire-jeweled girdle hugged her slender hips.

Ariane was a vision of pure beauty. The dress fit her as if it was made for her. She was far more radiant in it than Jane was the day he left her standing at the altar in St. Michael's Chapel.

By the cross, he heard the devil's cackle.

Twelve

I will call them my people, which were not my people; and
her beloved, which was not beloved.
Romans 9:25

HY ARE THEY STARING AT ME? ARIANE WONDERED.
A few moments ago the room hummed with
laughter and merriment, but when she stepped out of the
shadows all talking and laughter ceased. A flute in the corner
let out a wail that sounded more like a goose being
slaughtered than an instrument used to lighten the heart.

Despite the heat of the room, a chill slithered down
Ariane's back. Lady Catherine covered her mouth to muffle
a sharp cry. Smiles fell from cheery faces and were replaced
with frosted frowns.

Her head felt light when she looked into Julian's accusing
eyes. *What had she done?* Perhaps she was mistaken. Surely
he could not be upset with her? She looked about the room.
Many lowered their eyes when she met their gaze. Others
answered her questioning look with an icy stare. Some stood
together, shaking their heads and mumbling among
themselves. The only one who seemed as perplexed as she
was Brother Andrew.

A tall thin woman, wearing a golden beaded dress and
carrying a small dog, pushed through the crowd until she
stood before Ariane. With a targeted gaze, she examined
Ariane's face. The woman pursed her lips and her cheeks
sunk like shallow craters.

Ariane flushed as the woman's constricted gaze slipped down her body. Though she did not speak a word, Ariane could see she loathed her. A small, almost calculating smile tugged at the corner of her mouth while she placed the back of her hand across her forehead, gave out a loud cry and fell faint. The small dog yelped slightly as he scurried away from his mistress's arms.

The silent room came alive with shouts and screams. Many rushed forward to assist the fallen woman.

"Move aside," Hugh barked, pushing his way through the crowd. He knelt down and took one of her hands in his and gently patted it. "Jane, Jane." The woman did not respond.

The small circle that had formed around Hugh parted as Lady Catherine and Julian appeared.

"Bring us a damp rag and my healing box," Lady Catherine ordered as she bent down next to Hugh.

Julian towered over and glared at Ariane. "Where did you find that gown?"

For a moment Ariane's mind was a muddle, for his question came out more as an accusation than a query for an answer. "The dress belonged to Lady Catherine's late mother."

"Nay, 'twas not my mother's," Lady Catherine said, placing a rag on Jane's brow. "The dress must have been placed with her things after..." Lady Catherine shook her head and continued more to herself than those about her. "Oh dear, I should have ordered the thing burned."

"Jane, Jane," Hugh cried. "Wake up, my sweet."

His plead was answered by Jane's calm, relaxed breathing. Ariane watched the gentle, even rise of Jane's chest. Normal breathing. During the fighting in the Holy Land, Ariane had seen many faint. All had shallow or erratic breathing and pale waxy-looking skin. Jane's skin had a healthy glow. Ariane suspected that Jane's skin was not cool and clammy to the touch.

"I know not what came over her." Ariane bent down next

to Jane and reached for her legs. "Many healers back home say it helps to raise the feet."

"Do not touch her! Have you not done enough?" Hugh accused. "Be gone and take your heathen cures with you."

Lady Catherine placed her hand on top of Ariane's. "Go and change your clothing. Give the gown you are wearing to my maid."

Ariane knew by the warning edge in Lady Catherine's voice that she should comply without an explanation, but she wanted to know the cause of Jane's apparent distress. She looked at Julian who stood behind his mother. 'Twas evident by the stony features of his face no answer would be given by him now or later. Yea, she should leave. Go do as she was told.

"Why?" The word tumbled out of her mouth before she could call it back. She never seemed to learn to do as she was told. Abi Bin had said he was going to name his pit after her because she spent so much time in it. Perhaps Julian and his Templar brothers would name their prison after her as well, for surely if they had one she was going to it.

"Why?" Hugh seethed. "Why indeed. Why should you take off the gown that causes my wife distress? Why not parade around in the vile thing and remind all that Julian broke his vow to my wife. Why not gash open old wounds and let them fester?" Hugh turned his vindictive gaze on Julian. "Is this your doing? This is why I want you dead. Jane has never forgotten that day, nor does it seem that your little whore will let her."

"Hold your tongue," Julian warned.

Hugh looked down at his wife. "Nay I cannot. The garment pains me as well. Think brother, how my life is. I have taken your leavings. Jane wore that gown to marry you, not me. For me she wore an old drab servant's tunic."

Jane's wedding gown. Wed to Julian?

Nay, it could not be. The room began to spin. Colorful spots flickered before her eyes. If she did not leave soon she would be on the ground—next to Jane—and she was not certain Lady Catherine would place a cool cloth on her brow.

All sound slowly rushed away as she turned to flee. Her ankles felt like they were shackled to heavy chains.

Run. She would not swoon before their eyes. With determination she placed one foot in front of the other.

Run. She would not let Julian know how Hugh's revelation affected her. The door was but a few paces away.

Run. She never should have come here. With all her strength she focused on the egress. Her vision cleared, her pace quickened. Ariane threw open the door and ran into the black night.

She raced across the bailey. The brisk night air filled her lungs and cleared her head. In front of her lay the gatehouse and the only way out. Unfortunately two guards—one tall as a tree and the other round as a rock—stood fast before her.

"My lady, the sun has set. 'Tis unsafe beyond these walls this late," said the rock.

"Stand aside, knave. I need to think and do so best when I walk about."

"Yea, my lady, but ye can walk about the bailey and be safe all the same," the tree answered.

Ariane notched her chin and mustered as much authority as she could. "Nay sir, the air is foul here and does naught but cause my stomach to roll."

"My lady," said the stone, pointing to the walls. "The air up on the battlements is much more pleasant to a lady's nose, yet still provides safety from beasts and thieves which roam the forests."

The stone had a point. She should have gone up the stairs as ordered. There she could have thrown herself over the wall and ended this tragic trial. But she had no desire to walk through that crowded hall again. Nay, death by a wild boar would be much more preferable.

"'Tis all right, Conley. I will walk with the lady."

A chill raced through Ariane's body as she heard Julian's voice behind her. "I have changed my mind," she said quickly.

His hand caught her arm in a tight grip as she turned to flee. "Nay, my lady, the hall is not a pleasant place at the moment."

"Then I shall seek the privacy of my room."

His fingers bore into her flesh when she tried to pull away.

"Nay, you have made your decision. We will walk."

The tone of his voice was like sleet on a stormy night. Ariane could do naught but nod and walk mutely through the gate with Julian at her side.

"Slow your pace!" she cried as he dragged her across a harvested field. "I cannot breathe. My chest is about to burst."

"You wanted to walk. Therefore we walk." His words snapped like wheat stalks beneath their feet.

"Nay, we do not walk, we run. If it is your intent to kill me with exhaustion then lead on, butcher. 'Twould be a preferable death than to be pulled apart by a wild animal or run through with your sword."

Julian stopped abruptly near the edge of the forest. He ran his fingers through his hair. "By the cross, I forgot my sword."

Ariane took a deep breath and sighed. "Ah well, exhaustion it shall be. Run on, Brother Butcher."

"Enough! What nonsense do you speak? I am no butcher. I do not wish to kill you."

She pulled away from his grip and sat down on a stump on the edge of the clearing. Ariane rubbed her sore calves. "Too bad, for I would rather die than stay another moment in this withering country."

Unfortunately the night was too clear and the moon shone bright above their heads. She could see the hard lines of his face and his frozen frown.

"'Twas your choice to come here."

"Yea, but that was before I met your betrothed."

The frosty frown broke into a look of bewilderment. "Jane is my brother's wife. What came before is no longer."

"If this is so, then why does Jane fake a swoon?" For fake it she did. "She may be married to your brother, but her eyes are still for you."

Julian looked up at the moon. "Jane was a childhood friend. The marriage contract was an old one made between our families, made when we were both children. Neither of us ever thought to question it, but when the time came for us to be married, it felt to me like a betrayal of God."

"So you left her there…in the church."

He took a deep breath. "Aye, not very honorable, but feeling as I did, I could not go through with it. Soon after, she married my brother." His words were laced with pain and embarrassment.

A shiver raced over Ariane's shoulders as a burst of early winter air swirled across the field.

"You are cold. By the cross, I left my cloak as well as my sword!" Julian extended his hand. "We must go before you take ill."

Ariane rubbed her hands over her arms. "Why Brother Julian, you have sworn twice since we have been out here."

He sighed. "Aye, many things have changed since I've been home. I am no longer the saint, but a sinful man."

Ariane stood with her arms still wrapped about her, moving closer to him until she swore she felt the heat of his body. "I like you as a man," she whispered.

Julian enveloped her in his large arms and crushed her to his body. His heat seeped into her frigid joints and cold muscles, warming her all the way through. She felt protected. She felt secure. She felt as if she had always belonged here…wrapped in his arms.

"Know this, sweet Ariane, 'tis you who tempts me and bring forth feelings I have never known. Had you been standing at that altar, I would have pledged my life to you."

His lips were less than a hand from hers. His warm breath kissed her face. "Then for this brief moment," she whispered, "pretend that we have taken that vow and kiss me like a husband kisses his wife."

She heard his breath hitch and he gave her a slight squeeze. Ariane closed her eyes—

The bushes rustled behind them. "By all means, kiss the girl. I would never deny a dying man his last pleasure."

Ariane stumbled forward as Julian quickly released her and reached for a sword that was not there.

A shadowy figure appeared on the edge of the forest. "Darrin, can I slit his throat and take his lass? For even in this light she looks good to me eyes," said another ghostly figure standing next to the first.

Within moments a band of scraggly men circled around them. "A horse would look good to ya, Gouch," said another grubby man. The group laughed and made lewd comments about this Gouch.

"Enough." The one they called Darrin stepped out of the shadows.

Dressed slightly better than the rest, he held himself with a commanding presence. Though he was a head shorter than Julian, his body was lean and muscular. He circled around them, tapping a very deadly looking dagger against his shoulder.

Ariane gulped and looked at Julian. His face remained calm. How could he be at ease when these ruffians would probably tear him limb from limb? Even if he did have his sword, Julian would be sorely out numbered.

"Forgive me, my lady." Suddenly, like a gust of wind, Darrin whipped behind Ariane and brought the dagger to her throat. "But we need a few words with your benefactor."

Her breath came up short as the cold blade scrapped her neck. The muscles in Julian's arm twitched as he flexed his empty hand. His gaze met hers briefly; Julian held up his hands.

"I am unarmed. Let her go." Julian did not fight as four men grabbed hold of his arms and two more pointed their weapons at his chest.

Darrin lowered his dagger from Ariane's neck, and released his hold. He walked in front of her, his gaze raking her body. He raised his chin and shook back his short curly black hair. "Beautiful," he whispered, drawing his index finger lightly down her cheek. "Mayhap I keep this one for myself, Gouch," he said louder.

Ariane slapped his hand away. "Leave me alone you mangy dog."

His men roared with laughter, mimicking with slaps and punches of their own. Julian began to struggle against his captor's hold. Darrin raised his hand silencing his men.

He turned sideways so he could see both Julian and Ariane. "Cease your struggle, good sir. You cannot escape, and even if you did, my men would have to kill you and what help would ye be to the lady then, eh?"

He smiled at Julian. "You have nothing to worry about. Your lady looks at me as a dog, but she worships you as a god." He winked at Ariane and gave an exaggerated sigh. "If I thought she would ever look at me that way, you would be dead already, but that is not the case."

Julian stilled. "Then let us go. We have nothing to give you."

Darrin returned his dagger to its sheath and clutched his hands behind his back. "On the contrary you have much to offer me, Brother Julian."

The shock that crossed Julian's face was matched by the quick intake of Ariane's breath. This man knew who Julian was. He had seen them in each other's arms. Could he use this information against Julian? Nay. Templar or not, who would care if the great Lord Julian de Maury was having a dalliance. Unless he knew who she was and to what purpose she was brought to this land. If this information should reach the king or Prince John, then indeed, this could be trouble for Julian. Yet again, who would believe a common thief?

She had to find out his true purpose. "Kind sir—"

Darrin raised his hand. "Silence, my lady. I have come to talk to your lord."

"But he is not—"

Again the villain waved off her words. "What his

relationship is to you makes little difference to me. I have come to ask him about his forest."

"His what?" she said in bewilderment.

"Forest, my lady," Darrin answered. "I would have thought you would have been educated on titles and the ownership of English lands during your long voyage."

Her heart sunk in her chest. He knew of her. No good would come from this meeting, she felt it. Darrin meant to harm Julian.

"The land is no longer mine. I gave it to the Templars before I went to free Jerusalem. I can give you nothing," Julian said.

Darrin's gaze darted between Julian and Ariane. "Aye, the monks may own the land, but they have little interest in the forest other than providing them with game. The forest has fallen under the watchful eye of your brother. And for the most part, Hugh has been willing to share a few deer," a small smile tugged at the corner of his mouth, "as long as we do not irritate his lovely wife."

Hearty laughter rolled through the band. Again Darrin raised his hand to quiet his men. "We never take more than is necessary to fill our bellies. In turn, we have left his holdings and the monks untouched. Now that you have returned I fear that all may change. My men have families to feed. I must know where you stand."

At first, it seemed as if Julian was not going to answer Darrin. His features did not reveal his thoughts. He stood between Darrin's men like a stone pillar—staunch, stern, and strong.

Finally he began to speak. "I do not have control of this land nor will I ever again. When my mission here is completed, I will go back to the Holy Land. If my brother does not find fault with you then neither do I. Now tell your men to release me for I have answered your question."

Though she always knew the truth, his words were as sharp as a lance piercing her heart. He may desire her or want her, but he would never break his vows for her. For the second time tonight, Ariane wished she were dead.

Slowly Darrin nodded. "Release him." The band began to disperse and drift back into the woods. "I will hold you to your words, de Maury. For methinks you will have a change of heart. You will not be able to leave that which you love the most on this earth."

Before Ariane could make sense of Darrin's words, he was gone. She stood alone. With Julian. And for a brief moment she wished the poachers would return.

"We should return to the keep," he said flatly.

Ariane stared at the black forest, then at the clouds moving across the face of the moon. She looked at the frozen leaves at her feet. She saw his boots, then his legs, then his torso, then his chest. Please Allah, God, Mohammed, Jesus, anyone who heard her, please don't let me look into his face. But try as she might, her gaze seemed to have a mind of its own. Before she knew it she was staring at his unrelenting face. His expression was like a fatal blow to her already wounded heart. He would follow his duty to his king and to his God, because they held his heart—not her. She could not win his love. 'Twas foolish of her to ever think she could. She must run away. She glanced back at the dense forest.

And she knew just who would help her.

Ariane nodded. Julian took her elbow and guided her back to the keep, as a dutiful knight would help a lady.

Thirteen

Watch and pray, that ye enter not into temptation: the spirit indeed is willing, but the flesh is weak.
Matthew 26:41

ARIANE SQUINTED AS THE MORNING LIGHT SEEPED into her bedchamber. The yawn and loud sigh that left her lips reminded her of the restless night she had just spent.

"Good morn, my lady." Najila swept into the room carrying bread and a bowl of cheese. "Please forgive me for disturbing your slumber, but Brother Julian insisted you rise. You have much to do this day."

"Leave me rest but a little longer, for I did not sleep well last night."

"I know. Your tossing and turning kept me awake as well, but that does not matter. Brother Julian awoke before dawn, long before the other Brothers. He spent his time in prayer in the chapel. When he left, his first order was to have you up and about. He is concerned about your education. He fears you have much more to learn."

"Does he?" Ariane rubbed her eyes and rolled over to watch Najila scurry about the room. "How do you know all this? Did you see Brother Julian this morn?"

"Nay, Brother Andrew told me." Najila placed the bowl on the table near the fire. "And he said Brother Julian is in the foulest mood."

Ariane yawned. "Is he?"

"Yea, Brother Guy said that the bark of his orders sent the dogs howling."

"You talked to Brother Andrew and Brother Guy? You have been busy this morn."

"Everyone is rushing about—Brother Julian was that forceful. Arise quickly, my lady, I do not think it wise to slumber the day away."

"Very well, 'twould be wrong to stay in bed when everyone else has arisen." She swung her feet over and placed them on the chilly floor. Shivers coursed through her body. "My, 'tis cold this morn."

Najila handed Ariane a plain undergarment. "I do not care for this country. Nor, do I care for this drafty keep."

Ariane poked her head through the garment and then let Najila help her into a green grown. "Poor Najila, you are here because of me. You should be home with the glow of the sun and the warmth of your family."

"Yea, I miss the sun and my family."

The longing Ariane heard in Najila's words brought back thoughts of happier times. When her old nurse Raya, and her friend Isam were alive. But now there was no one for her. There were many who cared about Najila, but for Ariane there was no one...anywhere.

She made her way to the basin and splashed icy water on her face, then grabbed the bowl of food from the table and sat by the fire. "I will talk to Brother Julian and see if he will send you back to your home."

Najila rushed over and knelt at Ariane's side. "Oh no, my lady, I do not wish to leave! I miss my family, but I cannot leave."

"Why? You have just said you do not like this country. Would you not like to see your parents, your brothers, and your sisters again?"

"I would love to see them, but I cannot leave." Najila lowered her gaze to the fire, staring wistfully at the flames.

Could it be possible? Could Najila still believe she and Julian had a future together? At one time this thought would have sent Ariane into a fit of jealous anger, but now all she felt was pity. For Julian had already committed himself to his love, his God alone.

She placed her hand lightly on Najila's shoulder. "He is already married."

Najila turned wide eyes on Ariane. "Nay, my lady, he is not!"

Ariane patted Najila's shoulder hoping to settle her down. "Brother Julian is married to God," she said calmly.

"Oh," Najila said with relief. "'Tis Brother Julian you speak of."

Her strange behavior left Ariane wondering just whom Najila had been thinking of? Surely it could not be Brother Guy? Julian had told him to stay away from Najila. Brother Guy would do anything for Julian. Yet, love had a way of making one forget any promises. Many would sacrifice anything for love. She would sacrifice anything for love. Why would Julian not sacrifice for love?

"He does not love me, that is why," she whispered.

"What did you say, my lady?" Najila asked.

Ariane shook her head. "Nothing. 'Tis getting late and soon Brother Julian will be here for my lesson. I must get ready."

A short while later there was a knock at the door. When Najila opened it Brother Guy stood in the doorway with his hands full of scrolls and a prayer book.

"Brother Guy, what do you here?" Ariane asked.

"I have come to teach you, my lady."

"I thought Brother Julian was to instruct me now."

"Aye, but he has other pressing matters," he stammered.

"And what are those pressing matters?" she asked.

Guy's face flushed and he took an unbearably long time to clear his throat. "Lady Jane sent a message that she needed to see him post haste." Guy quietly added, "He left immediately."

Ariane felt like a fool. Last night in the woods, Julian had all but declared his love for her and this morn he ran off to see Jane, a woman for whom he declared he had no feelings. What game did he play?

Why, he was more fickle than the women in Abi Bin's harem. At least they would spend a fortnight professing love to one man. Brother Julian spent his night with God, and his morn with his brother's wife.

Her body began to shake with anger. She shoved Brother Guy in the chest with both hands. Scrolls flew everywhere as he stumbled about trying to catch his balance. Ariane bent and picked up the book, shaking it at Guy. "When will Brother Julian return?"

Guy swallowed nervously as he hustled about the room helping Najila pick up the remaining scrolls. "I-I do not know."

"You do not know! You do not know!" Ariane shouted. "Why do you always protect him?"

The confused look on Guy's face only heightened her fury.

"Do not look at me that way, for you know exactly what I mean."

Guy stopped his gathering and rose to his feet. "My lady, if I look odd 'tis because I do not know what you are talking about. From what do I protect Julian?"

"Aggh!" Ariane stamped her foot on the floor. "Tell Brother Julian that I will not take lessons from an insolent knave. Since he loves the chapel almost as much as he does a certain wedded lady, I shall wait for his return there!" Ariane tucked the book she held under her arm and left the room, slamming the door behind her.

Julian entered the great hall and was thankful for the roaring fire in the hearth. The winds were sharp and unyielding; 'twas not a nice day to go romping about the countryside. Yet he had no choice, after receiving Jane's idiotic letter. His journey to his brother's home, and the return trip, had left him frozen to the bone, and he wanted nothing more than to sit idle by the fire the rest of the afternoon. Near the fire he spotted Guy drinking ale and telling tales to Julian's mother while she worked on her embroidery.

With due haste, Julian made his way over to the pair. "Good day to you, Mother. I trust all is well with you?"

"Yea, Julian. It goes the same as it does every day. Come give your mother a kiss." She stopped her stitching and tapped her cheek.

Julian bent to give his mother a tender kiss.

She smiled warmly. "I am so glad you are home. Take off your mantle and sit by the fire."

He returned her smile. "I would like nothing better, but I must check into a few matters first." His smile faded when he turned to face Guy. Julian took off his gloves and began tapping them in his palm. "Is Ariane finished with her lessons already?"

Guy rose and belched. "I did not expect you back so soon."

"Apparently," Julian said dryly. "Where is Lady Ariane?"

Guy rubbed his beard, looking toward the fire. "She is in the chapel."

"In the chapel?"

"Aye, she was quite...agitated when I showed up in your stead this morn. She would have nothing to do with me. She stormed out of her room and waits for you in the chapel."

His mother shook her head. "The girl has been there all morn and will not leave. She is blue from the cold and ignores our pleas to come out."

"I have given her a cloak," Guy interjected.

Julian glared at him. "How generous of you. Why did you not drag her out?"

"Julian!" his mother admonished. "She is a lady. He cannot go around throwing her over his shoulder as if she were a prize stag from the forest."

"Besides, Lady Ariane has quite a temper," Guy added.

Julian shook his gloves in Guy's face. "She is but a feather of a woman. You are a knight, for God's sake."

His mother rose from her seat. "Julian! Do my ears deceive me? For I cannot believe what I have just heard. Is this what you have learned in the Holy Land? Using God's name falsely?"

"Nay, my lady. His language changed when he began associating with Lady Ariane." Guy shook his head.

Julian ground his teeth. "Enough of this. I will get Ariane myself." He turned abruptly to leave.

"Be kind, Julian. She has had a difficult start here," his mother called.

He did not acknowledge his mother's words for he was certain he would say something he would regret later. He threw open the hall door and walked out into the frigid afternoon.

Within moments he was at the entryway to the small chapel built in the bailey many years ago by his father. 'Twas a small humble building made of old wood that had been discarded when his father built the keep. Light filtered in through the warped shutters that covered the few narrow windows. The modest chapel's stone altar was graced by a wooden cross. Two chairs near the side of the altar were used by the visiting priest to hear confessions. His father said the structure was just temporary, sufficient until he had the time and resources to build a suitable chapel. But his mother had grown fond of the tiny church and begged her husband to leave it be. She said it represented the humble beginnings of Christ, born in a stable built for beasts of burden.

Julian smiled, remembering his father's protest to his mother's pleas. 'God will keep me in purgatory forever if I do not build Him a better chapel. I can hear his voice already demanding a better place of worship.' Yet in the end it was his wife he listened to. The chapel remained modest, a symbol of Christ's meek and lowly birth.

Ariane sat on one of the chairs holding a prayer book up in the dim light of a lone candle strategically placed on the other chair. She resembled some underworld being with her body hidden by the folds of the cloak. Vapors of her warm breath escaped the hood as she read quietly. Her body trembled when a gust of wind rattled the shutters and whistled through the tiny sanctuary.

He frowned. She belonged where the sun sat high and long in the sky. Where thousands of grains of sand caressed the bottom of her bare feet. Where the wind was warm and whispered through the palm trees. 'Twas wrong to pick a delicate flower and plant it into frozen ground.

Softly, he walked toward her. "Ariane, this is no place for you."

She kept her face buried in the shadows of the hood. "Nay that is not true sir, I find it quite refreshing. 'Tis a good place to be when one needs to clear one's head of foolish dreams."

Julian picked up the candle, placed it on the altar, and sat down beside her. "What dreams could you have that need clearing from your lovely head?"

The hood slid off her hair when Ariane raised it abruptly. "Do not call me lovely, you fork-tongued viper. Save your platitudes for your brother's wife."

"My brother's wife? Pray tell, what does Jane have to do with your loveliness? For truly, there is no comparison. Your beauty shines like the sun, and she is but a mute star in the distant sky."

Ariane pushed him away when he leaned closer. "What tales you weave. Have you been rehearsing these words with Brother Guy, or have you developed the art of deceit all on your own? Be careful how you answer, Brother Julian, for you are in a house of God."

"I know well where I am, my lady. I speak naught but the truth. These words are from my heart."

She put the hood back over her head. "What do I know of your heart? You profess to be a pious man. Yet I wonder, does a devout man run after another man's wife?"

"Is that why you are sitting in here?" He tried to prevent the smile from spreading across his lips, but he could not.

Ariane was jealous of Jane. 'Twould be the most satisfying thought...if he were allowed to have such thoughts.

She gave no answer.

Though he could not see her face, Julian knew she watched his every expression. He tried to reach for her hand, but she buried it deep in the cloak. "Ariane, I look at Jane as my sister, my brother's wife. There never was, nor ever will be, anything between us."

Again she said nothing. Instead she wrapped the cloak more tightly around herself and turned away from him.

Gently, Julian took her by the shoulders bringing her about until she faced him. He expected her to resist and look away, but she did not. "I would never lie to you."

A statue could not have been more still.

Carefully, he reached up and removed the hood from her head. Tears flowed down her cheeks. "Ariane, why do you cry?" he asked softly.

She shrugged her shoulders and lowered her head.

Julian gave out a deep breath. "Jane is bent on destroying her only chance at happiness. She has polluted my brother's mind with lies and now she wishes to spread these lies to my mother and to Prince John. I tried to show her how futile her claim would be. Yet, she seems bent on revenge. That is why I left this morn, not for a clandestine tryst."

Her head remained bent as if she did not hear a word he said.

Tenderly, he raised her chin until he could see her face. Her eyes were firmly shut. "Ariane look at me. You do believe me?"

She pushed his hand away and nodded without ever opening her eyes.

"Then why, Ariane? Why do you weep?" he asked confused.

"I cry because I do believe you. 'Twould be easier to hate you if I thought you were a deceitful cur."

"Nay, I am not a cur, I am the butcher," he teased.

"Do not try to humor me, sir. Before I met you I had to

fight for everything. I know deceit, aggression and betrayal, for they were the rules I was taught when I was young. But you changed all the rules. I have spent most of the day wishing to strangle you because of your deceit. Then you come here, tell me my thoughts are false and I know down in my heart you speak the truth."

"But that is good."

"Nay, it is not," she said, looking away from him. "Your deceit would have turned me to anger. Anger would then lead to my hatred of you, and with that I could live without you."

The sadness in her words put a longing ache in his chest. For he felt the same thing. Nothing would make him happier than to forget his duty to his king and his God and run away with her. Last night he spent hours in prayer searching for an answer, begging The Almighty to show him how allowing Ariane to marry Lord de Craon was the right answer.

God answered him by showing him all who would be hurt if he did not do his duty. His mother and brother would be at the mercy of the Templars and the king. Why, even the peasants and that bandit in the forest might find their existence threatened.

The fragile alliance with King Philip could crack; thousands of Crusaders could be left without the hope of any reinforcements. He knew what that was like; he had spent months in Acres waiting for reinforcements. Every day that passed the fear that no one would arrive increased. Nay, he could not live with the thought that he was responsible for the deaths of many men.

"Ariane," Julian said softly. "Look at me."

Slowly she turned her gaze back to him. Tears still hung on her long lashes. The urge to kiss them away was great, but he knew what he must do. What he must say.

"It is written in scripture that a man cannot serve two masters. He will love one and hate the other." A hard lump began to form in his throat as he tried to continue. "If I love and serve you, then I will not be able to serve God."

She reached forward and grabbed the front of his mantle. "I do not want to be your master. I do not wish to stand in front of your God, but behind him. Many Templars back home had lemans. I ask for nothing more than that."

Julian grasped her shoulders and pulled her up to stand. He cupped her face between his hands. "Do not say such a thing. I did not bring you here to fall into sin. You are here to learn to love God."

"I will believe anything you want me to if it will keep you by my side." She put her hands over his and turned her face until she could kiss the palm of his hand. "I will worship your God because it is what you wish."

As if her kiss to his palm was a hot ember he dropped his hands to her shoulders and shook her. "Never worship God for my sake! God should stand before me in your heart, your soul, your mind."

"You are my soul," she cried.

Her words were like a lash to his back. What had he done? From the beginning he wanted her. When she followed him in Marseilles he was overjoyed. Not because he would obtain his goal of becoming the youngest Marshall of the Knight Templar, but because she came with him, because she wanted to be by his side. Her mortal soul was in danger and 'twas his fault.

He felt his hands tighten on her arms. Despite the cold, sweat formed on his brow. "Nay, Ariane, say it is not so. I am not worthy to come before any man, let alone God. Please Ariane, I beg you, try to find God."

"I have tried, but cannot because He keeps me from you. I cannot bear the thought of you leaving. I cannot marry Lord de Craon. I cannot marry anyone I do not love. I love—"

"Stop! Do not say it!"

She pulled away from his grasp and stepped back from him. "Nay, I shall shout it to the roof. I love you." Then she raised her head and shouted upward. "I love Julian de Maury."

A storm of conflicting emotion raced through Julian's body. Her confession of love was a bittersweet prayer.

"I love Julian," she yelled again, twirling about.

He knew he should stop her, certain others could hear, but he did not have the desire. Her words sang like a joyous hymn. A tune he would never tire of.

Finally, she stopped in front of him. She wetted her lips. "I love you, Julian," she said.

He pulled her into his arms and kissed her. Hard and demanding, as if he were a thirsty man taking his first drink. Her lips were as sweet as lush berries. He wanted more. His tongue parted her lips and he found hers as warm as wine.

His head became light. Her body molded to his and he wanted more. He kissed her eyes, her nose, her mouth, and her neck. Slowly, he felt himself sinking to his knees bringing her with him. His mouth finding hers again.

His lips broke free for a moment. "Say it again," he asked.

"I love you," she whispered.

His mouth captured hers. The feel of her lips, her tongue, 'twas as if God had made them for him. He broke the kiss briefly to catch his breath. Then plunged into the blissful taste again. He departed from her warmth, wanting to see if she felt what he did. Opening his eyes, he caught sight of the crude cross standing on the altar. A lump of revulsion caught in his throat. His lips burned like acid.

He pushed Ariane away, shocked at what he saw. Her lips were bright red and slightly bruised. Her skin was flushed and her hair a mass of tangles. She looked like a woman who had been thoroughly loved, and that is what he would have done if he had not seen the cross.

"Ariane." He shook her shoulders lightly, she opened her eyes. "What we do is wrong. You are pledged to another and I am pledged to God."

He watched the reality of his words replace her dreamy expression, and he did not like what he saw. A coldness entered her eyes and her jaw set.

"Soon I will be gone and you will forget me. You will be wed and be happy," he pronounced.

"Nay, then I will kill myself, for I cannot live as wife of another."

He reached forward and shook her shoulders again. "Stop it! Stop it, Ariane! Nothing is worse than this sin, for you cannot ask for forgiveness once it is done. Do not jeopardize your soul. If you do such a thing then I will never see you in heaven."

She looked at him with empty tormented eyes. "Life will be like the fires of hell without you."

His chest could hardly bear the pain of his heart. His hands relaxed on her shoulders. "Aye, for me also, but you must remember our lives on this earth are short. Someday we will walk together in heaven for all eternity. Do not separate yourself from me. Promise me you will not do such a thing."

She dropped her head. "Nay, your God will keep me from you. Better to die and be done with it."

Julian squeezed her shoulders. "Ariane, if you kill yourself you will suffer forever. Live, Ariane. Live. Do your duty and in the end you shall have your reward. Promise me."

She raised her head and stared at him directly. Her face held a look of defeat. "I promise. I will not kill myself. I will not cut off myself from you for all eternity."

"Good," he said quietly. "Now come, let us leave this place."

Ariane looked about. "Aye, it pleases me no longer."

Julian nodded his agreement; this place no longer held love for him either. He had betrayed his Lord. God help him.

Fourteen

A man that beareth false witness against his neighbor is a
maul, and a sword, and a sharp arrow.
Proverbs 25:18

RIANE STOOD ON THE CREAKING TIMBER battlements watching the Templar flags whip wildly in the late winter wind. She stared across the barren fields, clutching her cloak tightly around her. 'Twas the same as it had been every day for the past four months, not a soul or creature insight. The days had grown longer yet a thaw seemed years away. A chill swept through her body. Would spring never come?

A guard standing off to her left coughed. "'Tis mighty cold out here, my lady. Perhaps you should go inside before you fall ill."

"'Tis as cold as it was yesterday. You may leave if you wish. I see no need for you to stand here with me," she said without turning her head to look at him.

"Now you know I cannot do that, my lady."

"Yea, I know," she whispered, more to herself than to the guard.

Ever since that day in the chapel those many months ago, Julian had a guard follow her about whenever he was gone doing Templar duties. 'Twas like it had been before; she was a prisoner. He still feared she would kill herself. Even though she promised she would not, he did not trust her, which angered her to no end. She was to believe everything he said, yet he could not extend the same courtesy to her.

She would love to tell him exactly what she thought of his boorish tactics, but somehow he managed to make sure they were never alone. He had passed most of her instruction to Brothers Andrew and Guy. Once a week, Julian would test her on her knowledge in the crowded hall. He would give a new list of instructions to Andrew or Guy, and then promptly leave.

But she had enough of this. She would seek Julian out and tell him she needed privacy. She needed time to be by herself. Though he would not know it, she needed time to think of a way to escape. Anything would be better than standing here dwelling on the kisses he had given her in the chapel. Yet 'twas the thought of those kisses that gave her the most pleasure.

She inhaled deeply, welcoming the chilly wind filling her lungs, pounding her face. Perhaps it would hammer away all memory of that day. She shook her head. How could she believe in such a fantasy? Ariane bit her lower lip. If she closed her eyes she could bring forth the feel of his lips on hers, the taste of his mouth, the feel of his strong arms about her. If nothing else, she wanted to be alone to savor the memory of that day without someone asking her if she was well!

Ariane fisted her hands on top of the wood battlement. She had to get away from here. Seeing Julian and not being able to talk or touch him was addling her mind. The only one who knew the countryside, and was not necessarily loyal to Julian, was Darrin. But would the thief help her? Even if she got word to him, would he risk leaving the sanctuary of the forest to come to her aid?

Abi Bin believed a woman held great power over a man if she used her feminine charms. That night in the forest Darrin claimed to be attracted to her. Did he speak the truth or 'twas it just a flattering platitude to provoke Julian into a fight?

No matter, she needed to get away before the weather ebbed, bringing her betrothed. She would rather die in the frozen forest than marry that Frank goat.

Ariane gave out a sigh of despair. There were no guarantees she would find Darrin even if she did get away. Not to mention the possibility that he wouldn't help her at all. She needed an ally, but whom? Andrew, Guy, and Najila would never turn against Julian. His mother? Never.

Ariane shook her head. From the noblest knight to the poorest peasant, there was not a soul in the region who would go against Julian's will. Perhaps she should offer up a prayer like Julian did when he needed help. The problem was, she wasn't sure to whom she should pray. Her prayers to Allah had all gone unanswered. So perhaps she should pray to one of the Christian's saints she had just learned about, but which one? There were so many: Peter, Paul, and Joseph... Ah now she remembered, she needed Saint Jude, for her petition was surely a lost cause.

She folded her hands and bowed her head. *Saint Jude, if you are there, please help me find a way out of here.*

A rumble of horses' hooves from the north drew Ariane's attention from her prayer. Four riders approached the gate at a vigorous pace. Could it be an answer to her prayers already? Two were clearly knights escorting what looked like a cloaked woman and a youth. Mayhap these strangers would help her. If she could get them to see her predicament, perhaps they would help her flee.

Ariane looked at her guard and headed for the steps. "Look lively, Lady Catherine has guests."

By the time Ariane entered the hall, Lady Catherine knew about the approaching riders. She rose to her feet and smoothed her gown. "My dear, perhaps you should go upstairs and rest awhile," she said to Ariane. An odd look traveled across her face.

"Nay," Ariane answered. "We have not had any visitors since the first day of my arrival and I mean no offense to you, but a change in company would be nice."

Catherine gave a nervous glance toward the entranceway. "Ah, but this company may not be to your liking."

Gently, Lady Catherine took Ariane by the arm and nudged her toward the steps.

Ariane resisted. "Please, my lady, let me stay. I will not get in the way and I promise not to make a scene."

"'Tis not you I fear who will start the ruckus. As sure as I stand before you, our guest will," Lady Catherine said nervously.

Her agitation only heightened Ariane's curiosity and turned her feet to stone. Lady Catherine gave Ariane one more healthy shove toward the stairs, but alas, it was to no avail. Jane entered the hall with a young boy in tow.

"Ah, there you are," Jane said, throwing back her hood, walking toward the pair. "I expected your usual greeting, out in the bailey, but now I see you have other more important things on your mind." Jane gave Ariane a pointed look.

"Oh no, Ariane was just feeling a little feverish so I was helping her to her room," Catherine said.

Jane gave Ariane a look over. "Yea, her cheeks do look a little red, but perhaps it is a permanent condition caused by living in that vile, hot country."

Ariane did not care for Jane's comment or tone. She spoke as if Ariane were a pot of poorly made stew. "I have been outside, for as you can see I am wearing a cloak as well; I stood upon the battlements before you came. 'Tis this country that has reddened my cheeks."

Jane gave out a strangled laugh. "Well, perhaps you should stay indoors in such wicked weather. We wouldn't want any harm to come to someone so valuable to the king."

"Come let us all get warm by the fire. I am sure one of the brothers will fetch some mead," Catherine said quickly ushering them toward the flame.

"How you can stand living among all these monks is beyond me." Jane relinquished her cloak to a second monk as the first retreated to fulfill Lady Catherine's request.

"They are diligent in their tasks and I never have to

remind them to change the rushes. They eat but once a day, which leaves more for the rest of us," Lady Catherine said, giving Ariane a small smile.

"I never thought of that," Jane mused, plunking herself into a chair.

A young lad peeked around Jane's chair. By the shape of his chin and the color of his brown hair, there was no doubt that he and Jane were related.

Lady Catherine reached out. "Simon, come and give me a hug."

He rushed into her outstretched arms. "Let us go and see if Brother Duncan has something for you to eat. Would you like that?" Lady Catherine turned to Ariane and gave her a wary look. "Are you sure you will not rest?"

Ariane lifted her chin and straightened her spine. "I am quite well. I would like to stay."

Catherine nodded and took the boy's hand. "Shall we see what the cook has for you?"

Simon grinned and nodded his head. They walked off hand in hand whispering and laughing to each other. 'Twas easy to see the love between them. The tender scene warmed Ariane and left a twinge of longing in her heart. She could never remember anyone looking at her with such affection. What did it feel like to be loved by someone? 'Twas something she would never feel.

Jane cleared her throat, disrupting Ariane's thoughts. "My throat is raw. Where is that monk with the mead?" Jane rubbed her neck and forced a cough several times.

Her question was answered immediately as young monk scurried over with the brew in hand. The bold look Jane gave the youth made Ariane uncomfortable, and the monk as well, judging by the color creeping across his face.

Jane watched the monk quickly retreat and sighed. "Perhaps having a few monks around would not be such a bad idea after all."

Embarrassed by the innuendo in Jane's comment, Ariane looked down at the mug in her hand.

"Sit," said Jane motioning to the chair across from her. "I would like to have a few words with you before Lady Catherine returns."

Jane's sharp words rang with an authority that demanded compliance. Unable to help herself, Ariane rapidly took her seat. "I have something to ask of you also, my lady." Then she wished she had said nothing for it was clear by the devious smile on Jane's face that what would come next would serve no good.

"Anything, my dear. I would help anyone whom Julian holds in high esteem." Her gaze darted about the room. "Is Julian about?"

"Nay, he left a fortnight ago to see Prince John and we know not when he will return," Ariane answered as sweetly as possible.

"Good. I mean, I will enjoy the chance to get to know you without Julian hovering about me." Jane gave out a fictitious laugh.

Ariane answered with a trite titter of her own. She wondered how Julian could have ever considered this woman his friend. Though beautiful, she was petty and contemptuous. An expert liar.

"I am sorry about what happened when first we met." Jane said, taking a drink. "'Twas just the shock of seeing someone else wearing the dress in which I was to be wed."

"Truly, I would not have worn the dress had I known the history behind it."

Jane leaned over and patted Ariane's hand. "Of course you wouldn't have." She leaned back in her chair and took another drink.

The silence made Ariane squirm in her seat. Would Jane help her? Was she the answer to her prayer?

"So you are to wed King Philip's cousin. I have heard that Lord de Craon is quite handsome," Jane finally said.

Ariane shrugged her shoulders. "I only saw the man once. I could not tell if he was handsome or not, for he was covered in blood. The blood of my people."

"Oh my, 'tis apparent you are not happy with this arrangement. I truly feel sorry for you." Jane took another sip of mead and tried to give Ariane her most sympathetic look.

'Twas easy to see through Jane's insincerity. There was no doubt in Ariane's mind that this woman did not know the meaning of empathy. Yet Ariane did not need her compassion; she needed her help.

"I know what it is to marry someone you do not love." Jane sighed. "But we all must do what we have to do for the sake of our children."

"Our children? I do not have any children," Ariane said puzzled.

Jane waved her hand flippantly in the air. "Of course you don't. I was thinking of myself."

"My lady?" Ariane asked bewildered.

"Well surely you have noticed my son, Simon."

Ariane nodded her head. "Yea, he resembles you."

"He looks more like his father," Jane corrected.

For the moment Ariane considered Hugh. The boy did have the de Maury eyes, yet the boy seemed to resemble Jane more. "I see your husband in his eyes," Ariane answered hoping the comment would satisfy her.

Jane gave out another fallacious snicker. Then she leaned closer. "My dear, Hugh is not Simon's father. Look close at those eyes. Who do you really see there?" She sat back in her chair, taking another long drink, clearly waiting to see the effects of her words.

A sharp pain rolled from her stomach to her heart. Simon, Julian's child?

Nay it could not be! Any questions she had were frozen deep within her.

Jane could not hide her elation at Ariane's predicament. "You know about the tragedy of our wedding day?"

Ariane's throat constricted, she shook her head.

"When Julian decided to run off to the Holy Land instead of honoring our parents' wishes." Jane leaned forward. "I had no choice but to marry his brother. I had missed my flow twice already. Of course, when Simon came early Hugh suspected who his sire might be, but in the end he still claimed the child as his." An all too evil, insidious innocence slithered across Jane's face. "Did not Julian tell you?"

Ariane could do naught but stare at the viper.

Jane placed her hand on her heart. "Oh, I see he did not."

I look at Jane as my sister, my brother's wife. There never was, nor ever will be, anything between us. The words Julian spoke in the chapel months ago raced through Ariane's mind. She knew as sure as she was sitting here that Julian had spoken the truth and Jane's words were nothing but lies.

More of Julian's words came to her. *She has polluted my brother's mind with these lies.* Now she understood why Hugh held so much hatred toward Julian. He thought his son was Julian's. Suddenly Ariane felt great sympathy for Hugh. What an awful burden to live with.

Yet Simon did have the eyes of a de Maury. Ariane gave her mind a mental shake. Nay, she believed Julian. Hugh would have not married Jane so quickly had there not been a reason. More than likely 'twas years of Jane's lies that caused Hugh to doubt what he knew to be true; Hugh was Simon's father.

A boy's playful laugh interrupted Ariane's thoughts. Simon entered the hall again, arm and arm with Lady Catherine.

Jane leaned forward and placed her finger over her mouth. "Shh, enough of this. Lady Catherine does not know the truth."

As the pair approached, more of Julian's words flooded Ariane's mind. *Now she wishes to spread her lies to my mother and Prince John.* So that is why Julian left in a hurry to see Jane that fateful day. He knew what Jane had planned in her twisted mind.

Sorrow for Julian consumed Ariane, an emotion she was not sure she wanted to feel toward him, but nonetheless she did. He had been forced to return home, forced to face again a woman who was set on destroying him and those he loved.

"Mother, Brother Duncan gave me a piece of mutton," Simon said, waving the meat proudly in Jane's face.

Simon's merry face twisted Ariane's heart. Did not Jane realize what such a lie would do to her son?

Jane pushed Simon's arm. "Get away from me," she said with disgust.

Ariane studied mother and son. Jane treated her son as if he were nothing more than a bothersome itch. Every time the boy opened his mouth, Jane waved him to silence. She scolded Lady Catherine for pampering him. Not once during Ariane's observation did Jane say one positive thing about or to the boy. In fact, the only subject Jane seemed to be interested in was herself. Yea, the more Ariane watched the more she pitied all the de Maury men.

But most of all she felt sorry for Simon. With each reprimand Simon became more sullen. 'Twas apparent that no matter what the boy did he could not win his mother's approval.

The sick feeling Ariane felt in her stomach matched her withering plan. At first she thought Jane would be the perfect person to help her to escape. After all, 'twas no secret that Jane viewed her as a threat to her future with Julian. Now after listening to her, Ariane knew all she would have to do is mention her plan and Jane would jump at it.

But that was before she learned Jane's vicious lie, before she saw the sweet boy with the sad eyes, before she realized what a terrible lie would do to a doting grandmother. Ariane didn't know how, but she would stay and help Julian protect the ones he loved from this maniacal woman.

"Mother, I—"

"Quiet, must you always interrupt me," Jane shouted at Simon.

"I—"

Jane waved her hand in the air. "I don't want to hear!"

Before Ariane could intercede on Simon's behalf, Lady Catherine took Simon by the hand. "Come, I have something I wish to show you in my chamber."

The boy rose without a word and followed Catherine toward the stairs. A tingling feeling went down Ariane's spine for she knew she had just witnessed a scene that had been played out many times before.

The moment the pair had left, Jane leaned forward again. "Now what was it you wanted to ask me?"

Tongue-tied, Ariane could not ask for her help. Not after what she had just learned. Why did her quick wit have to fail her now?

"Are you ill?" Jane asked

Ariane rose. "Yea, suddenly I feel quite peculiar in the head. Perhaps it is from sitting to close to the fire. Please excuse me."

Jane reached out and latched on to Ariane's arm. "Do come and visit me."

Ariane nodded. "I will."

"When?"

She was taken aback by the urgency of Jane's question. "Soon," she answered tugging her captive arm.

Jane held fast. "Say you will come at week's end. Promise?"

"I promise," Ariane said hastily.

An evil light flickered in Jane's eyes. "I know we can become such good friends."

Ariane raced toward the stairs as if the devil himself were chasing her.

"I will send someone to bring you," Jane called after her.

The hair on the back of Ariane's neck rose as Jane's monstrous laugh floated up the stairs behind her. She rushed into her room and slammed the door. Her heart hammering in her ears, she looked at the tapestry above the bed and for the first time realized the identity of the young lad with his hands clasped together and his eyes raised to the heavens.

Julian.

She walked over to the bed and ran her fingers across the threads. "I know what you prayed," she whispered. "You prayed for your freedom from this place. I am sorry I have brought you home to this. I am sorry. Someday I hope you will find it in your heart to forgive me." She fell on the bed and wept as she never wept before.

Fifteen

*Now the serpent was more subtle than any beast of the field
which the Lord God had made.*
Genesis 3:1

*A*S EXPECTED, THE DAYS DRAGGED UNTIL WEEK'S
end. The cold spell that held the land for months
had broken yesterday morning, bringing warm winds and
the promise of spring. Geese honked as they traveled
across the sky and birds chirped in yonder trees. Even the
somber monks became jolly. For every smile and heartfelt
greeting Ariane received, she became more and more
depressed.

Julian still had not returned.

She had told herself the desire to see him was solely
based on her need to discuss what had happened with Jane
earlier this week, but deep down she knew the truth. There
was no light in her life without Julian. How would she ever
live without him?

Ariane ran her fingers over the gold-trimmed green gown
she had draped across her arm. Lady Catherine had been
more than generous and gracious since her arrival. She never
mentioned the horrendous scene that had taken place the
night Ariane had arrived in this country. From her, Ariane
had learned the duties of a noble woman, and how to keep
her husband's home and lands running smoothly. Lady
Catherine often commented what a good wife Ariane would
make, a wife a husband would be proud of. Would she still

say those things if Ariane told her whose wife she really wanted to be?

Ariane threw the garment on the table. What good did it do to wonder about something that would never be? Best to think about what was at hand; a visit with Jane.

A knock at the door drew her attention. "Who is it?"

Lady Catherine poked her head into the room. "'Tis just me. I hope I am not disturbing you, but the men have arrived who will escort you to Jane's."

"So soon? I thought I would have more time."

"Seems Jane is anxious to see you."

Ariane picked up the gown from the table. "Yea, must be."

"Here let me help you," Lady Catherine said, taking the garment from Ariane. "Where is Najila?"

"She had some private business to attend to in the village. She seemed quite anxious about it so I let her go. 'Tis all right, I have dressed myself many times before."

"True, but things are different now. Soon you will be the mistress of your own household. Allow me to help you."

"My lady, no—"

"Nonsense child, raise your arms," Lady Catherine bunched the dress up to the neck opening. "Besides this will give us time to talk."

Ariane complied. She could see her fight would be useless. Since her arrival she had done many things that seemed foreign to her. As if she was playing someone else's role.

Lady Catherine slipped the gown over Ariane's head, then stepped back to take a look. "My son has good taste. Perhaps I should have him pick out the material for my clothing as well."

"Julian had this garment made for me?" Ariane said, running her hands over the soft material. "I thought it belonged to you."

"My gowns would be too short for you. Julian thought it would be best if you had garments that properly fit you, and

I agreed. I was amazed at how he agonized over picking out the cloth. Everything had to be perfect, down to your shift. I have never seen my son take such interest in woman's clothing before."

Ariane's body warmed. "Julian picked out my garments? All of them?"

"Yea, all. He said he had some experience in doing so. He claimed he picked out some lighter women's clothing in the Holy Land."

Ariane blushed. She glanced at the trunk filled with satins and silks Julian had given her.

There was a twinkle in Lady Catherine's eye. "But let us not discuss that now; there is something much more important that must be addressed. I think you should send Jane's men away. Does not your head throb?"

"Why no, my lady."

"Do you not feel a mood of melancholy coming on?"

What peculiar twist was this? Why did Lady Catherine think her to be ill? "Truly I am fine," Ariane answered.

Lady Catherine grabbed hold of both Ariane's hands. "I do not think it would be wise for you to go and visit Jane."

"But I have promised."

Lady Catherine gently squeezed Ariane's hands, as if the simple act could wash away the promise. "You do not understand what transpired here years ago."

"Yea, but I do."

Dropping Ariane's hands, Lady Catherine gave out a long sigh and walked over to the hearth and stared at the embers burning within. "Nay, you do not. There is more than Julian's rejection of Jane. There is a deep seed of rivalry that has bloomed in Hugh's soul. A seed I fear I had a hand in planting."

The fire crackled and hissed while Catherine's face took on a gloomy glow. "I cannot tell you of the joy my husband and I felt after Julian's birth, a son to carry on the de Maury name and secure the de Maury holdings for another generation. When Hugh was born a few years later, I was certain it was God's will that he be given to the church. I instructed both boys in the word of God while my husband educated them in the use of weaponry."

Once again Lady Catherine gave out a long jagged sigh; a look of pure anguish enveloped her features. Ariane wanted nothing more than to relieve the woman's suffering. "My lady, I can see this subject pains you. Perhaps 'tis best if you do not speak of it."

Without looking away from the flames, Lady Catherine shook her head. "Let me continue. It is my wish that you know all of it."

Ariane fell silent, dreading what would come next.

"As God would have it, Julian flourished on both planes. He was a master with the sword and the love of God shown bright in his eyes. Hugh, though talented with his weapon as well, had no love for the Word. 'Twas apparent he would never serve God as a monk or priest. He knew he was destined to be second to Julian in title, combat, and faith. 'Twas a revelation that did not sit well with him."

"My lady, please…"

Lady Catherine moved away from the fire and gazed at the tapestry hanging above the bed. "Julian, Hugh, and Jane grew up together. My husband and Jane's father thought a match between the two houses would be a wise decision. 'Twould unite our lands and lend defense against our enemies. Besides, Jane had great affection for Julian. I believe she thought of the match first and whispered the idea to her father. All believed time and Jane's great beauty would plant the seed of desire within Julian."

Lady Catherine paused, then slowly drew her attention from the tapestry to study Ariane's face. "But Julian was never one to fall for a pretty face. There had to be something more. Is that not right?"

"My lady?" Ariane asked, not quite sure what Lady Catherine meant by her question.

Lady Catherine waved off. "Never mind, my wandering

thought has naught to do with the subject at hand." She took a deep breath and continued on with her memory. "Though the seed did not take root in Julian, it did in Hugh. The knowledge his brother would have the woman he adored did not sit well with him. Adoration we all attributed to youth. We thought time would change all for the better. We were wrong.

"Trouble began when Julian wanted to go on a pilgrimage to the Holy Land. My husband wanted him to honor his commitment to Jane. Hugh took great pleasure in telling Jane that Julian's desire to visit Jerusalem overshadowed his willingness to be her husband. The thought inflamed Jane. She tried to gain Julian's attention by tempting other men, Hugh included."

The anguish in Lady Catherine's eyes wrenched Ariane's heart. How painful to have those you love pitted against one another. "My lady, you look so weary. Please sit down and rest a bit."

Lady Catherine accepted the seat, but pressed on with her tale as if speaking of the sad event could wash the hurt away. "Her actions did naught but push Julian away and attract Hugh. 'Twas the first time in Jane's life that she could not have what she wanted, and the revelation did not suit her. Soon gossip swirled about the keep that Jane was coupling with any man who looked her way. I feared Hugh's involvement, and spoke of the matter to my husband. Hoping time would set things right, we decided to grant Julian his request to go on a pilgrimage, and to send Hugh to my brother in Wales until the gossip ebbed.

"But fate was not with us. A plague swept over the countryside and took Jane's father. Her mother pressed for fulfillment of the marriage contract, saying it would ease Jane's loss. Unfortunately, my husband agreed."

Tears welled up in Lady Catherine's eyes. "The decision tore this family apart. Hugh became enraged and threatened to kill Julian. My husband banned Hugh from our home. The night before the wedding, Julian came to me with his doubts about the marriage and Jane's loyalty to him. I should have gone to my husband and stopped the agony, but I did naught but watch those I love destroy one another."

Tears slid down Lady Catherine's cheek as she placed shaking fingers over her mouth. Ariane knelt next to her and placed her hand on Lady Catherine's arm, hoping the simple act would lessen the pain that coursed through the older woman's body.

"Carry this burden no longer, my lady. You were but honoring your husband's wishes."

Lady Catherine patted Ariane's hand. "You are a sweet child. Here I am laying my troubles on your shoulders when your own life is being used in a game of power over which you have no control. But there is a reason to the telling of these woeful past events. Pray then, listen to the rest of it.

"The marriage day arrived quickly and the small chapel near Jane's home was filled. Jane glowed with happiness; Julian's face was a stone mask as they knelt before God's altar. Suddenly Julian rose to his feet and hammered his chest with his fist. He begged forgiveness from Jane and said he could not marry her because in his heart he had already pledged his life to God."

Lady Catherine's knuckles turned white as she squeezed Ariane's hand. She turned a tearful gaze toward Ariane and whispered, "I cannot tell you the relief I felt when he uttered those words. Jane began to scream, lashing out at anyone who came near. 'Twas a horrible day. Jane's mother shouted at my husband, demanding that Julian be forced to marry her daughter. Swords were drawn between the knights of both houses. Before cooler heads could prevail, my husband was slain. Jane collapsed at that very moment, ending the skirmish."

"My lady, no!" Ariane had never asked Julian how his father had died, assuming it had been a natural death. A sharp pain stabbed at the middle of her chest. Now she understood the painful look she had seen so many times in Julian's eyes whenever his father's name was mentioned. He carried this sorrow on his shoulders, and so did Lady Catherine. Ariane took the frail woman in her arms, as if she could shield her from any more grief.

But Lady Catherine pulled away and continued on. "The next morn, Jane was missing and none knew where she had gone. Two weeks later she returned as Hugh's wife. Julian left for the Holy Land within the month, giving some of our land to Hugh and the rest to the Templars, at my consent.

"Seven months later Simon was born. Julian had no knowledge of his existence until he returned with you. I wanted to protect him from Jane's deceit. You see, she was carrying Hugh's child that day of the wedding and had every intention of passing the babe off as Julian's. No doubt Jane told such a lie to her mother. That was why she pressed for such a quick marriage. Jane's mother never saw her grandchild, for she died of the plague two months before his birth."

Done with the telling, Lady Catherine's shoulders sagged. Tears trickled down her face and fell on to Ariane's hands. What suffering lurked in her heart after all these years. If Jane would make her lie public, it would destroy Lady Catherine.

Ariane could not stand by and watch Julian's family be ripped apart. The thought of Julian being devastated and alone tore her heart to shreds. Nay, he must never feel the pain of being alone, of having no one to dry your tears or calm your fears. He must never feel as she had. She loved him too much to let that happen. Ariane knew she had to stop Jane. But the question was how?

Lady Catherine raised her head and looked at Ariane through red-rimmed eyes. "Jane has already planted the seed of doubt in Hugh's mind. 'Tis sad, but he is rejecting his own child. How often he has heard Jane compare Simon to Julian instead of him, twisting her lie until it has choked any sense of reason from Hugh. I swear Jane takes pleasure in torturing my son, constantly reminding him that he is a poor second to Julian. Now you know the depth of Hugh's hate.

His wife has nurtured the feeling for many a year. I beg of you do not go and visit Jane. I fear she means you harm."

"My lady—"

"I have noticed how my son looks at you and so has Jane," Lady Catherine said strongly. "She sees you as the obstacle that stands in her way to winning Julian's heart. Please, do not visit her; send her escort away."

Ariane wanted to give into Lady Catherine's plea, but she could not. Someone would have to make Jane see reason before she destroyed everyone's life around her. Surely once she saw that Ariane was not a threat and Julian would never give up the church, Jane would put aside her lies. Ariane felt she had no choice in the matter; she had to see Jane.

"I think your fears are groundless. What would Lady Jane gain by harming me? We both know Julian is committed to God and surely Jane knows that also."

A look of doubt spread across Lady Catherine's features. "'Tis hard to know what a mad woman thinks. Jane fills her days with trying to make those around her miserable, a task she has crafted well. Stay clear of her, for one never knows what she plots."

A small chill of foreboding lingered at the base of Ariane's neck. Jane had blamed those around her for her loss of Julian instead of seeing the truth. 'Twas a strange way to protect a broken heart, but nonetheless that is what she'd done. Someone had to open Jane's eyes to the truth; perhaps then she would seek consolation from Hugh.

But what if she did not? What if Jane could not accept reality? The chill at Ariane's neck skidded down her spine. Lady Catherine was right; one never knew what a mad woman thought or what she might do. Yet, Ariane did not see any choice in the matter. If she did nothing, Jane would carry out her destructive scheme.

A plan began to form in Ariane's mind. She gave Lady Catherine a hug. "Whatever her plan, someone must stop the bleeding of this old wound. I will go and visit Jane. 'Tis time to start the healing."

Lady Catherine clutched Ariane's arms. "Then I shall pray for you. And for your safe return. God be with you," she whispered. "God be with you."

After Lady Catherine left, Ariane walked over to her chest and pulled out the dagger Julian had given her. She tucked it into a deep pocket within her gown. She tapped the side of her leg lightly. A little extra help in case God did not show up.

Jane danced around her solar, twirling this way and that, admiring the shine of her satin gown. Her fingers danced through the folds of the soft material, enjoying the luxuriant feel of the fabric.

"Stop that silliness," a voice hissed from one of the high back chairs near the fire. "You are making me ill. You look like one of the fools who prance about Prince John's court."

The dress swished about her legs as Jane halted in front of the intruder sitting in one of her beautiful embroidered chairs. Edward Baldwin. Her gaze narrowed on the slouching, brooding, bitter man. With Hugh gone on one of his regular hunting trips, she could have had the manor house all to herself, but then Baldwin had to show up.

Such a vile little man. If not for their partnership, Jane would have tossed him out on his bony behind. Unfortunately, she did not yet have the luxury to do so. Jane surveyed the room. Without Baldwin there would be no golden chairs. No ornately carved table to place her jeweled chalice on. No fluffy bed with silk linens to caress her body at night. Instead she would be lying on a hard pallet with a coarse blanket chaffing her delicate skin. No longer would she sip wine out of a golden goblet; she would be forced to drink weak ale from a wooden cup. A shiver crawled down her spine. Nay, no matter how much she despised the scrawny, hooked-nosed man, she would tolerate his presence and bide her time. For soon all she dreamt of would be hers.

"If what I do is so revolting then why not leave and return to the desert you came from," Jane said.

Baldwin slurped from the exquisite chalice. "Had not your precious Julian killed Brother Randall, you and I could have left this measly existents behind. The cargo Randall had was my largest shipment ever."

Baldwin slammed the cup on the table. "Blast Richard! 'Twas me who should have been entrusted with the girl. None of this would have happened. Instead, I had to convince Richard my services were needed in Cyprus. To cover up my real intent to desert and meet Randall in Marseilles. We were supposed to finalize our biggest trade. Plus, dispose of de Maury and Lady Ariane. But the fool wound up getting himself killed."

Baldwin leaned forward and poured himself another glass of wine. "Unable to go back to Richard, I had to follow. Finally, after spending months getting into Prince John's favor, I will make de Maury pay for my losses and Randall's death."

Jane put her hands on her hips and glared at Baldwin. "'Tis not Julian's fault. 'Tis Ariane's fault. She enticed Randall. When he came for what she offered, Julian did the honorable thing. He is innocent."

A breath of dismissal escaped Baldwin's lips. "What would you know about innocence and honor?"

Ignoring his words, Jane turned toward the fire. "The alliance Richard seeks with the Franks will be killed tonight with the death of Lady Ariane. Prince John will secure the throne, and the goods from the Holy Land will flow like sweet honey into our coffers."

Baldwin sat up and waved his bony finger. "Hold your tongue. The walls may have ears. Many here would take great pleasure in watching both of us swing from the nearest tree."

She shrugged. "These pathetic peasants live in fear of me. They would not dare defy me or they will find themselves out in the cold, scraping for their next meal."

Baldwin let loose a loud hoot; wine splashed on his tunic as he fought to contain his laughter. "Oh my dear, when was the last time you spent an eve in your hall? Your faithful servants stand before a few glowing embers and combat each other daily for the sparse pieces of bread you offer them. Aye, not one of them would dare rebel against such grand generosity."

Jane whirled about and lunged toward Baldwin with raised fists. "You are nothing but a simpering pig."

He grabbed her wrists and pulled her body close to his. "Now, now, my dear, we must not show our claws quite yet."

His fowl breath curled across her face and down the front of her gown. "Someday I will dance on your grave," she vowed.

Baldwin released his hold. "Just remember to play the gracious hostess when Lady Ariane arrives. Keep her in the great hall, do not bring her in here." Baldwin waved a hand about the room. "'Twill not be hard for her to figure out what goes on here if she sees your extravagance. Better to have her leave feeling sorry for Julian's brother and his poor wife. The less she suspects, the more unaware she will be when she meets her demise in the forest come eventide."

"I know what role I must play." Jane rubbed her hand against her neck, hoping the simple act would wash away Baldwin's touch. "You keep out of sight. 'Twill not be me who gives our plot away."

Baldwin's smile exposed his sharp-edged teeth. "Make sure all in the hall see you as the charming, gracious hostess. I want you to fawn all over the girl as if she were a sister to you. I will join you in the hall after she leaves. We will break bread with your loyal servants this eve."

"That is unwise. I never eat with the rabble. To do so would seem odd. I shall return to my solar. *You* can eat with them. Now get out. I wish for a few moments of peace before I must perform my role." Jane turned back to gaze at the glowing flames.

Like a serpent's strike Baldwin grabbed her arm, twisting her flesh in his grip, pulling her down toward him. "'Tis not wise to dismiss me so, Jane. Remember, I know all your secrets."

She coughed slightly to loosen the hard lump fear placed in her throat. How she wished he was the one riding out to his death tonight. "I am not the only one with secrets here."

He twined the fingers of his other hand through her braid, pulling her closer until his lips were a thin whisper from hers. She grimaced in pain and tried to turn her head to avoid the sour smell of wine that emanated from his lips, but an agonizing jerk on her braid prevented her from doing so.

"Do not threaten me. I can arrange to have my guards add another killing to their list. Who would care? Your starving servants? Your embittered husband? Your pitiable son, the daily target of your rejection? I doubt even he would shed a tear if you mysteriously disappeared."

"Julian would hunt you down and feed your entrails to the buzzards."

His hold on her eased. "Oh my, how I do enjoy your stupidity. The only death that will cause Julian to raise his sword is that of Lady Ariane's. In fact, I am counting on it. Think of it!" His voice fell to a sneering whisper as his eyes began to give off a hellish glow.

"Only a few of her escort will return, wounded and battered, stumbling into the bailey at Crosswind keep with another mount carrying the slain body of Lady Ariane. Why, within the hour Julian will be charging into the woods to avenge her death. And there in the deepest, thickest part of the forest will be my men with their bows aimed at his chest. Oh I cannot wait!

"But the best part," he continued, "is that Darrin and his forest droppings will be blamed for both deaths. The sheriff will not rest until every last man, woman, and child from that bunch are hanged. Then the threat of losing some of our precious cargo to that villain will be gone forever."

Baldwin let go of Jane's braid and traced her lips with his forefinger. "More coin for you and I. Is not that wonderful?"

Jane gritted her teeth. She needed him to fulfill her dreams. She would tolerate his pinching fingers and skeleton arms. For within the week she would be held in Julian's strong embrace and Baldwin would be dead.

Sixteen

The wicked walk on every side, when the vilest men are exalted.
Psalm 12:8

FOUL AIR FROM THE FILTHY RUSHES ALMOST CAUSED Ariane to gag as she entered Jane's manor house. The cold gray day filtered in through large gaps in the ceiling and walls, shedding light on the wretched life that lurked within. In one corner, two dogs fought with a young lad over tiny straps of discarded food. Ragged servants stood by a hearth trying to warm themselves by a dwindling fire. Ariane's spirits fell. Surely the poor conditions of Hugh's affairs also helped fuel his hatred of Julian.

And what of Jane? What went through her mind every time she came to Julian's home? Did she look around the warm, clean castle and think about what should have been hers? No wonder Jane kept up her lies. The austere conditions she lived in could only make her dream of a better life. These conditions would only make Ariane's mission harder. She would be asking Jane to give up on her dreams and accept the sparse life she had. Ariane knew that it would be a hard thing to swallow if the roles were reversed.

Jane entered the hall from an adjoining room, dressed in a drab gray tunic that ended below the knees and a yellowing white undergarment that continued to the floor. Both were made of very coarse wool. A plain white wimple covered her head. Where was the finery Jane had worn the night Julian returned home? Gone were the jewels that usually graced her fingers. Could all of those things been borrowed to hide her destitution?

One look at Jane and the servants scurried to the corners of the room while the dogs and boy fled out the door into the brisk day. Ariane tried to relax when all about her seemed on edge.

"Ariane, I am so glad you are finally here." Jane came forward and gave Ariane a hug. "I hope your journey was not unpleasant?"

"Though there is a slight chill in the air, the ride was quite invigorating." Ariane removed her gloves. "This is the first time I have been outside the keep since my arrival. My thanks for the invitation."

"Think nothing of it. You have no idea how lonely I get when Hugh leaves on these long hunting trips. Come, let us sit by the fire." Jane called a servant to stoke the meager embers within. She urged Ariane to sit in one of the hard wooden chairs that stood near the hearth.

Across from her, Jane settled into an equally poorly constructed chair that gave out a loud creaking wail when she sat. "I am sure your throat is dry from the long journey. Let us have some drink." A servant hurried forward when Jane raised her hand.

"That is not necessary," interjected Ariane before Jane could give her command. "I truly do not thirst." She could not bear to even take a drink from a household where each drop must be precious.

Her thoughts must have been imprinted on her face for Jane raised her chin in defiant dignity. A wave of despair rolled through Ariane. Offending Jane was the last thing she wanted to do.

"Well, I do. Bring forth two mugs of mead," Jane snapped at her servant.

The chair moaned as Ariane fidgeted. She searched for the words that needed to be said. Perhaps she could rely on a mother's love for her child to warm Jane's heart. "Where is Simon? He is such a fine lad."

Jane let out a low huff. "He is about. No doubt running around with some dirty peasants. There are times I do not see him for days."

A hollow ache filled Ariane's chest. How could Jane have so little feeling for her child? Oh, how grand it would be to have a son or a daughter to love and to receive their love in return, to protect from harm. But Jane gave no thought to that; she was bent on destroying her son by naming him a bastard. A title Simon did not deserve because there was no truth in it.

"Ah, our drink is here." Jane took the cup her servant offered and raised it to Ariane. "To our friendship."

Ariane slightly raised her mug and then took a small sip. The mead was sour and had an edge of rankness. She resisted the urge to spit the liquid on the ground.

Jane, on the other hand, did not. The amber liquid gushed from her mouth and landed on her coarse tunic and the floor. "What kind of pig swill is this?" she shouted. "I will not drink this. Bring us something of a finer quality and do not come back saying there is none."

"Nay Jane, I do not need drink."

A look of disgust traveled across Jane's face as she turned her gaze on Ariane. "Think you I cannot give better?"

She knew not how she did it, but once again she had put Jane on the defensive. "Nay Jane, please give pardon. I meant no offense. We must all learn to be happy with our circumstance in life."

"Ah, so you have come here to lecture me. You must glorify your son, you must heed your husband's wishes. Spare me, for I have heard these lines many times before."

"I only meant to soothe—"

"I need not your pity. You think I am impoverished. Come, I have much to show you." Jane rose from her chair and then pulled Ariane from hers. "This hall is too damp. Let us retire to my solar." Jane hooked her arm through Ariane's and led her through an adjacent doorway.

Thinking her eyes were playing tricks on her, Ariane blinked several times. The room before her was the complete opposite of the one they had just left. A roaring fire flamed in the hearth and before the fireplace stood two red and gold embroidered chairs. The arms and legs engraved with Islamic designs were etched in gold and silver. On a long, beautifully carved table stood two golden goblets and an intricately painted bowl done by the desert people. To the left of the table stood a large bed draped in fine silks and satins. At the foot of the bed was a chest painted in different shades of red and yellow. Over the chest lay a gown of red velvet. A gold belt studded with rubies laid on top of the dress.

'Twas almost as if she was back in the Holy Land. How could Jane have managed to obtain such beautiful things? And from where did they come? From the thief in the forest? Was Darrin somehow involved selling goods from the Holy Land?

The sound of a tiny bell drew Ariane's attention toward the bed. Behind the silk curtain lie a little white dog with a silver bell draped about his neck. Jane had held that dog in her arms the night they met. The night when she wore a beautiful gold beaded gown. From the appearance of this manor house and the condition of the servants, 'twas easy to surmise that Jane squandered most of Hugh's money.

"My lady, you live quite well," Ariane said.

Jane walked over to the table and broke a chunk of bread from a loaf sitting in the finely painted Muslim bowl. She offered a piece to Ariane. "Trust me, 'tis not easy to keep up such a life living on limited resources."

Ariane could not believe what she was hearing. Jane did not care about anyone, except herself and her own personal comfort. There were no other pallets in the room, which could only mean she slept here alone. Where did Simon sleep? She doubted Jane would share her warm bed with him. The boy probably slept with the servants. Once again she felt a deep ache in her chest for him.

Ignoring Jane's offer, Ariane moved toward the fire. "You seem to have accumulated many valuable items on such a limited stipend."

Jane lazily chewed the bread Ariane had rejected and watched her with hooded eyes. She swallowed. "Do I hear a note of sarcasm in your voice? Do these items from the Holy Land distress you?"

The wicked smile Jane gave Ariane confirmed her suspicions. None of these items were obtained by honest means. "Not at all. I just worry about your Christian soul. Is it not written in your commandments that it is a sin to steal from others?"

A foul frown replaced Jane's false smile. She then rounded the table and plunked down in one of the ornate chairs. The tiny dog jumped off the bed and rushed up into her lap. "I did not steal these things. They were given to me."

"Really, from whom?"

A sticky smile spread across Jane's face. "Why from Julian of course."

"Nay, you lie," Ariane retorted. "He does not care for earthly possessions."

Jane cocked her brow and continued to pet the dog on her lap. "Perhaps, but he loves to shower gifts on those he loves."

For a moment, doubt clouded Ariane's mind. She thought of the fine clothing Julian had given her. Surely what Jane said could not be true? Ariane examined the woman sitting across from her. Nay, Julian could never love a person with a heart so black.

"You lie poorly, my lady. Julian could never love a woman who seeks only to please herself. Nay, you received these from another."

Jane's hand stilled on the dog's back. In reply the animal stopped its panting as if he knew the sound would draw his mistress's wrath. Only the crackle of the fire gave evidence that Ariane's hearing had not failed.

The moments dragged under Jane's scrutiny. The skin at the corner of her eyes crinkled as she narrowed her gaze. "You are a smart one. Now I see why men are infatuated with you."

"Infatuated? What do you mean?" Ariane asked puzzled.

"Oh please. Do not play the innocent with me. What woman raised by a pack of evil infidels would come of age honest and pure of heart?"

Taken by surprise at the viciousness of Jane's words, Ariane could do naught but shake her head. She watched as Jane's beautiful face all but transformed into an ugly mask of wrinkles and folds, her tongue flicking out between her teeth like that of a searching serpent.

"Don't shake your dense head at me. You know what I speak of," Jane hissed. "You probably stole that trinket you wear around your neck from the real Lady Ariane. Royal blood, bah. What attracts Lord de Craon to you is your tie to King Richard and nothing more. Just think what Julian would do if he knew what a little schemer you are."

"Nay, none of what you say is true," Ariane defended. "You see things that are not there because Julian has rejected your love. Even if he had returned without me things would be the same."

"You lie!" Jane shouted, rising to her feet and pointing a wicked, accusing finger at Ariane. "We were to be wed. Had not Lady Catherine interfered we would be husband and wife today."

Ariane could not believe the terrible twist this conversation had taken. She looked into Jane's face red with rage. Lady Catherine had been right; Jane was beyond rational thought. A hard lump formed at the base of Ariane's throat. Somehow she would have to get this mad woman to see reason.

"Jane, 'twas not Catherine who prevented your wedding, 'twas Julian's love for God that stood between the two of you, and still stands there now. Not me, but God."

A large vein bulged in the middle of Jane's forehead, her lips curled in an evil bent. "Nay, 'twas his mother who put those thoughts in his head. She was jealous of me. She was fearful that I would have more control over Julian. She knew Julian and I were lovers and she hated the thought of losing her precious son to me."

Ariane drew a deep breath. "'Twas not Julian who was your lover, but your own husband, Hugh."

Jane flew out her chair and the little dog yelped at the sudden upset and ran behind the large red chest. "Liar," she shouted, shaking her fist at Ariane. "Look at my son. Anyone who has the eye to see knows who his sire is. Simon is Julian's son."

Though Ariane's heart raced, she knew she had to hang on to her composure. 'Twas the only way to handle a crazed person. "I know how grief stricken you were at the time; your father had just died. No one faults you for seeking affection. Hugh is a good man and his son resembles him well. Give up your tale and speak the truth for you have much to be thankful for. Hugh has given you a beautiful son."

Jane lashed forward and struck Ariane on the cheek. "Silence. Do you not think I know truth from falsehood? You are the one who refuses to see the truth. Julian loved me. He still loves me. 'Tis you and his mother who have poisoned him against me. Once the two of you are gone, he will turn to me again."

Ariane rubbed her stinging cheek and her soul went cold. Jane meant to hurt Lady Catherine as well. "You are wrong. What stands between you and Julian is his God. God comes before his mother, you and me. You fight a battle you cannot win, and you live with a dream that can never be fulfilled. Your God has given you a beautiful son and a husband ready to love you. Rejoice in the fact that you have a family to love. For surely, if you stay on this course you will find yourself alone, and I tell you this, there is nothing worse than going through life with no one."

Her heart grew heavy as she thought about the lonely years she had spent in Abi Bin's house. No one cried with her when Raya died. No one put a cold cloth on her brow when a fever raged within her body. No one comforted her as she sat in Abi Bin's punishment pit. She had survived the past ten years without caring and love. Did Jane realize what she was throwing away?

"Jane, I beg you, cease these actions for they will only bring sorrow."

A sharp shriek shattered the air. Jane lunged forward and grabbed Ariane about the neck, squeezing her breath from her lungs. "I want you to die!"

Ariane clawed at Jane's hands, struggling to draw a single sweet breath. She sank to the floor as her legs gave way. Her fingers shook as she searched the folds of her gown for Julian's dagger. The tips of her fingers felt the cold metal. Clumsily she withdrew her weapon. Colorful spots danced across Jane's maniacal face, then slowly her features began to fade. The knife fell to the floor as darkness closed in around her and Jane's voice becoming a distant echo.

Suddenly, the pressure around her throat ceased. Air poured into her lungs, causing Ariane to cough uncontrollably. Blurry images began forming around her; a rush of voices penetrated the silence.

"Why did you stop me? You want her dead just as much as I do," Jane cried.

"Aye, but not like this. Your shrieks could be heard in every dark corner of the hall," a strange voice answered.

"So you hung in the shadows spying on me."

"Of course, you dimwit. I stood nearby in case you did something foolish like this!" the voice hissed.

Nay, the voice was not strange. Ariane had heard it before, but where? She tried to turn her head, but her neck ached too much to move.

"The question is, what are we going to do now? We certainly cannot let her leave since you attacked her. We need the cloak of darkness to carry out my plan. Such a mess."

Yea, that was it, the hiss of the voice. But it could not be; the viper slithered in the Holy Land with King Richard.

With all her might, Ariane fought her screaming neck muscles and managed to turn her head toward the voice. The fuzzy image came into focus. Baldwin! Why would he be here, and with Jane? Her head began to throb as her vision cleared, and the moment it did she wished it would cloud up again.

Baldwin bent down and picked up the dagger. "Are you all right, my lady?"

Unable to speak, Ariane shook her head. She tried to push herself off the floor.

Bony fingers grabbed her beneath the arm and hoisted her to her feet. "Happy to see me?" Baldwin asked sarcastically. "No? Such a pity."

"How did you get here?" Ariane asked hoarsely.

"How I got here is of no importance. The question I think you should be asking, my dear, is why I am here?"

By the leer he gave her, Ariane was not sure she wanted to know the answer to that question. For the answer could only bring calamity.

"What no comment?" Baldwin examined the blade; the blue stone in its hilt glittered in the fire light. "Another lovely gift from de Maury?" Her heart raced as he took the tip of the knife and lightly ran it across the swollen skin of her neck. "Too painful to talk, hey?" He turned his attention to Jane who sat by the fire rubbing her arm as if she were the one who had been wounded. "Blast it, Jane. Look what you have done to her neck."

Jane peered over Baldwin's shoulder. "What care you what her neck looks like? She will be dead within the hour anyway."

"Thieves that have to fight off escort guards usually do not waste their time strangling their victims," Baldwin said turning his dark eyes back to Ariane.

"Then have her defiled body found away from the others, off the path. 'Tis not unusual to have thieves carry off their women captives. Choking the air from her lungs would seem to be a normal way to die in a ruffian's hands."

A slow, slippery smile splayed across Baldwin's face as he tapped the blade against his other hand. "For once, something intelligent has come out of that useless head of yours. The question now is, how do we get her from here to the forest without raising suspicion?"

They spoke of Ariane's demise as if she was a doll of rags with no feelings or understanding, but she would not stand by and let her life be snuffed out. Bruised throat or not Ariane opened her mouth and attempted to give out a loud scream.

Baldwin clamped his hand over her lips and held the knife beneath her chin. "No one will come to your aid. The moment Jane ushered you into her solar I knew trouble would be afoot, so I sent your men to the stables with a mug of ale. No one who cares can hear you. I am going to remove my hand and you will not make a sound. For if you do, not only will you die this very moment, but I will also kill the boy, Simon."

Slowly Baldwin removed the blade and dropped his hand. Ariane drank in the sweet air that replaced the odor of his filthy hand.

"You will not kill my son," Jane screeched. "I have need of him."

"How will Simon help you secure Julian's love? He knows Hugh is Simon's sire. I would think you would want both father and son out of the way. A sad suffering widow is such an appealing picture to many men and especially to men of honor. Why, Julian would see it his duty to wed the woman of his fallen brother and nephew," Baldwin said.

"Do not lie to me. You mean to kill Julian as well," Jane retorted.

"Perhaps not. If you think you can keep the brute under

control while we carry out our trade business I have no objection to letting him live."

With his back toward her, Jane could not see the insincerity in Baldwin's eyes. He winked at Ariane as if he knew she saw through his little scheme. But he did not care. This man would destroy any and all who got in his way, even a defenseless boy if it would further his plan.

Jane drifted back toward the fire. What type of mother would allow another to bargain with her son's life?

Simon was alone in the world, like her. Did he cry at night for his mother's love? Did he wish to have his brow kissed each day? Oh, how the boy must suffer.

If by some miracle she survived she would take Simon to live with her. The lad needed love and she had plenty to give.

Baldwin leaned close and whispered in her ear. "Now my dear, remember, if you give out even the smallest yelp I will send for the boy. Do I make myself clear?"

"What difference does it make if I yell or not if you plan to kill Simon anyway? Leave the boy alone. He is innocent."

Baldwin stood back and glanced over his shoulder; Jane was lost in her musings. "One can change his mind again, can he not?" he answered in a low voice. "Hugh and Simon have never been a threat. What would I gain by killing them as long as you do as I say?"

"Jane will expose you if you kill Julian," Ariane whispered.

"There are many greedy individuals in England; I can find another to replace her as well." Baldwin gave out a low sigh. "However, I will miss the pleasure she has given me."

Ariane looked away, for she could not stomach looking at evil any longer.

Baldwin grabbed her chin, forcing her to meet his reptilian eyes. His gaze raked over her body. "Too bad you must die, for it seems you have a few attributes that would please me. Alas, we cannot all have what we want."

Ariane's heart raced with fear as Baldwin's glided the tip

of the dagger down her bruised neck. With his other hand he circled her upper arm.

"Jane, go tell Lady Ariane's guards she has decided to spend the night. Offer them your best ale."

"I'll not give—"

"Shut your mouth and listen! Give them plenty. Thinking they have nowhere to go this eve, they will drink hearty. A few hours from now, when they are well in their cups, you will announce that Lady Ariane has changed her mind and wishes to leave within the hour. You will offer some of your finest guards to follow because of the late hour to insure Lady Ariane's safety."

Jane rushed over to stand in front of Baldwin, a wild look in her eyes. "I'll not provide escort to—"

"Blast you, hold your tongue! Do you want to accomplish this or not? These shall be my men dressed as your guard. You shall don Lady Ariane's cloak, hiding your face within. Because of her lady's fickle mind, I am certain none of her escort will care if my men ride in the rear while hers take the front."

"I'll not go out on a cold nigh—"

"You will do as I say, or I will slice your throat from ear to ear!" Baldwin fixed his cold eyes on Jane and squeezed Ariane's arm until she swore that blood could not flow through the appendage. His brows flicked up, leaving no doubt that he would make good on his word.

Ariane's spirit sank, for try as she may she could not think of a way to foil this monster's plan. All would be lost. Lady Catherine would lose Julian and perhaps Simon and Hugh as well. Her whole family gone. Destroyed by a crazed woman and avaricious man.

"With their backs protected, her men will be expecting danger to strike from the sides or the front. They will never suspect arrows will pierce them from behind. Of course, a few of my men must die in order to remove suspicion from us, but alas, sacrifices must be made.

"Aye, this will work quite well, I will follow far behind

with Lady Ariane. When the deed is done we will join the scene briefly." Baldwin leaned over, his hot breath close to Ariane's ear. "Then I shall drag you deep into the forest..." He gave out another loud sigh. "I am truly sorry, my dear, but there is no other solution. There is only one thing to think on at this moment and that is what I am to do with you until we leave? Order up the ale and see to her men's needs," he snapped at Jane.

Baldwin released Ariane and tapped his chin with the hilt of the knife, pondering his own question. Ariane slowly edged herself away from Baldwin's side. If she could put a little distance between them perhaps, when he least expected, she could make one last attempt to reach the door. Surely someone in the hall would come to her aid.

Ariane saw her chance when Jane lifted the latch. Briefly, Ariane glanced out of the corner of her eye at Baldwin. His stare gave clear assurance that his mind was focused on his devious plan. She dashed for the door.

Jane screeched as Ariane pushed her out of the way.

Cold steel stung her neck as the serpent coiled his arm around her waist. "There is no escape, my lady. Only death for the innocent if you persist on this course. What would Allah say if you came to him with the blood of poor Simon staining your soul?"

"Simon is a Christian. What care I if he dies?" she lied.

"Oh, very good. You are very entertaining. You may fool the others with your act of indifference, but I know full well that you could not bear to see the boy suffer, Christian or not. After all 'twas you who said he is an innocent. We cannot let the innocent die, can we?" He twirled the knife beneath her chin. "Such a pity. You would have made a good mother. Now, you will behave or I will send for the boy and end his miserable life before your eyes."

Ariane moved to a chair. She sat passively, hoping he would think she saw the situation as hopeless. But, make no mistake, she would try again. Simon and Julian's lives hung in the balance, and she would not go to her grave until she was sure both were safe.

Jane put her back against the door, her face contorting into wrinkles of pure hatred. "We should kill her now and forget your plan."

"Blast it, Jane, use your head. There must be a place we can keep her without raising suspicion." Baldwin grumbled as he ripped the bottom of Ariane's gown into two strips, wrapping one about her wrists and jamming the other in her mouth.

A flash of elation spread across Jane's features. She reached for her cloak on the ground next to the red and yellow chest. "I know the perfect place." She moved to the left side of the bed and pushed away a mass of silk draperies. Behind the curtain was a door so small one would have to crouch in order to go through it. "Follow me."

Ariane tried to remain calm and keep her wits as Baldwin pushed her toward the narrow opening, for no place could be as bad as Abi Bin's pit.

Seventeen

I sought the Lord, and he heard me, and delivered me from all my fears.
Psalm 34:4

HE HAD BEEN WRONG.

Ariane peered into the dark well that stood little more than a stone's throw from the manor house. The vines that twisted up from its depth looked like the devil's fingers come forth to grip the wicked. Ariane closed her eyes and gave herself a mental shake. Nay, 'twas just the Christian teachings addling her mind.

After taking a deep breath, Ariane opened her eyes again. Her view did not improve. The worn stones were covered with a murky, frozen mud, mixed with a moldering moss, a waxy oozing slime in the setting sun.

A shove on her shoulder made her stumble forward, stubbing her toe on the jagged stones that circled the ancient shaft.

"Hurry up. My feet are freezing and the wind cuts fiercely through these peasant clothes. Thank goodness I am wearing my heaviest cloak." Jane gave Ariane another spiteful jab in the ribs.

Baldwin moved to Ariane's side grabbing her arm and warding off Jane's next attack. "Hush up. You will be much colder before this night is over. Have you forgotten you have a long journey ahead of you?"

"Nay I have not, but before I must play this witch's part,

I plan to change into my warmest gown."

"You'll find a gown that resembles the one Lady Ariane wears. I will not have you drawing attention to yourself." The chilly spring air bit at Ariane's back as Baldwin grabbed her cloak from her shoulders. He tossed the garment at Jane. "Here, you will need this for later. Now give me yours."

"I'll not give her my fine cl—"

"Give it to me. She cannot freeze to death. Her death must be as we planned. I cannot drag a blue corpse out into the woods," Baldwin hissed.

"Why not? Your manly skills bore women to death anyway."

Baldwin waved the dagger he held in his hand. "Give me the cloak now or I shall cut it from your body."

Jane unfastened the garment and threw it in Baldwin's face. "'Twill be ruined. Look at that hole. 'Tis covered with filth."

"Cheer up. I am sure we can have a brand new one made for you once our position here is secured," Baldwin said as he dropped the lush cloak about Ariane's shoulders.

Jane smiled. "Yea, I am in need of a new one."

"Good. Now let us be done with this." Baldwin pulled Ariane over the rough stones to the mouth of the well.

From the pit rose the stench of musty foliage and rotting death. She shrank back from its dark depths. Who knew what lurked below? Some wild animal could have fallen in, waiting to devour her. She leaned back, pushing herself away. She met with Baldwin's shiny blade dancing before her eyes.

"I will remove the gag and free your hands. You will be good or Simon will suffer. Do I have your word?"

Fear swept through her. For she knew Baldwin would not think twice about harming the boy. She nodded.

Baldwin pulled the material from her mouth and slit the knife through the cloth about her wrists. "If my plans are ruined, I will make haste back to the house and kill Simon where he lies." He thrust a large rope into her hands. "Tie this about your waist. And tie it tight, for I would not want the knot to come loose and have you plummeted to your death."

She had never been a person given to prayer, but right now she gave up a petition to Allah and to all the Christian saints she could think of, for she needed the help of any who could hear. If only one of them would truly send her a savior. With shaking hands she fastened the rope around her waist. Baldwin checked the knot, and when he was satisfied the rope was secure he pushed Ariane to the edge.

"Over you go, my dear, and be quick about it, we do not have all eve." He stuck the point of his knife into the middle of her back, encouraging her over the side of the well.

The stones were freezing beneath her touch as she sat with her feet dangling over the abyss. The rancid smell of aged decay swept through her senses and sought to pollute her very soul.

A heavy shove pushed her over the edge. She twisted about grabbing a few heavy vines that had embedded themselves in the masonry around the well walls. The frozen weeds cracked under her weight. She began to shake. A deep moan rattled in her chest and echoed from the dismal abyss.

Spots of color began once again to dance and blur before her as her body dropped lower and lower into the well. 'Twas no use. She could not fight against the fear that twisted through her soul.

She had failed. Julian would die and she would be swallowed up in this hellish hole.

"Hold on to the rope." Baldwin's face loomed before her. "I will not let you drop. Besides the well is not that deep. Your distress is so unwarranted." He looked back over his shoulder as he held the rope with both hands. "Here Jane, give me some help."

Ariane reached for his forearms, grabbing at the fabric of his mantle. Jane appeared from behind, and with a smug smile slowly pried Ariane's fingers from Baldwin's sleeve.

"Give greeting to my unworthy servant that choose to kiss and tell. Unfortunately he fell into this nasty well last summer. Perhaps there is enough of him left to keep you warm."

She grabbed hold of the rope, watching the entrance drift further away as Baldwin left the rope slowly slide through his fingers. Chilling dampness stung her face and seared her lungs; she began to cough and gag as the putrid smell threatened to suffocate her.

From up above she could hear Jane's fiendish laugh become a thunderous roar as her voice bounced off the stone walls. The terror stricken faces of all the girls Abi Bin had put into his pit floated before her. Their screams mixing with Jane's maniacal laugh.

"Do you feel the bottom yet?" Baldwin called.

"Nay!" Her shout came out as that of a wounded calf.

"Oh, let her drop. So what if she breaks a few bones," Jane said.

"Enough. Hold the rope," Baldwin spat. "She must be almost there, I cannot see her anymore."

Ariane tightened her grip, the rough hemp scraping the palms of her hands. She would survive this. She would survive this. Ariane repeated the words over and over hoping to make them true. Her foot brushed against a hard damp surface. The rope slipped further; her legs gave way and she landed in a heap on the muddy well floor. Her slippers became instantly wet from the small pools of water that remained protected from the icy wind up above.

The rope relaxed in her grasp, she tugged sharply. Ariane smiled at Jane's sudden scream and the small tiny particles of vine and stone fell into the shaft.

"I almost went over," she heard Jane cry. "She meant to drag us down with her!"

"Stop your prattling," Baldwin's voice echoed. "Nice to see you have made it safely down, my dear. Now remove the rope from your waist."

She stood as stiff as stone. Ariane had no intention of

helping Baldwin the viper, nor did she want to give up her cord to freedom.

"I know you can hear me. If you do not give me the rope, then I shall have to throw it in and there will be no way of retrieving you. All will think the barbaric villains have carried you off never to be seen again. Is that what you want? I thought for sure you would like to have another chance to best me thus gaining your freedom."

The viper spit his venom well. With frozen fingers, Ariane labored at untying the knot at her waist. Even though she knew Baldwin couldn't see, with her dwindling strength she raised her fist. "Know this, snake. I will see you dead by my hand or by those that I love. This I promise you."

"I look forward to the feel of your hands, my lady, and the rest of you as well."

Once the cord was loosened she gave a healthy tug, sending more debris down upon her and enjoying the momentary yelp that drifted from above.

And then silence.

She was alone, in the deep dark well…in the pit.

By the cross of all that is holy. For a man who never swore in thought or deed, Julian certainly was making up for years of abstaining from the act. He clenched the hilt of his sword while he listened to his mother. How could she have left Ariane go? By her own admission his mother agreed she had her misgivings, but Ariane had been adamant, so his mother relented.

"Even though Jane sent guards, I gave her my personal escort as well. There is no harm in being too careful. I am sure she is fine," Lady Catherine said.

The wringing of her hands did not go unnoticed. Julian's anxiety intensified when Jane's messenger arrived informing them that Lady Ariane would be spending the night at Jane's.

If Hugh were in residence, all would be well. Even though Hugh blamed Julian for the outcome of his life, Hugh would never harm another to satisfy his anger, but if he was not dwelling there...heaven help Ariane. Jane had left the reality of her life long ago. She clung to a dream that would never be and she cared not who she dragged into her misery.

"You should have been with your mistress," Julian snapped at Najila.

Large tears spilled from the servant's eyes as she clutched her chest. "I am sorry, my lord, I-I had a certain matter to attend to."

"Was this matter more important than the welfare of Lady Ariane?"

Najila looked to Guy and Andrew. Andrew gazed at Najila with empathy, while Guy stared at Julian with censure. Julian winced. Perhaps he was being too hard on the girl.

In truth, he had no one to blame for the outcome of events except himself. He should have left Guy or Andrew behind when he went to see Prince John, but he believed the sight of the Avenging Angel with his holy knights would quell the prince's ambitions. Then he might heed Richard's orders.

John had grown powerful in the king's absence and had many allies. He truly believed that *Richard Couer de Lion* would never return. 'Twas a belief Julian did not share.

His actions had put Ariane at risk. He had suspected Jane would come sneaking about, but he always assumed Ariane would be safe within the walls of Crosswind Keep. Ariane proved to be a resourceful, bright woman. Why would she venture into the den of a she-devil? She knew it would be dangerous. She knew that Jane harbored only hatred in her heart for her, so why would she go?

Talons of foreboding scratched at the back of his neck; there could only be one answer. "Mother, you said Jane called upon you earlier this week?"

"Yea, she had Simon with her."

"Were you present through her whole visit?"

His mother gave him an odd look as she pondered the question. "Nay. Jane shunned the poor lad as usual, so Simon and I went off in search of a sweetmeat."

Giving Jane plenty of time to weave her deceitful web. Aye, he should have known better. To be certain, Ariane would not fall for Jane's trickery, but she would go if she thought she could right what was wrong. He had noticed how her eyes softened every time she saw a mother and child hug and banter playfully with each other. Ariane needed love and wanted to give love, a love she sought from him, a love he was not free to give.

Even though she protested against her marriage to Lord de Craon, she would find her love there. From what Julian knew of him, her betrothed seemed to be a fair man and he would give Ariane many children...children for her to love.

Children that should be his. Julian flinched inwardly. By the cross, he burned with desire. Aye, what had Baldwin said when first he laid eyes upon Ariane? '*Burn you shall. Not in hell's fire, but in a blaze just as consuming, just as condemning.*' Aye, he burned for Ariane, and he feared he would be too late to save her from Jane's twisted schemes. If Ariane died this eve, hell's fire would be a welcome fate.

"Make ready the horses," he said to his comrades. "We ride to Hugh's manor."

A sharp squeak came from the other side of the well, Ariane shared her quarters with vermin. She moved to her left, away from the rustling sound only to come in contact with a rigid object lying on the floor. She jumped back waiting for whatever it was to leap forward and rip her apart.

Nothing happened.

Cautiously, she slid her left foot toward the object, giving it a quick shove. The thing rolled slightly then came to rest on her foot. Ariane cried out, certain her leg would be torn from her body.

Whatever it could possibly be was covered with coarse fabric and held an awful stench. She began to gag and claw at the wall. She had to get out of here. 'Twas dark and full of demons. She tried to pull her foot free by wiggling her ankle. Twisting her foot upward she came to what seemed to be a gap in the thing.

Bile rose in her throat. Nay, 'twas not a demon. She screamed and yanked her foot free. 'Twas the corpse of Lady Jane's lover. Mohammed, Jesus, help her. She had to get out of this pit.

Ariane gasped and scrambled away from the bones. She tried to gulp air that refused to enter her lungs. Tears coursed down her face. She heard the squeal of rats scurrying in the corners, the wrapping of crooked vines against the stone walls, the trickle of slimy water seeping from the broken masonry.

Ariane fell to the ground and crawled to the opposite side of the well. How much longer must she endure this? Baldwin had lied. He sent her to rot in this pit. His laughter rang in her ears. Then his merriment mixed with the snickers of Abi Bin. He wouldn't let her out until she obeyed.

"I promise," she shouted, "I will obey."

She would never get out. Ariane pulled up her legs and locked her arms around her knees. She began to rock, and rock, and rock.

"*Do not be afraid. I am here with you.*"

A calm soothing voice broke through her terror.

"*My lady, my lady, can you hear me?*"

The fear inside Ariane ebbed slightly. Could the voice be real? She raised her head. "Who's there?"

"*A friend who wants you to know I am with you always. You are never alone.*"

Ariane released her legs and tried to stand on weak limbs. "Get me out of here!"

"*Be brave. But have no fear, no harm will come to thee.*"

Ariane raised her chin and squinted, hoping to get a glimpse of the person who owned the voice. "Please help me. I cannot stay here. I will die."

"*Nay you will not die, for you are with me,*" the voice answered evenly.

Despair rolled through Ariane. Did the man mean to make sport of her? He offered her no way out and then calmly told her she would be safe. Was he one of Baldwin's minions sent to torture her?

"Please, get me out of here," she begged.

"*Help is on the way.*"

The voice no longer came from up above, but seemed to be in front of her. Ariane strained her vision hoping to get a better look at the shadowy vision before her. She covered her eyes with her hand and gave out a loud moan. She was going mad and the devil had come for her.

"*Ariane,*" the form called. "*I am with thee. Always. Even unto the very end. I am not the evil one.*"

Slowly, Ariane dropped her hands. Before her stood an old man who glowed with a gentle light.

"Who are you?"

The old man gave a reassuring smile. "*Who I am matters not. That I heard your cries matters a great deal.*"

"How did you get in here? Is there a tunnel? I must leave this place. You will show me the way."

"*There is only one way out.*" He pointed heavenward.

Ariane's hopes plummeted. She felt her fear begin to rise again. "You got in here. How? You will show me the way out!" She reached forward to grab him, but she seemed unable to do so. 'Twas like grabbing thin air. He seemed to sway away every time she reached for him.

"You are not real," she cried. "I have gone mad."

"*You are not mad. I am real. All you need to do is believe,*" he assured.

Ariane leaned back against the wall and looked into the man's sympathetic knowing eyes. Her fear floated from her body. A strange serenity entered her soul. Perhaps she was dead, perhaps she was not.

Ariane looked around and heard the rats screech. What seemed unbearable a moment ago, seemed harmless now. She fixed her gaze back on the old man. "Yea, I believe you."

"*Good. Sit. Close your eyes. Remember I am with thee, there is nothing to fear.*"

Ariane's eyes became heavy, she relaxed against the wall and closed her eyes and slept.

"My lady, my lady."

Ariane opened her eyelids and looked about. The old man was gone. 'Twas no one there except the vermin and Jane's dead lover.

"My lady, my lady are you down there?"

The voice was faint, mayhap 'twas not there at all, but an illusion produced by her mind. Mayhap 'twas the old man from above again.

"My lady, my lady, are you all right?"

Nay, 'twas not the same voice. Another phantom had come to visit? "Aye," she answered timidly.

"They did not hurt you, did they?"

The high pitched voice cracked and lowered and then turned higher again like that of a lad near the beginning stages of manhood.

"My lady, 'tis Simon."

Simon? Mayhap she was mad after all, for surely the boy could not have stumbled on this spot by accident. "Simon, is it truly you?" she shouted.

"Aye."

"How did you find me?"

"I spend a lot of time helping out in the stables. I took rest for a few minutes near the entrance when I saw the door of my mother's secret passageway open. I was curious to see who her night visitor was. She has them often when my father is away."

The boy spoke as if Jane's infidelity was as common as the sun rising each morn. The poor lamb, he had no idea what a loving family was. For that matter, neither did she. But once she had. In the deep recesses of her mind she remembered her mother and father. Their affection for one another was openly visible and their love trickled down to her. 'Twas a memory she had spent years on erasing, for 'twas the only way she could survive in a world where no love was given and safety became her major concern.

If I live through this ordeal, I promise, Simon I will keep you safe and give you love. However, in order to keep this vow she must find a way out of this pit, and soon.

"That's when I saw you leave with mother and Sir Baldwin," Simon continued. "I saw them throw you in this well. Why would they do such a thing?"

He was not ready for the truth nor did she have any intention of giving it. Better to leave the explaining for later. "Simon, do you see a rope lying near the well?"

Tiny bits of stone and vine spilled about her as time dragged on, but finally an answer came. "Nay I see nothing."

So Baldwin had taken the rope with him.

"I could go back. I am sure I could find some in the stables."

By the time the boy left and returned Baldwin might very well be on his way back for her, and there also was the chance that Baldwin would see Simon lurking about and would make good on his threat and kill the boy. Nay, there had to be another answer.

"Lady Ariane, Can you hear me? What say you? Should I go back to the hall?"

"Nay, 'tis too dangerous. There must be another way. If only your father was about." She let her head drop to her chest because she had no other thought as to how to prevent the terrible outcome of this eve. Though Hugh hated Julian, Ariane hoped he would want to prevent the bloodshed of innocent people. If only Hugh were about.

"I know where he is. He's not far. He hunts with Darrin and his band."

Ariane's chin snapped up. Perhaps there was hope.

"Father goes there quite often when mother gets too hard to live with. I followed him once, just like I followed you. I wish he would take me, but he never does. They laugh and dance and tell funny tales. Sometimes I wish that was my home."

The loneliness in Simon's words squeezed at Ariane's heart. He roamed the countryside and no one cared. 'Twas as if he had no parents at all. She would get out of here, she would live, and Simon would live with her. But first she must foil Baldwin's plan. "Are they close? Can you get to them quickly?"

"Aye, their camp is secret, but I have been there often enough I could find it with my eyes closed."

"Good, now listen. Find your father and Darrin, tell them that Sir Baldwin plans to have my escort killed when the road bends into the forest."

"I never liked Sir Baldwin," Simon chimed in.

"Just go, Simon," she continued. "Have them save the men, and you make sure you stay out of danger. Do not return to the manor house. Do you understand?"

"Aye, but what about you?"

"Do not worry about me. If all goes well, I will be there as well. Now go!"

"Aye," he shouted down.

Ariane leaned against the cold wall as Simon's footfalls drifted on the wind. She closed her eyes and gave up a prayer knowing someone heard her. *Please let them believe the boy and save all those men and Julian as well. Dear God, let Hugh believe Simon.*

Eighteen

*Who will rise up for me against the evildoers? Who will
stand up for me against the workers of iniquity?*
Psalm 94:16

"WAKE UP, LADY ARIANE, 'TIS TIME TO TAKE A
little journey," Baldwin called sarcastically into
the well.

After being in this pit for what seemed like an eternity,
even his scratchy voice sounded like an angel coming to
deliver her from the depths of hell. She pushed off the wall
and gazed up into the blackness. Everywhere she looked, she
saw nothing but total darkness.

"I am sure you are sorry to leave such comfortable
chambers, but it cannot be helped. I say, are you there, my
lady? It looks as if the well has swallowed you up."

Dirt and bits of vegetation landed in her eyes. "Aye, I am
here."

"Oh, good I was beginning to think a beast lurked
in the shadows and quickened your departure from this
earth."

A slight rustling sound to her left sent a shiver up her
back. "Please hasten to get me out of here."

"Patience, patience, my dear. These things take time.
Your guard left only a few moments ago. 'Twill not take
long to get you out. I know you cannot see, but I have
brought a friend with me."

Ariane's heart almost skittered to a stop. Baldwin must

have caught Simon. How foolish of her to think a young lad could outwit a fiend like Baldwin. If it was Simon, she would have to find a way to get the boy safely away. "Is it anyone I know?" she asked with a shaky voice.

"I do not believe so, unless you saw him in the hall when you arrived. His name is Melvin. I know you cannot see, but he is quite a large fellow and comes in very handy now and then."

The beat of her heart began to slow in relief, 'twas not Simon, but some servant. "What does he do here?"

"Why, he comes to help deliver you from this vile well. You really did not expect me to drag you up did you? I would be too exhausted to finish up what needs to be done in the forest. Here, the rope is being lowered, make sure you attach it securely around your waist. We don't want a tragedy quite yet."

Ariane groped in the dark trying to find the rope, stumbling over Jane's lover and causing the vermin to scatter to the corners. Finally, the rough hemp hit her in the nose. Quickly she pulled the end of the rope down and knotted it about her waist. "I am ready," she called giving the rope a hard tug.

The rope ascended with each powerful tug and grunt Melvin gave. The blackness faded some as light from the moon shone above. Though strange as it was, she was actually glad to see Baldwin's pointed nose peering over the edge of the well. She grabbed onto the stones at the mouth. Suddenly she was being lifted over the edge in Melvin's large arms.

"My thanks, Melvin," Ariane said.

Melvin nodded and gave a loud grunt.

"You may go, Melvin. I will take care of the lady from here."

To Baldwin's command the large servant nodded again, then turned back toward Ariane. He stood there a few moments with a look of worry etched on his face. Finally, he bowed low before her, grabbed her hand and gave it a tight squeeze. Then he straightened and ran off into the blackness of the night.

"Don't look for any help from him, my lady, he lost his tongue years ago." Baldwin bowed low, mocking the poor mute's actions. "Your steed awaits you. Accept the hand of your humble servant."

Like lightning, the palm of her hand struck his face, but equally fast he grabbed her wrist, pulling a piece of rope from his tunic and twisting it rapidly about her wrist until the tender bones ached with pain. She tugged, hoping his grip would slip, but instead he jerked the rope toward him and she landed against his chest. He wound his free hand in her hair.

"You'll not escape me; there is no point in trying. Give me your other hand." He yanked on her hair until her knees buckled beneath her. "Now give me your other hand."

Slowly Ariane brought her arm about. 'Twas the smug smile that he wore that made her do it. She balled her fingers into a fist and smacked him square in his pointy beak. Baldwin stumbled back in pain, the rope slipping through his fingers. 'Twas the only chance she would get. She rose and started running toward the forest, but her legs were stiff from the night's chill and she stumbled often. Baldwin struck from behind, bringing her to the ground.

He straddled her back, then grabbed the rope that still hung from her wrist, pulling her arm behind her until she thought he would tear the limb from her shoulder. "You wicked wench, you'll pay dearly for what you have done. Unfortunately 'twill not be here. Your games have made our departure even more urgent." He squeezed his legs about her waist.

"Now turn over, slowly. For I swear, one more silly attempt to escape and I will take this rope and choke the life from you, then carry your limp body into the forest. No one will be the wiser and the deed will be done."

Gritting her teeth, Ariane turned over. His thighs dug into her hips. She stared up into his evil eyes while he bound her wrists and hands together. "This plan of yours is foolish; you will never succeed. Just like it is written in your holy words, *The weeds will be pulled out and thrown into the fire.*'

"Oh, very good. What a diligent student you are. Perhaps you can use what you have learned to bargain with The Almighty. You'll be meeting him shortly."

"And what of you? Thou shall not steal, thou shall not kill—are not these your commandments? If you die this day, will you not face God's punishment?"

Pulling her up, Baldwin nudged her toward his horse. "My, my, Brother Julian has taught you well. I think God will overlook my little transgressions since I will be ridding the world of one more infidel."

"Killing me may appease God, but what of killing Brother Julian? I do not think your God will like it if you kill the Avenging Angel."

Baldwin took a cloth from his tunic and jammed it into her mouth. "The truth is, like you I doubt that God even exists, and if he does, well, then I shall see you in hell."

She sat erect on the beast, not wanting her body to touch Baldwin's odious form. His long thin arms slithered about her waist as he reached for the reins. With a swift kick, the stallion took off for the woods. She could only hope and pray that Simon had found Hugh and that he would believe the boy. She tried not to think about the other possibility— that Hugh would not lift a finger to help, being glad that Julian and she would soon be dead. Surely there still was some brotherly feeling for Julian in Hugh's heart? Yet Ariane could not erase from her mind the words Hugh uttered the day of Julian's return, *'I wish you were dead.'* She had given up on any type of faith years ago, since everything she prayed for had never come to pass, but as she rode with the cold wind biting her cheeks and the viper's hot breath pressing her back, she prayed.

Dear Julian's God, please let Hugh see that Simon is his son. Have Darrin and Hugh swiftly come and deny the evil one his glory. She asked for a miracle and prayed it would be answered.

Baldwin slowed the horse as they approached the rendezvous point. He pulled up on the reins when he could see the rear of the entourage.

"Watch, my dear, as soon as your guard takes the turn in the path, 'tis the perfect spot for an ambush. The path curves and winds between high rocks and dense trees. I have planted men behind those rocks and in those trees. They will shower arrows down on your escort. My men, following in the rear, will give chase to those who may escape." Baldwin gave a long sigh. "Of course a few of those will die as well. But it can't be helped. We don't want others getting suspicious."

Ariane watched the last of Baldwin's men turn the bend and, as he predicted, loud voices and the sound of arrows leaving bows pieced the air. Her stomach began to roll; Hugh did not believe Simon. Darrin and his men would be blamed for her death and Julian would pursue them with his sword drawn, quite possibly killing his own brother in the confusion. He already blamed himself for the death of his father. What would the death of Hugh do to him?

She had been right and Julian had been wrong; there truly was not a God, but surely there was a devil. For he certainly triumphed more often than the so-called righteous.

Baldwin leaned forward. "Shall we join them for a few moments, or are you impatient for the end?" he whispered.

The skin on her neck prickled where his rancid breath fell. She straightened her spine even more; Baldwin just laughed and guided the horse forward.

However, things were not as he describe when they arrived. Touches lit up the night. Baldwin's men were heavily engaged with a band of ruffians. On horseback, Hugh and Darrin fought Jane's guard in the rear. Poor Jane sat crouched over her mount in the middle of the fray, shrieking loudly as arrows sailed above her head.

Taken aback by the scene, Baldwin swore an oath and his

grip on Ariane's waist sagged. She gave him a swift kick in the shin with her heel. Baldwin jerked their mount, which began to prance about. Ariane leaned sideways, causing the horse to stumble, sending both of them to the ground. Hands still tied, Ariane struggled to her feet and took off into the fight still gagged. She dared not look behind, certain Baldwin gave pursuit.

Pandemonium reigned in front of Julian when he arrived on the scene. Who was friend and who was foe? He raised his hand holding his men.

"What goes here?" Guy shouted.

"'Twould seem my suspicions were right, but 'tis unclear who is the good and who is the evil."

Guy pointed to the left. "'Tis the bandits who fight a group of knights. Surely the villains are the enemy."

"At first glance one would think so, but look, there is my mother's guard. They fight both." Julian's blood raced in his veins. If his mother's men were here then so was Ariane, but he could not spot her through the fray. She was the target of this raid; he only hoped he was not too late to save her.

Guy's horse danced forward. "What say you then, who should we attack?"

Julian drew his jeweled sword from his sheath. "Stand with our guard. Those against us will scatter when they see us charge. Julian jabbed his heels into the destrier's sides and raced ahead.

'Twas the cloak that caught his eye as he sliced his way through the fight; the rich, rust, fur-lined coat he'd had made for Ariane. The sight almost caused him to lose his breath. She sat in the middle of the battle hunched over on her palfrey.

His sword slashed through another attacking knight. Then came another knight and still another, when a veil of red hair came running toward him.

Ariane!

Trussed up like a festive pig, she ran with her hands bound and a filthy cloth protruding from her mouth. 'Twas not her who sat on the palfrey. The moment of relief quickly turned to white-hot anger. Whoever did this to his Ariane would pay dearly. He raced his horse forward, vowing he would give his life if need be to keep her safe.

To the back of the column he spotted his brother and the outlaw standing back to back, fighting off some of Jane's own men and the other unknown knights as well. Julian knew not what went on here, nor did he care. His one goal was to reach Ariane's side.

He pushed onward. She was near. Close. He could almost feel her wrapped in his arms. Safe.

The woman on the palfrey reached out and grabbed Ariane by the hair. The hood fell back. With eyes red and wild, Jane pulled a dagger from beneath her cloak. *His dagger!* The blade glittered in the torch light.

Julian raised his sword. A fiery pain raced through his arm. He looked down. An ax had been wedged into his shoulder. He swore under his breath, pulling the ax free and slicing off its owner's head. He looked up; the dagger Jane held making its descent. His heart fell to his stomach; he had failed Ariane. He had failed to save the woman he loved.

A sharp zing pierced the air. Jane lurched forward giving out a frenzied cry. She fell from the palfrey, an arrow lodged in her back. There with bow in hand stood Hugh, his features gaunt with deep anguish.

With Jane dead, the unknown knights and what was left of her men retreated into the forest. A small nudge against his leg brought Julian's attention downward. With a dirt-smudged face, twigs stuck in her matted golden-red hair, and wreaking of a smell uncommon to a lady, there stood Ariane with a filthy rag stuck in her mouth.

She was beautiful. His lady was safe.

Her brows furrowed as she knocked her head against his

leg, clearly not happy with his immobile state. He dismounted quickly, pulling the gag from her mouth.

"You are injured," she said urgently.

The concern that flickered in her eyes and the warmth of her voice warmed Julian. He would never leave her alone again. Never again would she fall into danger.

"Julian?" she questioned when he had not answered.

"Nay, sweet lady 'tis nothing but a flesh wound."

Ariane frowned, looking at the trail of blood that oozed from his shoulder.

"I have had worse," he assured.

She stumbled into him. Her bound hands thumped against his chest. Raising his eyes to the heavens, he asked God to excuse his stupidity. He took his sword and cut her hands free.

Her palms came to rest against his beating heart. His pulse quickened as she lay her head there as well. He wrapped his arms protectively about her. He had no intention of letting her go.

The rough clearing of Guy's throat brought Julian's attention back to his surroundings. "We have lost only two men, but many of the others are dead. Come, I wish to show you something."

Julian wrapped his uninjured arm around Ariane's waist, and followed Guy over to one of the fallen knights.

With his boot, Guy rolled the knight over. "See who this is."

"'Tis Harold." Julian exclaimed.

"Aye, and yonder lies Warren. These are all men who came to the Holy Land with Richard."

Julian stiffened. "They landed with Richard, but they took their orders from another."

Guy nodded ready to give voice to the name Julian had long since formed in his mind.

"Lord Baldwin." Ariane confirmed.

Rolling red rage raced to every part on Julian's body. He saw the bruises on Ariane's face.

Baldwin.

The angry welts forming at her wrists.

Baldwin.

Her soiled clothing, her hair covered in dirt.

All Baldwin's doing.

His heart fell to a hollow pit in his stomach. He pulled her closer to his side. "What did he do to you?" he asked softly. "Did he harm you?"

Ariane shook her head. "He meant to, but only after my guard was killed. He planned to kill me and blame the whole attack on Darrin and his band."

A small shiver went through her body. Julian gently rubbed her shoulder.

"Baldwin put me into a well, until the time was right for the ambush. 'Twas not so bad."

'Twas not so bad! The anger bubbled ten times over at the timid sound of her voice. The one thing Ariane feared above all else was to be locked away in bowels of the earth. He had seen her wild eyes when she was expected to remain below ship, or the shake of her body when she talked about her time in Abi Bin's pit. How often had she said any punishment would be better than to be locked away.

His hand gripped the hilt of his sword, a fierce pain leapt up to his torn shoulder. Injured or not he would seek the viper out and cut his malevolent heart from his body.

Julian squeezed Ariane's waist then released her. "Guy will see you back safely to the keep."

She pulled on his tunic as he turned to leave. "Where do you go?"

Lines of worry marred her beautiful face, her head shaking as if she already knew the answer.

"Nay, you cannot. You are wounded. Your brother needs you."

He looked over to where Hugh stood rigidly above Jane's body, his face void of color, dull like a lifeless shadow. Darrin put a hand on Hugh's shoulder.

225

"He has others to see to him right now," Julian answered turning away again.

Ariane pulled on his healthy arm. "I need you."

He turned back, her pleading look tearing his insides to shreds. "I know this snake, he will come after you again."

"Yea, but you will be there to protect me. You will be stronger. I have nothing to fear."

She stood determined and he could do no less but take her in his arms again and kiss the top of her head not caring who looked on. "I will not let you out of my sight."

"Yea."

"You will never leave me."

"Yea."

"You are mine." The revelation lifted something deep within him and rang true even though it couldn't be.

"Yea. Now go and see to your brother."

Julian did not want to leave her. Yet Ariane gave him an insistent nudge toward Hugh. Slowly he walked over to where his brother knelt next to his slain wife. His head hung low, his shoulders slumped, Hugh held on to Jane's hand, wringing his fingers over and over the lifeless flesh as if in doing so he could undo the agonizing deed he had committed.

"Brother," Julian said softly. Hugh slowly lifted his head. The hollow, haunting look in his eyes ripped through Julian's chest. *How much more, Lord? How much more must my brother suffer?* "I am sorry for your loss, but—"

Hugh raised a shaking hand. "Please. Please do not tell me there was naught I could do. Just go and leave me in peace."

Julian hesitated and stepped back, uncertain what course he should take.

Darrin came up beside him. "Simon came to our camp and told us of Baldwin and Jane's plan. Hugh was the first to grab his bow and sword. We found Baldwin's men lurking in the trees ready to attack." A small sad smile slipped across Darrin's lips. "We changed their plans."

His expression hardened as he looked down at Hugh. "He was the only one who could prevent the death of your lady; Hugh had a clear shot. There was no other choice, he knew that."

"My thanks," Julian said, giving Darrin a firm handshake.

"'Tis nothing, I helped my friend's brother. Stay. Talk with him. Deep in his heart he still loves you."

If only Darrin's words were true, but there had been so many years of pain. Pain not caused by Hugh or Jane, but caused by him. He knelt down next to Hugh and placed his arm around his brother's shoulder.

"I am sorry, all this is my fault," Julian said in a grave voice. "Had I done the right thing and married Jane none of this would have come to pass. Father would still be alive, Jane would still be alive, and you would have found another who would have loved you. I was selfish and thought only of my own happiness."

Hugh raked his hands through his hair and shook his head. "Nay brother, 'twas I who was selfish. I took what should have been yours. I took Jane's maidenhead. We joined so often there is no doubt that Simon is my son. Had I known she was with child the day of the wedding, I would have stopped it myself. However, Jane did not tell me until after you rejected her and father was dead."

He paused taking a deep ragged breath. "After we wed and you had left, I thought things would right themselves, but I was wrong. Jane took great pleasure in pointing out all the ways I was second to you. Especially that you were the better lover, and 'twas you who planted Simon in her womb. 'Twas easier to believe her lies than to face the truth. Easier to reject my own son than to face my own failure."

Julian patted Hugh's shoulder. "You did not fail Jane. I did. I could never love her and the knowledge of that twisted her mind."

Hugh gave out a weak laugh. "You are wrong. Jane loved herself and the vision of being the grand lady of the

Crosswind Keep. She had a very healthy appetite; she would have cuckolded you also."

"Perhaps you are right." Julian dropped his arm from his brother's shoulder.

"My jealousy of you fueled my anger. Forgive me, Julian."

"There is naught to forgive."

Hugh stood and looked across the path to stare at Ariane. "At one time I would have sold my soul to the devil if Jane would have looked at me the way that one looks at you. I have also seen the way you look at her. Do not lose her, brother."

Julian stood. "She is promised to another, and I have my commitment to God."

"This may all be true, but that does not make it right. Perhaps God wants you to spend your life with her and not as a Templar in the Holy Land."

Dumbfounded, Julian stared at Hugh. Could he be right? Would God want him here with this woman? He rubbed a hand above his brow. "I-I do not know. I will give it some thought."

"Search hard, Brother, and you will see that I am right. I have one more thing to ask of you. Will you take Jane's body back to the manor house? Simon is waiting for my return at Darrin's camp."

"I am surprised the boy did not insist on coming along," Julian said.

"He did, but I would not hear it. If something happened to him—" Hugh paused. "I could not bear it. Now I must go and tell him what I have done."

Julian watched the pain and hurt flicker in his brother's eyes. "You do not have to give him every detail."

Hugh cocked one eyebrow. "What is this? The saint is telling me to state a lie of omission? It does not suit you. Nay, Simon needs to hear the truth and I will have to live with his judgment."

Julian nodded. "Aye, the truth will set you free."

Hugh hugged Julian. "May God bless you, Brother."

Tears stung at the back of Julian's eyes, his throat tightened. Until this moment he did not know how much he had missed his brother. Hugh turned his back and headed into the forest. "God's peace, dear Brother," Julian murmured. "God's peace be with you."

Nineteen

Though I speak with the tongues of men and of angels, and
have not love, I am become as sounding brass, or a tinkling
cymbal.
Corinthians 13:1

LOUDS DRIFTED OVER THE BRILLIANT MOON CASTING
an eerie, calm darkness over the countryside. A
steady sleet stung Julian's cheeks as he drove his steed hard.
The task of laying Jane's troubled soul to rest had taken
longer than he expected. Each order given, each pull of the
shovel, each hour that passed seemed like a decade. He
feared that his mind would grow feeble with age and his
body would be weak with disease before he saw his beloved
Ariane again. For surely a century had passed since the last
time he held her.

His urgency to reach home matched the rapid tempo
of his mount's hooves slamming over the hard ground.
Huge puffs of mist bellowed from the beast's nostrils; his
head rose and fell like that of an oar pushing through a
turbulent sea. Tree limbs cracked above, giving off a sinister
cackle.

Just like Baldwin's depraved laugh.

The frigid air stilled in his lungs. His heart plummeted.
The monster still lived. Ariane. He had to make sure Ariane
was safe. Julian dug his heels into the horse, pushing the
animal onward. The clouds overhead broke briefly, and the
moonlight revealed his home in the distance. All appeared to

be quiet, but Julian did not pause. Fear and trepidation compelled him onward.

Impatiently, he waited as the portcullis groaned open. Templars rushed forward, plaguing him with questions. He had no time for this. He needed to find Ariane. Thankfully a young boy pushed his way through the group and grabbed the reins of Julian's horse.

Julian dismounted. "The others are not far behind. I wager they will be here within the hour." Wager. Never in his life had he wagered on anything, nor would he speak such words for fear of offending God. But all that was before he met Ariane...when life was different. When life was simple and the truth seemed so clear.

The boy gave out a low sigh, his shoulders drooped. "There will be no sleep tonight."

Julian patted the boy's shoulder. "No good deed goes unnoticed. What you do here tonight will be remembered and rewarded later."

Doubt settled across the boy's face. "Aye, my lord, my rewards will be in heaven, but right now I wish my reward was here. A little sleep and a warm bed would do for me."

Julian understood the lad's words. To see Ariane safe this very moment would be enough reward for him. The desire grew to the point where Julian thought his heart would give out if he did not find her this instant. He rushed to the great hall and threw wide the door. His mother sat near the fire with embroidery on her lap, and Guy stood staring at the flames. Many servants and a few monks were nestled into the corners of the room, most fast asleep. Nothing seemed amiss except for the simple fact that Ariane was not present.

He crossed the room in long strides. "Where is she?"

Both Mother and friend looked up.

"Julian!" Guy opened his arms.

His mother rose from her chair. "We feared something happened to you. What has kept you?"

"Where is she and why are you not with her?" Julian bellowed at Guy.

Guy dropped his arms. "All is fine here. Ariane is safe."

Uncertainty twisted Julian's gut. Though all looked serene, something was terribly wrong. Lady Ariane should be here and Guy should be standing guard instead of resting by the fire. "I'll ask you but one more time. Where is she?"

Before Guy could answer, his mother put a calming hand on Julian's arm. "She is in the chapel."

Julian whirled about and made for the entrance. Guy let her go to the cold dark chapel in the middle of the night? Where was his thinking? Baldwin was still on the loose. He could easily slip into this castle and harm Ariane.

"She has a guard with her. You really should let your mother look at your wounded shoulder," Guy called.

He clenched his fists and ran to the chapel, fear chipping at his soul and compelling him onward. The guard Guy had sent with Ariane sat slumped on a barrel, fast asleep.

Julian grabbed the front of the man's tunic and pulled him to his feet. "Why are you not inside with Lady Ariane?"

The soldier's eyes widened. "B—Brother Julian, my lady wished to be alone. So insistent was she that she kicked me in the shin."

Julian gave the guard a healthy shake then shoved him aside. Entering the chapel, he scanned the dimly lit room. Nothing. Empty. He gasped for air as if the devil had taken his breath away. Baldwin, the beast, had taken her. By all that was holy he would find the animal and slaughter him if Ariane was harmed. As he turned to leave, a tiny sound made him pause his retreat. Julian gazed back into the chapel. Hidden in the shadows of the altar knelt a huddled form draped in black.

His first impulse was to rush forward, but years of battle had taught him caution. With soft steps he approached the murmuring figure and drew his sword while pressing his back against the chapel wall. As he moved closer, the whispers of the low voice became clear.

"Our Father who art in heaven…"

Prayers. The person muttered prayers. Julian's grip tightened on the hilt of his sword. These were not Ariane's prayers.

"Thy will be done on earth as it is in heaven..."

With one great leap Julian rushed forward, pulled the cloak from the figure's face and raised his sword. A pair of moist green eyes stayed his hand. All air gushed from Julian's lungs. He fell to his knees beside her. His sword clanked to the floor as he opened his arms and wrapped them around Ariane.

She was safe. In his arms.

He kissed the top of her head. "What are you doing here? You should be in the hall with the others. Baldwin still roams about and who knows what evil terror he will unleash next."

Ariane lifted her head; tears flowed down her cheeks. "I waited and waited and you did not return. You were hurt and I feared the worst. I would have gone mad if I stayed in the hall. Was it not you who said, if you pray without ceasing, God will answer?"

Even though she was in his arms, he tried to draw her closer. "Aye, but..."

"You were right. I prayed all the prayers you taught me and added a few of my own words and here you are. You have returned!" She pulled away slightly to run her gaze over his body and brush her fingers over his injured shoulder. "Except for this wound, you are unharmed?"

"Aye."

"Then my prayers have been answered." She paused, her eyes downcast. "I will follow your God."

Had Ariane said those words two weeks ago, he would have rejoiced. But now they rang hollow. He loosened his hold and raised her chin.

"Look at me Ariane. Is your desire to serve God coming from here?" Julian placed his fingers over his heart.

Ariane shook her head.

"You cannot bargain with God. How can you serve him if you do not believe in him?"

Ariane pulled away. "But I do believe. For the first time in my life I do believe God does exist. When I was first captured, I remember praying to God for deliverance, and he did not answer. Then when the Muslims made me learn Islamic ways, I prayed to God in a different way. Yet there were no answers. Today I prayed in the old way of my youth." Ariane's brow furrowed. "And here you are. I now know there is a God."

"Ariane, it is a start. Your prayers were answered because you did not doubt His existence. God will direct your life if you listen and open your heart to His will."

Julian's own words stung like an arrow to his own heart. 'Twas as if he was breathing for the first time. When he rejected Jane and went to the Holy Land, he believed it was God's will. But it was not. 'Twas his own will. 'Twas always about him. The great Avenging Angel. He had said he did not want fame and power, but that was exactly what he was seeking when he went to see the master that fate-filled day he met Ariane. All his life he had done what he wanted to do, ignoring the wishes of others. He gave his mother's home to an order of questionable honor because he wanted to look righteous, because of his pride. Not because of God's will.

Julian looked into Ariane's green eyes. She searched for acceptance and he searched for truth. Aye, in spite of himself, God did direct his life. He directed him to Ariane. Together they could both find what they needed. If only he could be sure this was what God wanted. If only there was a small sign.

Ariane wrinkled her nose then nodded. "Yea, I know there is a God. For I am certain he was in the well with me."

"What?" A chill swept through Julian. The stress of being left in that dank hole must have addled her mind. He tried to pull her closer, but she placed her hands on his chest, stretching out her arms.

"I know you think I am mad, but I swear 'twas real."

He could not fight the fear that swept through him. She spoke like many Crusaders who had been in the desert too long. They screamed of images that did not exist.

Ariane took one finger and tapped her chin. "Well mayhap he was an angel, but are not angels young? This one was old and had a gray beard."

Did his ears deceive him? An image immediately formed in Julian's mind. Many months ago he, too, had an encounter with a mysterious old man. Nay it could not be. "Ariane, did this man wear a gray traveler's cloak?"

She looked at him as if he were the one who had gone mad and mayhap she was right. The old man he had seen in Tyre could not have miraculously appeared in the bottom of the well in England.

And yet, he could not shake the feeling her angel and his traveler were the same man.

Ariane tilted her head slightly. "Even though the well was dark, I could see him plainly. He wore a cloak, but it...but he...glowed."

Julian knew he should reason with her, tell her it was but an image of her frightened mind. "What did this man say to you?" He watched her ponder the question for a moment.

"He told me I would be safe and no harm would come to me. After a while my fear left and I slept. He came at a time when I could not bear it anymore."

Though 'twas foolish he believed her. The old man had come to him too when he needed answers, when he could not bear the thought of leaving the Holy Land.

Ariane shook her head. "Perhaps he was not an angel, after all, and just a vision of a mind crazed with fear."

"Nay!" Julian's denial came out even though he knew he should be agreeing with her. "I believe you saw the man."

Ariane looked up at him and let her arms relax against his chest. "It does not matter. You are here with me; that is all I care about."

Surely this was the sign he had asked for. God did want him to be with Ariane. There would be no Frenchman in her future. There would be only him.

He brushed a few matted curls off her forehead. "Ariane, do you know what God wants you to do?"

"Yea, marry Lord de Craon."

Julian lightly touched his fingers to her smooth lips. "Nay, God does not want that."

"He doesn't?"

Julian smiled when he heard the quiver in her voice. "Nay." He tipped his head and gently kissed her trembling lips. "He wants you to be with me."

Salty tears raced down her face and lingered on both their lips. He parted her lips, willing her tongue to mate with his. Yet, her tears increased and a soft sob bubbled from her throat. Though the kiss held ecstasy for him, 'twas obvious by the flood that rained down her cheeks she did not feel the same desire.

He released her lips and kissed her wet eyelashes, but the tears rushed over her flesh like a raging rapid. Perhaps he was kissing her too hard. Perhaps she cried because his kisses were too clumsy. Perhaps they were tears of laughter at his inexperience. He pulled her from his arms. Her eyes remained closed amidst the flow of tears. "Ariane, do my kisses displease you?"

"Nay."

"Then why do you cry so?"

"Because you want to protect me."

"Aye."

"Because you want me."

He nodded his ascent.

She wrapped her arms around his neck and drew him closer to her. "Because you love me."

"Aye." His voice shook with the need his admission gave him.

She leaned forward and gave him a kiss filled with passion and promise. "Let us leave here."

"Let us leave here," he said in a choked voice, rising to his feet and lifting her up into his arms. He held her fast, fearing what he had felt in her kiss was just a lie or, worse, a love not returned.

She pushed against his chest. "Put me down. 'Twould not be wise to let the guard outside see us this way and think of your shoulder!"

Julian tightened his hold. "'Tis a small wound already forgotten. I know another way that will shield us from prying eyes." Carrying her, Julian pressed his back against a panel behind the altar. The board opened to a dark passage that wound underneath the castle.

"Where does this lead?" Her fingers dug into the flesh of his arm.

The musty air rose from the bleak corridor and sent a shudder through Ariane's body that tore at Julian's heart. He promised Ariane comfort and love, but fostered her fears instead. "Do not be afraid; you are in my arms."

Her finger's relaxed against his chest, then she slid her palms upward and wrapped her arms around his neck. "Lead on, dear angel, for in your arms I fear nothing."

With due haste he plunged into the darkness and weaved his way through the narrow passage he had taken so often as a youth. Then he came to a set of stairs heavily draped with cobwebs. He smiled to himself as the cobwebs tickled his face. In all these years the monks still had not discovered his private entry nor had his sainted mother given up the secret.

He raced up the stairs, raised his foot and slammed it several times against a familiar worn stone. The wall groaned and opened slightly. Julian pressed his good shoulder into the cold stone, causing it to move further. With Ariane carefully secured in his arms, he turned his body sideways and made his way through the narrow opening into the light.

He saw her eyes widen with surprise when he placed her feet on the floor. She whirled about. "That tapestry, that table. We are in your room?"

"Aye, and I am glad that your maid is not here."

A cloud of worry flashed over her face. "Najila still has not returned from the village. Brother Andrew has gone in search of her."

Julian pulled Ariane into his arms and kissed the tiny lines of concern from her face. "Fear not she will be found, for there is not a more diligent knight than Brother Andrew."

"But Baldwin lurks."

"Nay, she is safe." He pressed his lips to hers deepening his kiss.

She pulled back. "We should go look for her." Her cheeks were flushed, her lips damp from his kisses.

"Najila will be all right. Do you believe me? Do you trust me?"

Ariane answered by placing a soft feather kiss on his neck. The air in the room became heavy. He drew in the heady scent that spoke of the need for fulfillment. He wanted her, but not this way. He placed his hand over hers. "Wait here."

With two strides he was at the door. Confusion and fear flickered across her face. He rushed back to her side and kissed her once more. "Do not worry, I shall return."

Her hand gripped the red cross on his chest. He kissed her once more, then made his way to the door.

"But where do you go?" she asked.

"To get a priest. We shall be wed this eve. The stunned look on her face made him laugh. "You do want to be my wife, do you not?"

She rushed over and circled her arms around his waist. "More than anything but let me tend to your wound first."

He kissed the top of her head. "Then do so quickly so I can find a priest. Then you can hold me tight for the rest of your days."

Her eyes showed bright with love. She cleaned and bandaged his arm and within the hour they were wed, in the small chapel, before the humble wooden cross.

During the night Julian had been pleased to discover his wife's purity. But before morn, the devil came and sat firmly between them.

"You were a maid."

Ariane looked down at the linen spotted with blood and at the same red marks that marred the fabric in Julian's hand. "Aye, I have fought off many waiting for you."

He dropped the cover. "You truly were pure. I have taken what was promised in good faith to another."

"Nay, you have not. Lord de Craon thought I was soiled. 'twas only the political power he could gain from our union that he truly desired." She stretched out her hand to him. He backed away. "You are my husband."

"You gave to me that which was promised to another. I have no right to this."

Ariane watched in horror as Julian turned and grabbed his clothes from the floor and made for the door. "Julian, don't leave me."

A cold bland look met her plea. The creak of the hinges followed by a hard slam was the only answer given. Ariane curled into a tight ball and wept. She could not control the sobs that tore from her throat and exposed her soul. She was alone again. This was the price she would pay for stealing a man of God.

Twenty

A false witness shall not be unpunished, and he that speaketh lies shall perish.
Proverbs 19:9

SHARP SUNRAYS FILTERED THROUGH THE TINY window, bringing in the cold, cruel reality of the day. Ariane lay in bed, waves of despair washing over her. She had gotten what she deserved. For months she had teased Julian and led him to believe she was something she was not. She should have told him the truth.

She drew her legs up tightly and cuddled the pillow to her chest. Yea, she knew why. Had she told him she was a virgin, he would have lightly kissed her on the forehead and walked away, giving her to her betrothed. 'Twould have been the honorable thing for him to do. But she destroyed his honor with a lie. Now she must learn to live with the consequences.

The clatter of another day beginning at the keep seemed exceptionally loud this morn. Ariane placed the pillow over her head. Nay, she was not ready to face the day or, to be more truthful, to face Julian. A loud rumble of horses' hooves echoed from the courtyard followed by earsplitting shouts. Could they be planning a hunt? Good, then Julian would be gone all day and she would not have to face his wrath, or worse, his stony silence. But then where was the baying of the hounds?

Boisterous bellows echoed from the yard to the hall

below. A single set of footfalls swept up the staircase. Ariane sat up in bed. What goes on here?

Guy burst through the door. "Lady Ariane, You must arise quickly. I know Julian said to let you sleep, but he is not here and they are but a breath behind me."

Ariane tried to wrap the sheet about her to conceal what had happened last night.

Guy hurried further into the room. "Forgive my intrusion, but time is of the essence… What happened here?"

Ariane felt her face flame as Guy's wide eyes took in the soiled bedding. "You were a virgin? Who did this to you?"

Pink fire flew to every inch of her skin. She wrapped the cover more securely around her and brushed one hand nervously through her disheveled hair. Hard as she tried, she could not answer, for the truth could not be known and a lie did not readily form on her lips.

"'Tis Julian. Isn't it?" Guy asked.

A flood of tears rushed from her eyes. The commotion from the hall seemed to being drawing closer.

"By the saints," Guy rushed to close the door. He made to lock it, then stopped. He came toward the bed and stripped off his shirt. "Do not ask questions. Remember we do this for Julian."

"What are you doing?" Heat washed over her face as she looked away from Guy's naked torso.

"You want to protect Julian, save him?"

"Yea, but this is foolish," she said feebly.

Guy tore off his breeches. "I too."

"Have you gone mad? Julian will kill you!" She pulled the covers over her shoulders.

Before she could protest further, Guy ripped the cover from her body and crawled into bed next to her.

Nay, this could not be happening. This was Julian's friend. He could not be so foul. A fearful cry bubbled up in her throat.

Guy clamped a hand across her mouth. "Listen to me.

241

They are right outside the door. Tell them it is I who did this to you. Not Julian."

"I did this to you, not Julian. Understand? We must protect him."

The room seemed to bend and sway as Guy propped up the pillows behind them and threw his arm around her shoulder. A tunnel of colors spiraled before her eyes.

The door slammed against the stone wall. Ariane gasped. Baldwin rushed into the room followed by His Highness, Prince John.

Julian stood on the crest of a small hill. His face raised to the bright noon sun. He had spent the morn on his knees in prayer. First asking God to strike him dead and then begging God for his forgiveness. But no mercy or death came Julian's way. He stood there a hollow man, not saved by grace, not condemned to hell's fire.

Empty. His sinful pride had caused destruction once again. His pride had killed his father, had eaten away Jane's mind, and now put Ariane in danger. He fell to his knees again, and pounded the earth in frustration.

How could he have been so wrong? Damn his pride, it had gotten in the way of God's will. How could he right the wrong? Heaven help him, he knew not what to do.

A sharp cough and low mutterings caused Julian to look up. Yet, he saw no one approach. His battle sense took over his feeling of woe. He reached for his sword. His hand came up empty. Once again he had left without his weapon. A common occurrence since he had met Ariane. She had a way of muddling his mind, of making him do things he had never thought possible.

A wave of guilt swept through him. She was pure. She deserved better. Now she may well suffer because of his desire. He hoped whoever ascended the hill would bring along swift death.

Yet what appeared first was not a sword, but the top of a staff followed by a gray cloaked figure, deeply out of breath.

"Is there some reason why you must always pray on the tallest mound?" a familiar voice asked.

Julian rubbed his eyes, for it could not be. Before him stood the same traveler he had met in the Holy Land many months ago.

"There is nothing wrong with your eyes," the man said.

"Who are you?" Julian asked in disbelief.

The man removed his hood. "I believe we have had this conversation once before. Who I am matters not. Now let us put that aside and discuss your plight."

Julian shook his head. He must have lost his wits in order for him to be speaking with an apparition. "Unless you can undo what I have done last night, there is naught you can do to help me."

"Really? Is that what you want? To undo your marriage?"

When he looked in the man's knowing eyes Julian felt his shame creep through his body. The man's gaze pierced into Julian, to the very core of his soul. This was no ordinary man. He knew Julian would not change what happened last night. He loved and cherished Ariane.

The old man stood before Julian blocking out the sun. "I ask you again, do you wish to change it?"

Julian lowered his chin, shaking his head.

"I thought not." The old man took a deep breath and looked about. "Now where would be a good place to have our meal? Come, Julian, break bread with me. After, we shall talk."

From the familiar sack the man withdrew a loaf of bread and a skin filled with wine. He placed both in front of Julian and sat down.

The man stretched out a hand. "'Tis not comfortable to eat on your knees. Come. Sit. We will talk."

Julian quickly complied and sat down with his legs crossed in front of him. Yet he could not manage to say a word. After all, this man could not be real and 'twas foolish to talk to a phantom.

The old man broke off a hunk of bread and offered some to Julian, he then did the same with the wine. Julian sat there with both wine and bread in hand, watching the man eat.

"Come, eat. And this time drink with me. For both are needed to clear the mind for the truth."

Julian found himself obeying the ghost's wishes. "Are you real?"

The old man stopped eating and raised his brow. "I have never seen a ghost eat. Have you?"

Julian shook his head again. Then this man must be an angel from heaven or *a demon from hell.*

The old man wiped his mouth with a small cloth. "Would a demon help calm your lady while she sat in the well?"

By the cross, the old man had read his mind! He spoke of Ariane. He knew her fears. Julian wanted to believe this man came from God. Yet the devil could be cunning.

"Eat. Drink. It is right to do so. The true answers will come," the old man ordered.

Julian took another bite of bread followed by a healthy swig of wine.

The man pulled the wineskin from Julian's hand. "The wine and bread will show you the way, but the answer is in your mind and heart. Why do you doubt me? Do you believe God is only pleased by a pious monk? Did not God make both man and woman? Do you not think that together they can please him?

A sudden serenity swept through Julian as he pondered the man's words. His mind began to clear and understanding began to take root.

The old man nodded. "All that has happened was for a purpose. 'Tis time for you to serve God in a different way."

All doubt left Julian's mind and the truth shone like a bright beacon before him. "She was always meant to be with me. All that has happened was meant to be. To open my eyes. I shall dedicate the rest of my life to loving and protecting her. 'Twas always what God wanted."

A smile spread across the old man's lips. He gathered the rest of the bread and wine placing both back in his sack. "My work here is done and you must return to your lady."

Julian grabbed the man's staff and handed it to him. "My thanks. Shall I ever see you again?"

The man gave Julian a warm smile. "Someday, perhaps someday. Come we have tarried enough. Your lady needs you take your sword and go."

Julian meant to tell the man his sword was not there, when a glint caught his eye. Nay, how could this be? He could have sworn he left his sword behind in the keep. Yet there it lay, not more than two hands from him.

He rose and picked up the sword. He closely examined the blade and hilt, which carried the blue de Maury stone. Aye, the weapon was his.

He turned to question the old man, but found himself to be alone. There were no footprints in the dust? The ground was smooth, no evidence that the man had ever been there.

No matter. There was not time to ponder his disappearance, for something from within urged him to return home quickly.

Ariane found herself standing in the hall in front of a seated Prince John. The slippery snake Baldwin lounged at his side. He wore a slick smile as if he had just swallowed a mouse whole.

Though the room was filled with people, the only sound that could be heard was the wind whistling through the cracks in the hall doors. Lady Catherine stood stiff next to Brother Andrew and Najila, who had mysteriously appeared this morn. Thankfully, Julian was nowhere in sight.

Guy stood beside her, the chains around his neck, hands, and feet so heavy he could not even straighten his back. Everywhere she looked accusing eyes met hers. Not one sympathetic face among the whole assembly. They all believed she had seduced Brother Guy, that she was a wanton. After all, that was the impression she had purposely given to everybody for months.

Arian groaned inwardly. Guy wanted to protect Julian and so did she, but not at the expense of destroying Guy. Somehow she must let the prince believe this was her sin alone and Guy was a helpless victim. What could they do to her? Make her marry Lord de Craon anyway? Or perhaps they would kill her.

Yea, death is what she deserved for making Julian break his vows to God and for remaining silent while Guy took a punishment he did not deserve.

The prince, not an uncomely man, sat silently staring at Ariane. He brushed his fingers under his chin against his tightly clipped beard. Casually he lowered his hand and motioned her to come forward. Determined to undo the mess she created, Ariane took a deep breath and stepped toward him, her legs shaking.

"Lady Ariane, did this man take advantage of you?" asked the prince pointing toward Guy.

"My liege," Guy interrupted, rumbling forward in his chains. "I would not have touched her had I known she was a virgin."

"Silence! No one gave you leave to speak. What you thought is not important here." John turned his attention back to Ariane. "Well, what say you?"

Ariane felt the temperature in the room rise at the crowd's grumbling anticipation. She cleared her throat trying to find the courage to foster a believable lie. "Your Highness, I-I did not want to marry a French pig, but yet that was what I was being forced to do. Even though I had no control over whom I was supposed to wed, I still had control over my body." Ariane wetted her lips. "I lived in a harem for a long time and was eager to try out all that I had learned. Guy is known for his way with women. I wanted to have a real man before I married a smelly French fish."

"Lie!" The word echoed forward from the back of the hall.

All turned about to search out the accuser. Voices erupted in the room and the crowd parted to let Julian, followed by Hugh and Simon, through. Ariane's heart sank. Julian would not let her lie stand.

"Ah, the Avenging Angel," Prince John said.

Julian came forward and bowed before the prince. "Forgive me, my liege, for not being here when you arrived."

Ariane shuttered at his cool confident tone. John would surely order his death once the truth came out. Yet, Julian acted as if he were the one in charge.

Prince John waved him up. "Arise, Brother Julian, What say you on this matter?"

"Guy had nothing to do with this. 'Twas—"

"He aims to protect me, he always has," Guy interrupted.

"Silence, fool. I wish to hear what the Angel has to say," Prince John clipped.

At the wave of his hand, one of John's knights came forward and bashed Guy in the head with the hilt of his sword. Guy's knees buckled.

Julian quickly grabbed Guy under his shoulders breaking his fall. "'Tis not his fault, Your Highness."

"Your actions are admirable, Brother Julian, but with my own eyes I saw this man naked in bed with Lady Ariane."

Murmurs raced through the crowd. Ariane wanted to run screaming from the room, but found herself unable to move or utter a sound.

After John's words, Julian dropped Guy into a heap on the floor. "He is not the one who took Lady Ariane's maidenhead, 'twas I."

Najila screeched. Brother Andrew caught Lady Catherine as she swooned. Guy struggled to his feet. Hugh put his hands over Simon's ears while Baldwin gave out a loud hoot.

Ariane stood like a prized roasted boar, her mouth stuffed with a giant red apple, unable to speak.

John rose from his seat and raised his hands. The hall grew quiet. He stared at Julian with disbelief in his eyes. "A lie, from the lips of Brother Julian? I have heard that is not possible." He turned to Ariane. "Which one of these men defiled you?"

Ariane swallowed to dislodge the large lump that sat in her throat.

Guy struggled forward trying to divert John's attention. "He protects me. He always has. All know Julian took me in and gave me friendship when none other would. In the Holy Land he constantly watched my back. He cannot help it. Even now he will sacrifice himself to save me."

"Nay, he lies," Julian protested calmly.

The room exploded with voices. Everyone speculating both men's words.

John clipped a hand through the air. "Silence. What think you, Lord Baldwin? You dragged me here saying the great Avenging Angel conspired against me. Perhaps 'tis Brother Guy who speaks the truth and the Angel who lies. Tell me, what think you?"

Baldwin slid next to Prince John's side. "Perhaps they both speak the truth. Perhaps she welcomed both of them. Her actions have always been brazen and bold. I think she has a wanton appetite and once that appetite was awoken, she hungered for more." Rumbles of agreement raced through the hall. "Brother Guy probably saw Brother Julian leave so he went to investigate and took the lady's invitation. What would any man do in that case?"

Heat infused Ariane's body as whispers of concurrence circled the hall. They all thought she was to blame and why shouldn't they? Had she not paraded herself in front of Julian, trying to arouse a carnal thought in his head? Had she not teased Brother Guy, trying to invoke jealously in Julian?

Yea, she was to blame, but she had to make sure she alone bore the punishment.

Ariane's gaze searched the room. Najila's strained features were focused on Brother Andrew. Brother Andrew's concern rested on the weak Lady Catherine. Lady Catherine's pale face watched Julian. Julian's accusing gaze fell upon Guy. Guy's pleading countenance landed upon her. She would have to find a way to save all.

Prince John tapped his lips with his finger. "An interesting theory. Only the lady, herself can clear up this delicate matter. Which is it, Lady Ariane? The Angel, the wayward monk, or both?"

The chance to clear up this mess and save all stood before her. Yet she could not muster a decent thought that would not condemn someone. She took a deep breath. "Brother Guy is mistaken."

Mumbling again circulated through the hall. John stamped his foot. "If anyone so dares to make a sound again I shall clear the hall. Continue, Lady Ariane."

The silence weighed like a heavy yoke on Ariane's shoulders. "Brother Guy assumed it was Brother Julian who slept with me. He created what you saw when you entered the room. All was an act, none was truth."

"What of your blood?" Baldwin snapped.

Prince John sat back down and casually began to rub the base of his chin. "Answer Sir Baldwin's question, my lady."

Guy moaned. Ariane felt Julian's heated gaze, though she dared not look at him.

"We wait, Lady Ariane," Prince John urged.

"He...he touched me briefly," Ariane said timidly.

A hundred horses' hooves could not have matched the explosion of voices that filled the air. John rose and stamped his foot over and over again.

"Quiet! Quiet! Guards, clear the hall of all except Brother Julian's family, the maid, and the monk," John said, pointing to Najila and Brother Andrew. "Remove the boy, as well. 'Tis not the place for him to receive this education."

Within moments only the crackle of the fire gave proof this was a place in which to live, and not a tomb. Ariane glanced at Julian. His hand held tight the hilt of his sword. His stony eyes fixed on Guy. No matter what the outcome here, she feared a friendship had ended.

Prince John moved away from his chair until he stood inches from her. "Lady Ariane, 'twas only a brief indecent touch you received from Brother Guy?"

Ariane nodded.

"She lies to protect me," Guy protested. "She loves me, can you not see that? You saw us naked in bed together. Do you believe her words or your eyes?"

Ariane winced. Why did he prattle on? Did Guy not see the anger that radiated from Julian?

John cocked an eyebrow. "Brother Guy, I have learned that often what you see can be deceiving, but fortunately we have someone here who knows the truth." He turned his attention back to Ariane. "If Guy did not soil you, then what of Brother Julian?"

Tears begging to be shed stung her eyes. Julian stood cold, unyielding like a fortress unable to be breached. This was not the man who had given her ardent kisses or utter foolish words to make her laugh. This man had hard cruel lines that marred his handsome face. This was not the man she married. This man did not love her.

Ariane bowed her head. "This is not the man who came to me last eve."

Prince John stepped back and steepled his hands under his chin. "Not Brother Guy, not the Angel. Then who?"

She did not answer; she would not answer.

"She lies to save me," Julian said harshly.

John cocked an eyebrow. "Lady Ariane, I'll ask you once again, is Brother Julian the man who stole your virginity?"

She clutched her chest and tears rolled down her face. She shook her head once.

"No one here then?" John asked.

Again she shook her head, knowing in her heart that

Julian would never forgive her for denying their vows. Yet this was the only way to set him free.

"What of you two?" John pointed to Najila and Brother Andrew.

"We know nothing. I left to search for Lady Ariane's maid yesterday. We only arrived back this morn," Andrew said.

"I suppose none of you have any words to enlighten us?" John looked at Lady Catherine and Hugh.

Lady Catherine fell to her knees before the prince. "Your Highness, Julian would never do such a dishonorable thing."

A flash of pain crossed Julian's face before his stony mask returned and he gripped the handle of his sword all the more.

John stood nonplused. "Arise madam. You wish to view your son the young saint who left years ago. Mayhap he has returned to you a sinner." He moved back to his chair and sat down giving out an exhausted sigh.

"Your Highness, what will happen when Lord Jacques de Craon and King Philip hear of this?" Baldwin asked, a note of satisfaction in his voice.

John flung a leg over the arm of his chair. "Perhaps he will be glad I broke the marriage contact a fortnight ago."

"What?" Baldwin gasped.

A flicker of hope rose in Ariane's heart. If the contract was broken then mayhap all would be well. She looked into Julian's now chilling ice-blue eyes. Nay, 'twould make no difference. The memory of their one night together would have to be enough.

"Forgive me, but will we not have problems with the French with the marriage contract broken? This union was to bring peace in the realm while King Richard was away. The king will not be pleased." Baldwin frowned and looked at his fingernails.

A slow smile spread across John's lips. "There are other ways to make alliances. I have it on good authority that the king, my dear brother, has been taken captive in Austria. I understand he was traveling in disguise. Were you in Acre when he offended the Austrians, Brother Julian?"

Julian's jaw tightened. He shook his head.

John gave another loud sigh. "Pity. Richard should have stuck to the sea, but alas we all know his apprehension of the water."

"Jerusalem is free then?" Julian asked coldly.

"Nay. Seems he had it in his sights too. He fought all the way to it, slashing and killing, killing and slashing. Had Saladin on the run, but alas, when it came time to take the city most of his resources were spent. If he took the city, how would he hold it? Such a waste."

Ariane wanted to run over to Julian and throw her arms around him in consolation. Although his emotions were unreadable, she knew what torment he must be going through. Once again he had missed the battles. No doubt he believed the outcome would have been different if he had been there. Instead, he was forced to be here because of her. Another thing he could lay at her feet.

John straightened in the chair and rose to his feet. "So the king's fate is unknown for the moment. Therefore, the burden of rule is totally in my hands for the time being." John's smile widened. "Which brings us to the delicate matter at hand."

Twenty-one

*Who knoweth the power of thine anger? Even according to
thy fear, so is thy wrath.*
Psalm 90:11

ARIANE SHIFTED HER FEET AND GLANCED UP AT THE
ceiling, trying to divert John's intense gaze. Yet
every time she peered at him, his steady stare remained on
her face. If Richard were here he would bluster and bellow
and act immediately, using his great size to intimidate all.
John, on the other hand, was a different matter. She had been
told he was a stupid, spoiled, conniving man, unfit to rule
and the cause of great poverty in England. But watching him
now, Ariane knew such reports were false. Stupid men did
not weigh and measure every situation before them like John
did.

Nor did he seem spoiled. He did not strut around the room
like a painted peacock; his clothes were plain and dark and his
manners were reserved and prudent. Nay, not spoiled, but
conniving? Aye, that she could see in his deep set eyes, in his
tightly drawn lips, in his rigid stance. This man had but one
goal—to sit permanently on the English throne. Woe to all
who got in his way. And that is where she stood, so much in
his way that his eyes would not glance elsewhere.

John folded his hands behind his back. "Lady Ariane, do
you remember where you lived as a child, before your
unfortunate capture?"

She had buried her past so long ago that little of it

remained. She bit her lower lip and tried to search her memory. "Sometimes before I go to sleep I can see my mother's beautiful green eyes."

"No, No," John said impatiently. "We all know who your parents were. Think of where you lived, the weather, the countryside."

A sharp pain shot through Ariane at John's scolding. Mayhap all of England knew what her family was like; she remembered none of it. As far as she was concerned, her father and mother could have been barbarians from the high country. Ariane startled at her own thought. Nay, at her memory. From deep in her mind she could hear her father's voice.

She tilted her head. "Your lordship, I remember my father always being worried about the barbarians from the north. I remember piercing winds singing through the hall. 'Tis one of the reasons why my father wanted to go on a pilgrimage, to get away from the cold."

Smiling, John shook his head. "Is that what he used as an excuse? Kirkridge, Lady Ariane, does that stir any memories? Kirkridge is located near the kingdom of Scotland. 'Tis a large holding that is constantly under attack from the barbarian clans. Your father became weary of defending it so he decided to take his family on a long, maybe even permanent, pilgrimage, which it did prove to be.

"From there it was up to the crown to find a suitable lord for the holding, which has proven time and time again to be an impossible task. The area is crawling with unsavory intruders and is the back door to the throne of England."

John came forward and took a lock of Ariane's hair in his hand and twisted it around his long, narrow finger. "If King Philip ever decided to make an alliance with the lord of this land, Philip may well become the next king of England, and his cousin, Lord de Craon would be looking at you for his leman instead of his wife."

His Highness released the lock and walked over to Guy,

circling him once. The Prince's gaze swept to Julian and then returned to Guy.

"Release this man from his bonds," John ordered. "Lady Ariane, for your crime of silence and your immoral act I give Kirkridge back to you."

Ariane let loose the breath she did not realize she held. With John's announcements the tension in the room seemed to ease in all, except one. Julian. His knuckles grew white as he grasped the hilt of his sword; he stood primed and ready for a sudden attack.

Julian's firm stance brought amusement to John's eyes. "However, a slight lady such as you will need a strong protector. Someone who can hold onto you and Kirkridge at the same time. Before us we see two fine, strong, virile, men. One or both may know the lady intimately." John slowly moved until he stood in front of Julian. "What does God's Word say, Brother Julian? 'The truth shall set you free.' I seek the truth and God shall give it to me."

Her heart hammered in her chest. John meant to have her marry. He stood before Julian. Would he make their marriage public or would he remain silent?

Prince John moved back until he stood before his chair. "Since both men claim they have broken their vows, both men are no longer protected by the church, both are outcasts, and both deserve to die. But, I need a powerful man to secure the north." John's eyes narrowed. "Give Brother Guy a sword. Only one can have the prize; the other must die for his sins. Brother Julian and Brother Guy will fight to the death for the hand of Lady Ariane."

"Your Highness, nay. You must not let friend fight friend," Ariane shouted.

"I must object also," Baldwin agreed. "Neither man is worthy to have Lady Ariane's hand. Both are disgraced by the statements given here. The lady needs a man of honor who can restore her good name."

John gave out a light chuckle. "And I suppose you are that honorable man?"

Baldwin bowed his head.

"Was it not you who said the lady and Brother Julian meant to murder me and rule England under the king's proxy? What is this, Lord Baldwin, has the possibility of title and property swayed your opinion about Lady Ariane?"

"Your Highness, I think you would want a man you could trust."

Now John gave out a hearty laugh. "And I suppose you think that is you?"

Again Baldwin bowed his head in submission.

"I trust you less than I trust these men. Both know as long as Richard is held prisoner I hold the power here, so neither would gainsay me. But if you truly want the hand of Lady Ariane, your request is noted and you will be allowed to fight the winner."

Baldwin paled at John's decree and made to protest further, but John raised his hand to signal he was done with their talk.

"Nay, no one will fight for my hand for I am already wed." Ariane's admission flared wildly in Julian's eyes. Guy raised hands in protest.

"Ah, now we have a confession from the lady and an interesting one indeed." John sat down and motioned for Ariane to come forward. When she did so he bent his finger to bring her face close to his. Ariane lowered her eyes. "Look at me, my lady. I am assuming you speak of Brother Guy?" John's face twisted in a sardonic grin.

"Aye, I am that man," Guy shouted to the roof.

"Nay, he lies," bellowed Julian. "She belongs to me."

"Julian? What is going on here?" Lady Catherine asked.

"Enough," shouted John. "I shall decide this matter."

Ariane watched as Hugh cradled his mother in his arms. Loud sobs pierced the air as Najila threw herself into Brother Andrew's chest. Julian stood like an unmovable fortress. Ariane closed her eyes briefly; she caused all this sorrow. "Please," she begged. "You do not understand."

"Lady, if you cannot hold your place I will have you removed," John declared.

Ariane glanced at Julian, wildfire danced in his eyes. All his anger was directed at Guy. He truly believed Guy had...

"Julian, he did not touch me," she cried. Yet his attention would not wavier.

Guy refused to take the sword handed to him. "Julian, do not do this. Don't let one brief moment of lust ruin your life."

Every muscle in Julian's body looked like hard granite. His mad gaze did not leave Guy. "Pick up the sword, silver tongue."

John crossed his arms over his chest. "Aye, the time for true confessions is over. I will have the strongest man defend my interests and the devil will have a sinner."

The knight within Guy came alive. He set his jaw and reached over to pick up the sword without taking his eyes off Julian.

Metal smashed against metal as broad swords met. Screams of protest were lodged in Ariane's throat. She could do nothing to stop this absurd fighting. Guy advanced only to be blocked by the swift lift of Julian's sword.

They shifted right, they swayed left and each time they both anticipated the others move. Beads of sweat lined Guy's forehead while perspiration moistened Julian's tunic. Neither seemed to be holding back, both seemed bent on destroying the other.

Madness reigned. Ariane glanced around the room. From Lady Catherine to Hugh all were pale and grim. None saw a positive outcome from this fight.

Guy grunted and fell on one knee as Julian charged forward. With a deft move Guy raised his sword and pushed off Julian's attack. Julian stumbled backward and Guy came to his feet.

The tears fell heavy from Ariane's eyes. No matter who lived and who died the outcome would destroy them all. Neither man would ever forgive himself for killing his friend. Guy would become the scoundrel he was before Julian met him and Julian...

Ariane's throat became tight and a tingle of apprehension skidded down her spine. Julian would let Baldwin kill him. What better payment for killing his friend and to atone for the death of his father than to pay with his own life. Either way she was certain Julian aimed to die this day.

Suddenly both men stopped, their gazes locked, each seeming to assess the other's strength. A strange smile slipped across Guy's lips; with great force Julian bolted forward and once again the swords clashed. Guy stepped backward and Julian assaulted him with an onset of blows until Guy had retreated to the stairs.

'Twas more than Ariane could take. She could hardly bear to watch. Her cries were muffled by metallic thunder. Guy ascended the stairs backward. Julian advanced rapidly without mercy.

The swords met and crossed high in the air, then dropped to regroup. Near the top Guy stumbled. Julian rushed forward. The swords impacted again. Guy faltered. His footing lost, he tumbled down the stairs.

Cries swept the room. Guy laid on the ground, his sword arm twisted above his bent neck.

Brother Andrew broke free and rushed to his side. He placed his hand on his chest. He glared at Julian. "He is dead." Quickly Andrew removed his tunic and placed it over the body. He then rose and turned to John. "Your Highness, I beg you to excuse me to tend to my friend's body."

John rose. "You have my leave and the assistance of my knights."

"Nay, if you please, I will tend to him myself." Andrew lifted Guy's body in his shaking arms. He turned to Julian. "Was she worth it, Brother? Was she worth the death of your friend? Go to the devil. 'Tis where you belong." Andrew lowered his eyes and made his way to the door.

Julian dropped his sword and fell on one knee, pounding his fist against his chest. Lady Catherine ran to her son's side to offer comfort. Ariane wanted to do the same, but she stood still, knowing very well that comfort from her was the last thing Julian would want. She was the true killer of Guy. If she had told the truth from the beginning none of this would have happened. *The truth shall set you free.* Were those not the very words Julian had told her time and time again? Oh why did she not heed them? If she had spoken the truth this whole scene could have been avoided.

He rose to his feet and patted his mother's hand, then he motioned for Najila to take Lady Catherine from the hall. Once his mother had left, Julian picked up his sword from the floor and straightened his stance before Prince John. "I am ready to continue."

"I am sure Sir Baldwin will give you a few moments to grieve for the loss of your friend," John said.

Julian raised his chin. "A false witness has perished. For that I cannot grieve."

"Ah, once again you are a repentant monk, but I am afraid it is too late. Your destiny is either with Lady Ariane or in death with your friend." John waved to Baldwin. "Pick up your sword."

"Nay," Ariane shouted, "Brother Julian will not defend himself. He will let Sir Baldwin kill him. He means to make payment for killing Brother Guy. My lord, I beseech you, do not let them fight."

John looked at Julian. "Do you plan to sacrifice yourself as the lady says?"

"Nay, I will fight." Julian then turned a cold gaze on Ariane. "I will fight with all my God given strength. If I die it will be God's will, not mine."

"There you have it, Lady Ariane. Brother Julian will fight with all his might. Do you doubt his word?" John asked.

Ariane watched Julian turn and set his jaw while he fixed his gaze on the wall past John's shoulder. "Nay, Your Highness, I do not doubt his word."

"Good, then let us see an end to this business. Sir Baldwin take your stance," John ordered.

Baldwin slowly moved to the middle of the floor, but did not raise his weapon. Instead he looked to those about as if expecting someone to come forth and do the job for him.

"Fight or I shall run you through where you stand," Julian said, keeping his deadly eyes fixed on the leaner man.

Baldwin gave no move, and Julian charged forward, his blade aimed at Baldwin's chest. Swiftly Baldwin raised the sword and fended off Julian's attack. He then whirled around and cut Julian in the left arm. Julian stumbled back.

Baldwin laughed. "Surprised? You did not think someone of my size could wheel a broad sword did you? Remember, I too fought in the Holy Land."

He leapt forward, his sword aimed at Julian's head. Julian deflected the attack, but Baldwin advanced again, swiping his blade low. Julian jumped back to avoid Baldwin's sharp slice.

Why did not Julian fight back? Ariane wanted to run forward and put herself between Julian's body and Baldwin's sword, but her feet stood rooted to the spot. Baldwin charged again and Julian did nothing, like a lamb to the slaughter.

A cruel smirk crept across Baldwin's lips as he sized up his opponent. Blood oozed from the wound in Julian's arm and traveled down to his hands. He fought to hold a tight grip on his sword. Though he tried to hide it, the torture of the day's events were written in the lines that creased his weary face.

Ariane whirled away. She could not watch. Baldwin knew that in spite of Julian promising to fight to his fullest, he would not protest long. He would welcome Baldwin's blade and his own death. A few more moves to satisfy Prince John and then it would all be over.

A sharp shriek shook the rafters. Ariane's gaze shifted to the source. Baldwin swiftly sped toward Julian like a deadly arrow in pursuit of its mark. Like a flash of bright light, Julian's blade connected with Baldwin's, sending the sword upward. Baldwin spun about, confusion registering briefly on his face. Julian's heavy sword struck deep into Baldwin's chest. He fell like a house planted on sand.

John clapped. "Well done, Avenging Angel. It seems the righteous have won out." He motioned to his knights. "Take care of Sir Baldwin's body."

Ariane looked away. Julian. who usually was in control, had let his full wrath fall upon Baldwin. A wrath she knew Julian directed toward her, for she had lied to save him.

John fixed his gaze on Ariane. "Come here, girl. Come stand by the man who has won you and your land."

The chill in John's eyes was nothing compared to the winter that swirled in Julian's. At one time they were bright with love. Or was that just a dream of a silly girl who wanted to conquer a great man? His hand shone white on the hilt of the bloody sword. Oh, that he would use the blade as swiftly on her as he had done on Baldwin, but he would not. He would fulfill his duty and travel north with her. Her husband. The thought brought no joy, only despair. He did not love her. She had murdered that love as sure as she had murdered dear, sweet, loving Guy.

"Come forward, Lady Ariane. I mean to have this business settled before this day is over. "Lord de Maury is your husband, is he not?"

She nodded.

"I knew this before this whole charade started."

Despair washed over her and John smirked.

"The priest who married you offered a full confession after some gentle persuasion. He told me all even before I stepped into your chamber this morn. You can't imagine my shock when I found Brother Guy in your bed instead of de Maury. 'Twas an entertaining turn of events. Brother Guy was a fool. I planned to pardon Lord de Maury and you for disobeying my brother's command. But Brother Guy complicated things. Your honor had to be set right. Is that not true, Lord de Maury?"

"Your Highness, please. Lady Ariane has suffered enough today."

Ariane dropped to her knees in front of John. "Forgive us. The marriage was a mistake. Julian will always belong to God. I wish to join the holy order at Wynnhurst Abbey. Then Lord de Maury may return to the Holy Land to finish God's work. Please find another lord to take the northlands."

Shock, mixed with amusement, flickered across John's face. "Has not your meddling caused enough sorrow for one day?"

Ariane bowed her head and placed a hand over her heart. "Aye, my lord, 'tis why I make this one humble request."

Julian sheathed his sword. "Listen not to her, Your Highness. Her words are given in confusion."

"Nay, I speak them in all sincerity." Ariane lied.

John said naught for a while. He just stood there, a glow lacing his dark eyes. Finally he moved toward Ariane until his tunic brushed against her chest. He leaned forward and whispered in her ear, "I know what you are planning to do. He will not leave. He fancies himself in love with you. Why else would he kill his friend? He is honor bound. He will see it through. Give up your folly and accept the wonderful gift God and I have given you."

John stepped back and gave her a true smile. "It is done. Lord de Maury and his lady will leave for Kirkridge in three days and I wish to be on my way on the morrow. Come let us break bread for I am famished from all of the day's excitement."

Ariane's stomach rolled. If she touched a morsel she would be ill.

John turned and placed his hand on Julian's shoulder. "Cheer up. All will take place as God sees fit."

Julian nodded without comment.

Twenty-two

*And these three abideth faith, hope, and love. But the
greatest of these is love.*
Corinthians 13:13

"MY LADY, YOUR PACING IS CAUSING MY HEAD TO
throb," Najila complained. "There is nothing to
worry about. Julian will not forsake you."

Ariane reached the bare wall of Julian's room, turned,
and began all over again. It took only fifteen paces to the
opposite wall; Julian could probably make it in two.

"That is the problem. I wish he would. I would do
anything to ease his pain. Now he is forced to stay where he
does not want to be."

"And where does he want to be?" Najila asked.

"In the Holy Land, of course," Ariane answered without
breaking her step.

"Nay, I think not."

Ariane stopped and glared at Najila. "Why not the Holy
Land? That is where you want to be."

Najila bowed her head.

"Agggh!" Ariane threw her hands up in the air walked the
same path again. There was no hope. Julian would not even
speak to her. The moment Prince John departed, Julian
stormed from the hall, but not before he leveled her with his
frozen eyes. Her pleas had been answered by the slam of the
door.

If Julian would not leave or listen to reason, then so be it.

She should leave this place, but where would she go? There were many at court who were unhappy that Prince John had seized power. While here, she had heard the whisperings that John had a hand in King Richard's capture. Mayhap those who were still in allegiance with King Richard would give her aid.

Ariane stopped suddenly and stared at Najila.

"My lady?" Najila asked.

With a brisk turn, Ariane made her way to her small trunk at the foot of Julian's bed. She flipped open the lid and pulled out a worn sack. "Many in this land despise Prince John and would certainly give aid to a lady so poorly used by him." She began stuffing the sack with clothing, discarding the colorful tunics and gowns for those more well worn. "We cannot draw attention to ourselves."

Najila rushed to Ariane's side. "My lady, what are you doing? Of what do you speak?"

Ariane ignored the alarm she heard in Najila's voice. "We must work quickly, for soon it will be night. With luck we will not be missed until the morn."

"My lady, we cannot leave."

Ariane jammed a pair of leather slippers into the bag. "If I flee, the only person who will be surprised is the prince. It is his misfortune to trust someone of such poor character."

"My lady, your character is not low. You but said those things today to save Julian and Guy."

"Yea, and look what came of that. Guy is dead and Julian cannot bear to look upon my face. To run is the only solution. Julian will have his freedom back. And Prince John will find another worthy soul to take my lands, for I do not want them." Ariane swept her cloak about her shoulders. "Come, let us go. We have not a moment to waste."

Najila stood firmly planted to the floor. "Nay, I will not go with you. What you attempt to do will only cause more suffering."

"What are you talking about? Do you not want your freedom? I will make sure you get back to your family. If we do not leave now you will never see your homeland again. You will be forced north with me."

Najila threw her hands in the air. "Think of your husband. Do you really think Prince John will not hold him responsible for your disappearance? Do you believe Lord de Maury will not give pursuit? You know as well as I, he will follow you until Judgment Day comes to us all. Where is the freedom there? Do not add to the misery he already feels."

Ariane dropped the latch and leaned her head against the door. Najila was right about Julian. His foolish honor would force him to search for her and he would not stop until he found her. 'Twas hopeless.

She made her way to the bed and dropped back upon it. Her gaze traveled to the worn tapestry above the bed. There he was, the young Avenging Angel on his knees, praying to God.

Ah Julian, such a look of purity and serenity you had then. But no more. She had made certain of that. She had stolen his purity and destroyed any chance that he might find serenity again. "I am a liar and a thief. I lied and stole Julian's future."

"Nay, you are none of those things."

Ariane sat up abruptly, certain her ears had betrayed her. 'Twas not Najila's voice she heard, but that of Julian. Oh, what pain he must be suffering from the death of his friend. And she had no choice but to add to it. She must force him away from her.

"Blast you. You are always sneaking about. A big clod like you should be heard like a stampede of wild elephants."

Taking a deep breath, Ariane narrowed her eyes and turned to look at the love she must give up. She expected to see a devastated man destroyed by today's events and further hurt by her cruel words. Instead he stood in the doorway with his arms and legs casually crossed.

Smiling.

"What are you doing here? I wish to be alone."

Slowly, a frown marred his face as he saw the stuffed

sack on the floor. His scowl darkened as he noticed the cloak she still wore. "Are you going somewhere?"

Najila ran forward with her head bowed. "Yea, my lord, she plans to run away. Taking me with her."

Ariane fixed her gaze on Najila. Blast again. After all these months, Najila's loyalty still belonged to Julian. "Leave us," Ariane ordered. "I wish to talk to Lord de Maury alone."

Julian nodded to Najila and she scurried from the room. "Now, I will ask you again. Are you going somewhere?"

"Aye, I am waiting for my lover to take me away from this place." She swallowed hard, hoping her tone carried enough bite in case her words did not. She meant to drive him away and by every saint that Julian saw in the heavens, she would do it!

A slight raise of his left brow met her false admission. "Ah, but my lady, your lover stands before you."

Ariane raised her chin. "You are such a fool, I have many lovers. You were... You were..."

"The first," Julian supplied.

She kept her eyes averted knowing that if she met his gaze he would see her lie. "Yea, you were but the first. I found I truly did enjoy being in a man's arms." She rushed on, "After all that is what I was trained for, to give a man pleasure."

In two steps Julian came to the bed and pulled Ariane to her feet, shaking her slightly. "Stop it. Stop the lies. You and I both know that until me you were as chaste as the Virgin Mother. You wish me to believe that in a day you developed a depraved appetite for men? No more lies, Ariane. No more lies."

The desire to throw her arms around him and tell him she loved him and wanted to be by his side for all eternity welled up within her and begged for release. Ariane struggled to hold back the tears that threatened to spill over her lashes.

"Look at me," he demanded.

Slowly, she met his gaze. "Guy is dead because of me."

Her soul all but cracked in two at her words. She stared out the window. The day shone bright, filled with a promising spring sun. It should be black, filled with clouds of bereavement.

She expected him to be gone when she turned around, but there he stood with that stupid grin still etched on his face. Ariane shook her head. He had gone daft. Guy was dead.

"Go back to the life you had before you met me. It is the right thing to do," she said.

Julian came forward and grasped her arms. She tried to break free from his hold, but he held her firm until her gaze met his. "You love me. You said so in the chapel."

Ariane rolled her eyes hoping the simple act would set him against her. Julian wrapped Ariane into his arms.

She struggled again to free herself. He must go back to the Holy Land where he could forget his pain. "Let go of me. Go back to your God. Go back to the Holy Land."

"Nay, I will not. God is here and I cannot leave the woman I love."

Ariane stopped her struggle. Did her ears deceive her? "What did you say?"

He kissed the tip of her nose. "I love you. I saw a man two days ago. The same man I met in Tyre. The man you saw in the well."

Ariane shook her head. Grief had addled his mind. "The man was a dream—"

Julian gently put one finger to her lips. "Nay he was real. A divine messenger from God. All that has happened was God's will. I was just too blind to see. God wants me to protect and love you, Ariane."

"Nay, this is madness." She knocked his hand away, putting space between them.

"Think, Ariane. You said so yourself. After seeing him, your fear left. I do not belong in the Holy Land. I belong here. With you. With the woman I love. The past will be washed away and made anew with our love. Let us make merry."

He loved her. Her heart and soul soared to the heavens; he loved her. He would love and protect her forever, but behind her joy lurked a darkness. Julian believed the man from the well was real.

Ariane ran a tender hand over the side of his face. "Your grief over Guy's death has twisted your mind."

He grabbed her hand and placed a soft kiss on her palm. "Did the man not say you had nothing to fear?"

Do not be afraid. I am with you. The old man's words echoed in her memory. He could not be real, and yet she did find peace when he was there with her in the well.

Ariane searched Julian's face. He simply nodded as if he knew her thoughts.

"The man was real. Believe," Julian said softly.

Perhaps Julian was right, but it did not matter. He would never be able to forget the grizzly details of Guy's death. The memory would destroy what love there was between them. Their love would decay just like Guy's lifeless body. An eerie sensation settled over Ariane. Julian had not once acknowledged Guy's death. He only wanted to make merry.

She took a hard look at his face. Nothing but love and contentment rested there. Oh nay, his senses had slipped. First, he thought the man was real and now avoiding any thought or memory of Guy's death. "Julian, do you think it is wise for us to be so joyous when we have lost our beloved Guy."

Julian gave her an odd look. "Guy? He is not dead."

'Twas worse than she thought. Julian's senses had not slipped. They had tumbled over a tall cliff into a deep ravine. Somehow she must make him remember the awful events of the day, though she knew full well that the knowledge would kill his love for her. She cleared her throat as she searched for the right words.

A loud screech pierced the silence and emptied Ariane's mind. The unending cry came closer, accompanied by the sound running feet. The door flew open to reveal Najila as pale as a celestial spirit.

"Have mercy, the devil has possessed Guy's body," she cried.

Ariane swayed into Julian, shocked.

"Guy?" she whispered.

Guy rubbed his neck and shoulders. "Had a hard time knocking it back in place. Must have been falling from the stairs. Usually I just fall to the ground."

"Usually?" Ariane muttered, too stunned to say anything else.

Julian rushed over and embraced his friend. Najila screamed all the louder from the farthest corner.

"A grand performance as usual. The Saladin Scare does it every time." Julian slapped his friend's back, then threw an arm over Guy's shoulder.

"Performance?" The astonished word tumbled from Ariane's mouth as she tried to take in the scene before her. Perhaps her senses were the ones that had fallen off the cliff. For either Najila was right and a ghostly vision stood before her, or two rats had sneaked about to fool a prince.

Ariane clenched her fist. She should be happy, Guy was alive. She should run over and throw her arms around the pair. Mayhap not.

She ran up punched Guy in the stomach and followed it with a firm sock to Julian's jaw. "You lead me to believe you killed your friend! 'Twas all an act. Then you fought Sir Baldwin. I thought you would sacrifice yourself... You were in charge all the time!" Ariane took another swing at Julian, but on his guard he ducked and the blow landed squarely on Guy's face, who still clutched his stomach from Ariane's last attack.

Guy stumbled back against the wall. "For mercy's sake, Julian, grab the she-devil before she does me in."

Julian grabbed Ariane's wrists. "Calm down, my love. 'Twas the only way to ensure your safety and achieve the correct outcome."

Ariane twisted in his grasp. "Correct outcome? I'll show you the correct outcome." She pulled back her leg and swung just as Julian moved sideways. Her foot shot into Guy's shin.

"Owww," Guy cried. "Tame the hellcat before she kills me."

Julian pulled her into his arms and covered her mouth with his, not releasing her until his kiss vanquished her anger. "All is as it should be. I am your husband and I will protect you. And you will be my wife who will love me forever."

Ariane tried to hold onto the anger but it dwindled away. She tried to hide the smile that begged to be released. "Will I?"

Julian squeezed her tightly in his arms. "Aye, you will."

"Aye, I will." Ariane placed her head against his chest. He loved her and wanted to be with her, and she loved him and wanted to be with him. Surely only peace and happiness would fill their lives now.

Julian dropped his arms from Ariane and turned to face Guy, who was rubbing his shin vigorously. Without warning, Julian launched his fist into Guy's chin. "That's for crawling into bed with Ariane."

Guy howled and staggered back toward the doorway. At that moment Andrew ran into the room, knocking Guy forward. Quickly Julian pulled Ariane to the side. She cringed as Guy stumbled into a small table and stubbed his toe. He danced about, grabbing his foot, until he landed on the bed. "Swords and Crosses, how did I survive battle after battle against Saladin's mighty army only to die in a lady's chamber?"

"This is my chamber," Julian said.

"Even worse," Guy answered rolling back on the bed.

"I heard the cries and came straight away," Andrew said, "I thought someone needed help."

"Oh aye, I really needed *your* help. You injured my toe," Guy mumbled.

The room erupted in laughter at the perplexed look on Andrew's face. Julian grabbed Andrew by the shoulder. "My thanks for getting Guy out of the hall quickly."

"I knew he could not play dead forever and was afraid John's men would soon hear his shallow breathing."

"You knew of this too?" Najila stepped to Andrew's side.

"Aye, I have seen these two play this game many times before on the battlefield, but then Guy always raised up behind his enemy's back and cut him in two."

"Like Lazarus rising from the dead," Najila said.

"Aye, my lady, like Lazarus rising from the dead," Andrew agreed.

"Well, Lazarus just might die now." Holding his head, Guy tried to sit up.

Again laughter rang out.

"Brother Guy, you are such a silly man," Najila said.

The laughter left Ariane. What of Najila? Surely she would want to go home. She made this journey for her family's sake. She expected to return home after Julian's mission was done. "Najila, Julian will see to it that you return home. I am sure you miss your family."

Tears welled up in Najila's eyes. "My lady, I know you mean well by offering me the chance to return home, but I cannot. My family would be shamed."

"But why? You have done nothing wrong. Why would your family not be happy to see their lovely daughter again?" Ariane asked.

Najila lowered her head. "I am with child."

Julian made his way to the bed, ready to lay his fist in Guy's face again. Guy raised his hands. "Leave off, Brother, 'tis not my seed that grows within her."

A small cough drew everyone's attention to where Andrew stood. "The child is mine. Najila and I are wed too." Andrew took Najila in his arms. "Her smile, her eyes, her sweet disposition drew me like a bee to a flower's nectar. We were in the village at the midwife's home making certain of Najila's condition the night Jane died. I am sorry I was not here when you needed me the most."

"You were here at the right time. But what of the situation at hand?" Julian frowned.

Andrew turned to Julian. "We would like to follow you to the north. Since I am no longer acceptable to be in the Templar order."

Julian nodded. "Nothing would please me more."

Guy loosely waved his hand at Andrew then at Julian. "The great Avenging Angel and the pious Andrew wed. And what of me? I have decided to become a true monk in word and deed. Guy threw himself back on the bed and laughed. "How has this happened? I am the only sainted one here."

The room again exploded in laughter. "Aye, Guy, you are the true saint," Julian teased.

The bailey bustled with activity in preparation for their departure. 'Twas Julian's hope that they would be underway before the sun rose too high in the sky. He surveyed the heavens; the brilliant blue sky bespoke of many promises. He had forgotten how beautiful spring could be; a warm breeze heated the crisp air. 'Twas a promise of the bright summer that lay ahead. Aye, there was nothing finer than a bright summer day, or for that matter, a bright future.

"'Tis a fine day to be traveling," Guy said.

Julian turned his attention to his friend. Guy was dressed in a drab monk's robe, pulling a mule burdened with a large sack. "So you will see this through?"

"Aye, I finally have the calling. I have heard there is an order of Benedictine monks on the other side of the king's forest. I am sure they will welcome a fellow brother."

Julian rubbed his chin. "The Benedictines are a strict order. They will not put up with certain things that the Templars would."

Guy raised a hand in defense. "Fear not, I am a changed man. I seek a life of service and prayer."

Julian cocked an eyebrow. "This remains to be seen."

"And where is the fair Lady Ariane on this fine morn?"

"Probably taking some poor unsuspecting monk to task over a piece of scripture."

Guy began to adjust the bag on the donkey's back. "Julian."

"Aye?"

"I know your faith is still an important part of your life."

"Aye."

"Well, Ariane is new in hers. Be gentle with your instruction and give her time to grow." Guy ran a hand through his hair. "There, I have said it."

Julian put a hand on his friend's shoulder. "Fear not, I believe God has given me Ariane so I can finally learn to be humble and patient. I love her. 'Tis God that has joined us together. It is a vow I will honor until death."

Guy covered Julian's hand that sat on his shoulder. "Then Brother, go in peace."

"Julian, Julian," Hugh shouted as he ran up to the pair. "Thank God, I have not missed you."

Julian turned to greet his brother. "Nay, I have learned traveling with a woman takes double the time of preparation."

"Aye, they are so involved in worldly things," Guy added.

Julian smiled. "This from a man who wore brightly colored hose while dancing up the hill where our Lord was crucified."

Hugh coughed to hide his laugh.

"Well, a man can change." Guy smoothed out his robe.

"I had thought Mother would be here to see you off? Is she around?" Hugh asked.

"Nay, she is resting. She said to watch me leave this time is harder than the first. I said my farewell earlier this morn. You will watch after her when I am gone?"

"Aye, more so than I did the last time. I promise you, I will be a better son and father."

Julian hugged his brother. "I know you will. I am sorry for the grief I have caused you."

The brothers clasped arms. "Nay, 'Twas I who was hell bent on making everyone miserable, but all is changed now. I will spend the rest of my days making amends. This I promise you."

"Do not make amends. Make yourself happy, then your joy will flow to others."

"Godspeed, Julian."

"God's blessing unto you, Hugh."

With one last hug the brothers parted. "I shall seek out Mother. Give my joy to your lovely bride."

Julian watched as Hugh made his way through the crowded bailey. For the first time in Julian's life, he felt close to his brother.

Ariane came up from behind him and circled her arm in his. "Is that Hugh?"

"Aye."

"I had wanted to bid him farewell."

"He gives you his joy."

"Does he? I would give the same to him. I wish he could be as blissful as I am."

Julian looked down upon his beautiful bride whose hair matched the sun-filled rays of heaven. "Then pray he finds a love like ours."

Ariane smiled up at Julian. "I shall do that."

"I am sorry to intrude on this tender scene, but I must be off," Guy said.

Ariane turned to give Guy a hug and a kiss. "We shall miss you. Will you not go with us?"

"Nay, Prince John does not need to hear that a dead man is walking about."

"We could change your identity. Perhaps you could become the Dark Knight, whom the barbarians fear," Julian offered.

Guy shook his head. "We have been through this before. I have a calling now."

Julian shook his friend's hand. "Then may God go with you."

"And also with you," Guy added.

Ariane gave Guy one last hug before he turned to leave. They watched him make his way to the gate.

"Do you think he really will become a true monk?" Ariane asked.

Julian watched his friend cross the gate's threshold. "He claims he wants a life of service and prayer."

"And you believe this?"

"Nay, but I do believe he will find fulfillment."

Ariane leaned into Julian. "Then I shall pray for him also."

Julian folded his love in his arms. "Aye, pray that all find the joy, the peace and the fulfillment we have found in each other."

'Twas a promise Julian sealed with a kiss. And the angels above smiled, for they knew soon these prayers would be answered.

If you enjoyed this book,
please consider reviewing it where you purchased it.

Excerpt from

REDEMPTION

THE SWORD AND THE CROSS CHRONICLES

One

Deliver me, O Lord, from the evil man: preserve me from the violent man.
Psalm 140:1

England, September, 1193

"PLEASE, FATHER, HELP ME. SAVE ME!"

Guy Ashton tried to dislodge the boy's grip, but the lad squeezed his legs to the point he could do naught but throw his arms about his mule to keep from crashing to the ground.

"Let go, boy, or we both will be beneath the donkey's hooves," Guy shouted.

"Better there than to be dragged back to feel the lash on me back."

Guy wiggled one leg free then pushed his foot against the boy's shoulder. The lad tumbled backward and grabbed at his grimy hood pulling it low over his forehead. He crouched down with one hand extended outward.

"Please, Father, I beg you. Do not let them take me back."

"I am not a priest," Guy hissed. "Who is after you, lad? What have you done?"

The boy remained mute, taking tiny steps backward as best as he could given his crouched position. Guy knew what fear could do. He had seen it often enough on the faces of Crusaders during the ten years he had spent in the Holy Land. Some charged half-crazed to their death, others stood

277

still like marble statues, but most likely this lad meant to bolt. The worst thing you could do was give your enemy your back.

Guy decided to change tactics. "My child, I will not harm you. I seek only to learn the truth."

The boy dropped to his knees and folded his hands. "I swear, Father, on the holy words of God, I did nothing. My master is cruel and I cannot bear the lash any longer."

A rumbling as loud as thunder turned Guy's attention. Horses. At least four, maybe more. The boy gave out a chilling cry and rose to his feet.

"Listen. Not more than five paces ahead of you is a fallen tree. 'Tis hollowed out near the ground. Big enough for you to hide in. Go!"

The boy took off like a frightened deer. Guy reached inside his pack on the mule's back until his hand gripped about the hilt of his sword, but before he could withdraw the weapon he found himself circled by six well-armed knights. They wore Prince John's colors. For five months he had eluded the prince and his guard. He should have gone straight away for the Benedictine monastery as planned. There he would have been safe, cloistered away from John's clutches. By the cross, they had discovered his charade. He relaxed his fingers and withdrew his hand, raising both of them in submission.

"Monk," one of the knights shouted. "Have you seen a skinny lad slip by here?"

Guy let out his breath. He had been smart to grow the thick beard; they did not recognize him. "Nay, but I did hear the leaves rustle not more than a pace or two back from here." Guy pointed to the right in the opposite direction from where the boy had run. "I thought 'twas only a deer, but 'twas loud, like the sound of a running man."

"Heaven's gate," the knight cursed, "The scamp has doubled back on us. My thanks, monk."

The knight nodded to another who threw a handful of coins at Guy's feet. Within moments Guy found himself alone in a cloud of dust. 'Twas a close call. Had any of the knights recognized him, the bony boy would have been forgotten.

He brushed his foot over one of the shiny coins and shook his head. Only Prince John had enough gold to throw about. He bent down and picked up the gleaming pieces, dropping them one by one into the small purse he had concealed in his robe. The last coin he flipped between his fingers. This one he would give to the lad, after he put the fear of Jesus into him. The boy was either a ninny or full of courage thinking he could outsmart John's men.

"Moses, I think 'tis time we end this journey before both of us become a meal for Prince John's dogs."

The mule lifted his muzzle and pushed against Guy's worn brown robe. He answered Guy's question with a loud snort.

"By the saints!" Guy picked up a few fallen leaves and quickly wiped his shoulder. "How many times do I have to tell you I am not your personal handkerchief. He threw the leaves away and patted the animal's neck. "You can come out now. They are gone," Guy called.

The boy crawled out and brushed decaying leaves from his clothing. "My thanks, Father. For certain they would have nabbed me. I never knew a priest could tell a lie."

Guy grabbed the lad by the arm. Had the knights recognized him, he would be standing before John this very night explaining why he still drew breath when he should be buried in the grave that bore his name. "Why did you not tell me, 'twas Prince John's men you fled? By the cross, I should whip you myself."

The boy twisted against Guy's grip. "I never knew a priest to swear before."

Guy shook the lad until his hood fell away. "I told you I am not a priest. Why would the Prince send six knights to capture one scrawny whelp?"

The boy raised his head. The coin slid from Guy's fingers and thudded onto the hard ground.

He had his answer. Two of the deepest azure eyes and a face framed in short midnight curls gazed up at him.

"May God save me, you're a woman."

Guy released her immediately and stepped back. "And just who might you be? Someone of great importance, I wager if Prince John is interested in you."

"Good sir, I thank thee for saving me."

Gone was the garble talk of a peasant. Her speech was clear and soft of that of a lady's. Guy shuddered and ran a hand through his hair. What had he done? He'd meddled in something that wasn't his concern. He needed time to think. His gaze fixed on the satchel on Moses' back. "Are you hungry?"

She looked at him as if he were thicker than a piece of dead wood. "Should we not keep going? The knights could return."

Oh that they would. He'd turn her over without another thought. "I doubt it. They have no cause to believe a monk would lie to them."

Guy pulled out a loaf of bread and a wine skin from the pouch, carefully adjusting the pack afterwards, making sure his sword was concealed. He made his way over to the hollow tree and sat. After taking a healthy swig form the wine skin, he offered her some.

"I've never seen a monk drink spirits before." She took a step back.

Good. Maybe she would run. 'Twould solve a lot of problems. *Would you abandon another defenseless maid?* His mind chided.

Sara. His sister's face floated before him.

He offered the girl the skin again. "Mayhap I am not a monk."

Tentatively she raised her hand and took the wineskin, taking a small drink. She patted her lips with a delicate finger. "This I believe. You look more like your mule's tail than a man, let alone a monk."

Guy glanced at the donkey's backside and chuckled. She had wit. "I guess Moses and I have a few things in common." He held out the loaf to her.

She smiled and took the loaf from his fingers.

"What is your name?"

She sat down across from him and began to eat. "I'm not telling you," she said between mouthfuls. "You might ransom me."

Guy rolled the thought through his mind. He could use the coin. What was he thinking? He must remember he was supposed to be dead and dead men do not ransom damsels.

"My lady, if you do not tell me your name I will never be able to help you. I will be forced to leave you in these woods to be devoured by wild beasts."

"Like you," she retorted.

"My lady, I am no beast."

She wrinkled her nose. "You smell like one. You are filthy and hairy. Like a beast."

Her insult wounded him, he knew not why. He had always considered himself a handsome man. Women used to loved him.

A sweet smug smile crossed her face. "I wager you wear all that hair because you are quite ugly."

Ugly! No woman had ever thought him ugly. Did not at least a dozen women weep for him when he left Palestine? But that was a different time. Now...he was but a shadow of that man. He stood. "This nonsense gets us nowhere. Your name, lady or I will leave you here alone this very moment."

She gave out a long sigh. "Very well. My name is Lady Grace de Melun and I was traveling to be wed."

Guy shook his head, an angry bridegroom would not stop the chase. Things could not get any worse.

"I guess I should give you my thanks. I truly did not want to wed the man." She took a bite out of the bread. "But Prince John decreed that I should."

He stood corrected; things could get worse. Once again he had saved a damsel from marrying a royal's choice. Not just any royal, but Prince John. The one man he needed to avoid most of all.

"The prince was going to be at the ceremony."

Guy groaned. He had to get rid of her quickly.

"I have heard he enjoys attending them."

Guy raised his hand. "No more, Lady Grace, I wish to hear no more."

She leaned forward, a lively glint sparkled in her fair eyes. "Why? Do you think Prince John will slice open your naval when he finds out you have aided?"

If Prince John found out Guy's bones still held flesh he would do more than that. "My lady, cease."

She crossed her hands over her chest and batted her eyes. "You could help me."

Guy vehemently shook his head. "Nay lady. I will take you to the nearest town and be done with you. I do not need Prince John's men on my back."

She narrowed her eyes. "Mayhap I will wait for the knights to return and tell them you had your way with me. Then no lord will take me to wife and I would be free to find Edmund."

Guy jumped to his feet. "Now see here. I will not have my neck stretched for something I did not do. Besides you'd be surprised what a man would overlook for John's favor."

Before he could rise, she was at the mule's side, rummaging through his bundle, drawing his sword. Her hands shook as she tried to steady the blade.

"How the devil did you know..."

"I knew you would not travel unarmed, in truth, I thought you had a dagger, but this is even better. Now you will see me safely away from Prince John's men."

He moved slowly to the left of her; the way Grace kept whipping the weapon about she was more likely to kill herself than him. Yet another sin he had no wish to bear.

She stumbled forward. "Do not move. I swear I will kill you if you try to disarm me."

Guy stopped and raised one hand. "My lady, let us be cautious. That is not a sewing needle you hold."

"Aye, I am well aware of that." She wobbled backward yet her gaze never dropped from Guy's. "I know not who you are, but I can tell you are a very dangerous man. Mayhap a renegade knight."

He wondered if she realized how close she was to the truth. Not many men, let alone a woman would draw a sword against him. For one so young she had a lot of courage. Most women would be weeping and wailing, but not this one.

She moved forward then veered to her left, bumping into Moses, who brayed and kicked the air until the bundle fell from his back. She twisted right, the sword pointed straight up into the air. Grace tripped over his pack and the blade slipped from her fingers. It curved up in an arch above her head. Guy's heart froze. He dove forward knocking her sideways to the ground. The sword slammed into the dirt less than a hand from her shoulder.

"Get off of me, you hairy oaf."

Guy rolled to his side and gasped for air. "Your thanks would have been enough."

She scrambled to her feet, but Guy was faster. He grabbed the sword before she could steady her stance. The look of defeat on her face tugged at his insides. "You fought well, little warrior."

She crumbled in a heap next to his bundle. Tears flooded from her eyes and spilled over her cheeks. "'Tis no use. You will return me to John, who will force me to wed a man I do not love and Edmund will be lost to me forever."

Her sobs rang to the heavens. Guy dug the tip of his sword into the earth. "Surely it is not that bad. I am sure your father has made a very good choice for you. In a few years this Edmund will be forgotten."

She shook her head. "You sound like papa. I have not forgotten Edmund and he has been gone for nearly five years. My father says he is gone forever, but I know he will come back."

Guy shook his head and leaned on the hilt of his sword. Mayhap she was as stupid as most women. "You would waste away your life on a man you have not seen for five years?"

She notched her chin and wiped her eyes with her fingers. "He fights in the Holy Land. He is a Knight Templar."

Guy's pulse quickened. He did not like where this tale was going and he did not care to hear the end of it. Mayhap he even knew her precious Edmund. Last thing that he needed was to become entwined in this woman's love dreams. Especially when they involved a Templar.

He looked up into the sky; heading west would take them out of the forest. There had to be a town close by. "Come. We must go. The sooner we find your father the happier both of us will be." The tears washed over her cheeks in earnest again. "My lady, stop your weeping. I am sure all will be well."

She placed an elbow on top of Guy's sack and began to play with a white cloth protruding from the side. Before Guy could stop her, she pulled the garment out and dried her eyes.

She gasped as the tunic marked with a red cross floated freely from her fingers. Her tears stopped instantly, a bright smile swept across her face. "You are a Templar. You can help me find Edmund."

Guy raised his eyes heavenward. So this was his penance for his many sins.

Dear Reader,

The Crusades began in 1095 with the goal of restoring Christianity in the Middle East. By the Third Crusade, (1189-92) much of the royal Christian European coffers were empty. Many believe King Richard didn't have the resources or the alliances needed to lay siege to Jerusalem. Instead he signed a peace treaty with Saladin, the Muslim leader at that time. The treaty didn't last long and more unsuccessful Crusades followed.

During the Third Crusade, when Richard arrived in the Middle East he marched his troops south. But what if, just for a brief period of time, he headed north to deliver a very special package which might have changed the course of history. This is the idea that gave birth to Julian's and Ariane's story and also introduced us to Guy Ashton.

Please join me on Guy's crusade to find forgiveness and peace in *Redemption,* Book Three in *The Sword and the Cross Chronicles.*

Until then...abundant blessings,

Olivia Rae

Olivia Rae spent her school days dreaming of knights, princesses and far away kingdoms; it made those long, boring days in the classroom go by much faster. Nobody was more shocked than her when she decided to become a teacher. Besides getting her Master's degree, marrying her own prince, and raising a couple of kids, Olivia decided to breathe a little more life into her childhood stories by adding in what she's learned as an adult with her first Christian romance series, *The Sword and the Cross Chronicles.* When not writing, she loves to travel, dragging her family to old castles and forts all across the world.

Contact Olivia at Oliviarae.books@gmail.com

For news and sneak peeks of upcoming novels visit:

Oliviaraebooks.com

Facebook.com/oliviaraeauthor

44476214R00166

Made in the USA
Middletown, DE
07 June 2017